# falling
### for your
# Best Friend's Twin

# falling for your Best Friend's Twin

**EMMA ST. CLAIR**

Copyright © 2020 by Emma St. Clair

All rights reserved.

No part of this book may be reproduced in any form or by any electronic or mechanical means, including information storage and retrieval systems, without written permission from the author, except for the use of brief quotations in a book review.

Contact emma@emmastclair.com for more info.

Cover design by Stephanie of @alt19creative

Interior formatting by Jody Skinner of Skinner Book Services

*To: Morgan & Elizabeth Moore, Kim A , Abby Reese, Jordan Truex, Kelli, Berly, Cassie Payne, and Gabby!*

*I appreciate you all SAM LEVEL much. Thank you!*

# one

*Abby*

WHEN I FINALLY MAKE IT to the restaurant, I'm only ten minutes late. Three of my friends don't even blink as I slide into the last empty seat, panting slightly, but Zoey gives me the patented Abramson death glare. My best friend and her twin brother, Zane, probably came out of the womb throwing this look at the nurses in the hospital.

I've learned to ignore it, but Zoey used to put the fear into me when we met our freshman year of college. The few times I've seen Zane do it, my body has an entirely different reaction. One I would never admit to Zoey, what with the whole twin thing and all.

I'm less bothered by her dirty look than the fact that my friends have decimated the contents of the bread basket. There's one lone breadstick, which I wave. "Hey, ladies! Sorry I'm late. Did I miss anything? Besides the bread, obviously."

And the butter. The little silver butter dish has been totally cleaned out too, I realize as Sam, Harper, and Delilah say their hellos. The waitress stops by and I scramble to choose a sandwich with ingredients I can recognize and pronounce.

"Could I also get a coffee?" I ask, handing over my menu. "And more breadsticks and butter?"

"You wouldn't need to ask for more butter if you'd been on time." Zoey raises one perfectly manicured blonde eyebrow.

"Save your speech, *Mom*. I got caught up at work. Well. My extracurricular work."

"Lateness forgiven. Oh! That reminds me. I've got a potential job for you. I'll tell you after lunch," Zoey says.

For the past six months I've been trying to build up a client base so I can quit my day job. I want to be a systems analyst or working in cyber-security, but I'm stuck doing basic IT work in a soul-sucking office. Tech geeks like me are almost as common in Austin as singers trying to catch a big break. There are lots of jobs, but even more people trying to fill them.

Today I was helping my brother, Jason, who founded a company that has been massively successful designing video games. Every time I talk to him, he offers me a full-time job. One that would be a dream compared to my current situation. So tempting.

But I was never into gaming the way Jason always has been. Sure, it would beat this stupid IT position, but I'd have to move back to Katy, just outside of Houston, because Jason wants me on site. As much as I miss my parents and love Jason, Jessa, and my nephews, no way am I leaving Austin unless I'm being dragged.

Sam lightly taps on her water glass to get our attention.

When we are finally quiet, she clears her throat, then smiles in a way that makes me nervous. "The reason I called you all here today—"

A collective groan rises from the table, drowning Sam out. We all know what a *Sam lunch* means. Usually something to do with her alter ego, Dr. Love, needing us to do her a favor.

Zoey pokes me in the shoulder. "Abby, I thought you planned this lunch!"

"Me?" I shake my head. "I mean, I told you about it, but—"

Harper cuts me off, glaring in my direction. "Abby invited me too."

Zoey's evil eye might not work on me anymore, but Harper, with her dark hair, intense eyes, and muscular physique, still terrifies me. She looks like a beautiful but evil queen from a fairy tale. One who does CrossFit and could toss a giant tire at your face one-handed.

"Same," Delilah says, her honey-sweet Alabama accent somehow extending that one syllable into four. She pats my hand and gives me a *bless-your-heart* look.

I narrow my eyes at Sam. "You tricked me into inviting everyone for you?"

She has the audacity to wink. I remember now—Sam made it sound like I was reminding everyone of a lunch that had already been planned. Normally, I would have seen right through her. But Sam took advantage of the fact that I've been distracted lately with all the extra freelance work. I'm pretty much running on fumes and caffeine.

Sam grins, looking purely Machiavellian. "What do they call it in computer-speak ... I used a back door?"

Everyone is still directing their dark looks toward me. I hold up my hands. "Hey, I'm a victim too!"

"You should know better," Harper says.

I should. After all, the five of us have been roommates in various configurations for the past five years, since we all met freshman year at the University of Texas. I know Sam is tricksy, as Gollum would say. *Tricksy hobbit.* And now, thanks to my unwitting help, she suckered us into a lunch with an agenda. Fantastic.

Sam raises her voice and continues. "As I was saying, I called you all here today because I've got a big opportunity and—"

"You need our help," Delilah, Harper, and I all chorus. We know this script by heart.

"Guys, if you'd just listen!" Sam starts speaking faster now, as though she knows we're about to mutiny. "I got a book deal. Which means lunch is on me!"

The table erupts into cheers and hugs and basically chaos. For now, the irritation with Sam is forgotten. We give each other a hard time, but the five of us will always have each other's backs. This book deal has been Sam's dream for as long as I've known her.

Our waitress appears, waving her hands as though wanting to shush us. Zoey, who's standing at her full Amazonian height to hug Sam, glares. The waitress scurries back to the kitchen like she's being chased by a pack of Dementors from Harry Potter. I hope she's not too scared to bring back my butter.

When we're finally all seated and somewhat quiet again, Harper pins Sam with a look. "We're all super happy for you. But the question is: what do you need from us?"

Sam fidgets with her silverware. "I need to bolster my online presence leading up to the launch. Longer blog posts with relationship advice. Plus, stories I can use when writing the actual book."

"So, you need us to write more fake advice emails for you-know-who?" Zoey asks.

Sam gets tons of emails as Dr. Love, but they don't all make for good entertainment, which is what sets her column apart: solid advice in a snarky package. For years now, she's asked us to send in emails under anonymous usernames with fake relationship issues. She doesn't know which ones are real and which ones are from us—though if she guesses correctly, we owe her dinner.

"Keep it down," Sam says, glancing around the restaurant.

Abby started Dear Dr. Love as a local column on an Austin news site but grew so wildly popular that it's syndicated in big cities all over the United States. The more successful she becomes, the more scared Sam is of her identity being revealed. She says that Dr. Love gets as much hate mail as requests for advice, probably because of all the breakups she's instigated.

"Definitely keep the emails coming, though some of you are getting sloppy at hiding your identities." Sam gives me a pointed look.

I shrug. "The DC-versus-Marvel rivalry is a potentially real issue in a relationship."

That earns me eye rolls around the table.

"For the book, I'll need bigger, more substantial stories, not just questions. Preferably *real* love stories." Sam plays with the end of her dark braid.

Harper raises an eyebrow. "And you're asking *us*?"

Sam is the only one in a relationship, so I totally understand Harper's skepticism. Overall, we seem pretty unsuccessful as far as love goes. Cursed, if I'm being honest. Especially considering the fact that we're all attractive in our own ways and no one has a mustache, a tail, or some kind of weird habit like collecting dryer lint.

Zoey is totally career driven and swears she doesn't have time to date. Harper is beautiful but terrifying. I haven't made it past the second date with a guy in years. And I'm not sure about Delilah. The former beauty queen has no lack of guys chasing her down. I've seen two trying to get her attention just at this lunch. But other than one long-distance relationship while we were in college, she hasn't dated seriously.

If Sam is counting on us, she might be in trouble.

The waitress arrives with our food, careful to avoid eye contact with Zoey. She wins bonus points from me by bringing out two containers of butter and coffee that smells amazing.

"What's the angle?" Zoey says, as we start eating. I half expect her to pull out her phone and start taking detailed notes. "Is there a theme to the book?"

"Love clichés. You know, like common tropes."

I raise my hand. "You lost me at tropes."

I can speak fluent computer code, but the only way I passed my English classes in college was with Sam's intense tutoring. Which involved late nights and chocolate truffles as rewards for correct answers, like I'm a dog. I didn't even care, because: chocolate. And I passed with a flying C.

"Tropes are like the core story in a rom-com or a Hallmark movie."

"Like the Christmas one y'all forced me to watch?" I ask. "The one where the girl doesn't know the guy she meets online is actually also the Santa at the mall where she works?"

"And a billionaire," Delilah points out. "Handsome to boot. Who knew Santa could be hot?"

"Yes!" When Sam laughs, I feel like I've earned a chocolate truffle. "That movie had a secret identity trope. Mixed with the online dating trope and the billionaire trope, which can be a lot like a rags-to-riches story."

"Those plots are all so fake," Zoey says. "You expect us to date secret Santas or find billionaires?"

Sam holds up a finger. "The tropes are exaggerated, sure. But there's a reason they're popular. They're common. Almost universal. Think about it. How many of you know someone who's fallen for their best friend?"

We all look at Harper. Her olive skin flushes, but she pretends not to notice us all staring. We've been trying to tell her for years that her best friend, Chase, is in love with her, but she won't hear of it. I think she's in love with him too, but she most definitely isn't ready to face that truth.

"Or their boss?" Sam asks.

We all try *not* to look at Zoey, who for sure will strike us all dead with her laser eyes if we even bring up her hot but much older and very off-limits boss, Gavin.

"There are tons of these things." Sam begins counting them off on one hand. "Fake relationship, second chance romance, cowboy, enemies to lovers—you get the picture."

Harper rolls her eyes. "Yeah, but how about a fake relationship? That's ridiculous. Just like most of those storylines. They're predictable and totally not real."

"I had a fake relationship," Delilah says, biting her lip to hold back a smile.

"You would," Harper says with a laugh.

"Actually," I say. "So did I."

Now everyone's laughing. If they weren't my friends, they'd all be dead to me. Dead.

"You did? We need details," Zoey says.

"It was at coding camp the summer before seventh grade. There was major beef between the two teams about our source code, and so to distract the other team's best programmer—"

Zoey holds up a hand. "Enough said. I should have known it would have to do with computers."

"Most of my life has to do with computers. Don't forget who fixed your laptop when you got a virus from opening that attachment with—"

"Anyway! Back to Sam's big book news!" Zoey shouts.

I smile, loving this tiny bit of leverage over Zoey. No one would think less of her for trying to open an attachment showing secret photos of a certain Hemsworth brother in a Speedo at a private beach. If I had a nickel for every person who got that virus, I'd retire and buy my own island.

It's nothing to be ashamed of, but Zoey doesn't want to admit that underneath her all-business front, she's got another side. She's like a mullet, business up front but a lot of fun hidden out back. Wayyyyy out back, behind a chainlink fence with razor wire. I've seen the out-back side of Zoey only a handful of times, and it's like a unicorn sighting. I've often wondered if Zane, equally as uptight and all-business, has the same fun side hidden somewhere. I'd pay good money to see it.

"Why don't you use your own relationship," Harper suggests.

"That would be perfect!" Delilah says. "Y'all are adorable."

"They're too perfect," Zoey grumbles.

She isn't wrong. Matt, Sam's boyfriend, is about three seconds from being her fiancé, and they do have one of those perfect relationships. While we're all happy for her inevitable proposal, the first one of us to get married will be like the first domino to fall. It's going to disrupt the delicate roommate and friend balance we've kept up for years.

More importantly, because of the cutthroat Austin housing market, without all five of us, we can't afford the rent for the house we've lived in for the two years since graduation. It's an amazing location in the trendy South Congress area. The historic craftsman-style home has been updated and renovated, so we each have our own room, even if they're tiny. Until our circumstances change, or unless the older woman who owns it dies and her kids hike up the rent, it's the perfect home.

"I know I'm asking for a lot," Sam says, leaning back in her chair. "I'm not trying to force you guys into something. Just do what you're already doing, and if you *happen* to run into one of these love clichés or tropes, let me write about it. Your names will be changed, obviously. I won't share things that make you uncomfortable."

"What's in it for us?" Zoey asks.

I nudge her shoulder. "Besides helping our good friend, you mean."

Zoey nods. "Right."

Sam leans over the table and lowers her voice. "My advance was pretty high. Like, six-figures high."

This takes a minute to sink in. Aside from Delilah, who has tried everything from dog walking to modeling, we're all doing pretty well. But not six-figure-advance well.

"I need this to work," Sam says. "I need my book to sell to earn back the advance and secure me another deal. So, I have an idea for a thank-you to my amazing roommates who helped me get here. If Matt proposes—"

"*When* Matt proposes," Harper interrupts.

Sam grins and crosses her fingers. "*When* Matt proposes, I'll keep contributing to rent for the first year after our wedding."

We're all stunned into silence. That's a *huge* gift. Shocking, especially coming from Sam. Not that she's selfish, exactly, but she's not the first of my friends I'd go to for help. This is a bad deal for *her*, but it's great for *us*. I, for one, am not about to say no.

"Sold," I say. "Do we need to shake or sign something in blood?"

Zoey touches my hand. "This is a big deal. Maybe we should slow down and think about it."

Sam shakes her head. "I've thought about it. I wouldn't have been as successful without your support. I want to do this."

"Sam wants to," I say.

Harper smirks at me. "Are you sure about this? It might mean you have to go on more than one date with a guy, Abs."

"Ha ha."

I try to stuff down the hurt. Because it does bother me. I simply haven't been interested in any of the guys I've dated. Still, what I call my first-date curse (really, a first-and-second date curse) feels like my fault somehow. I'm like the girl who gets sent home the first night on the Bachelor, who doesn't even get a write-up on a recap blog.

Under the table, Zoey grabs my hand. She knows how much it secretly bothers me. And how, ever since my older brother started having kids, I've dreamed of having a family of my own. Somehow, people get the idea that because I'm sarcastic, a total computer geek, and dye my hair (it's currently blonde with the bottom half pink), that I don't hear my biological clock ticking like a time bomb. Even in a city like Austin, which has a much more artsy vibe, people carry a subconscious idea of what a mom should look or act like. And that idea is definitely not *me*.

Delilah wrinkles her perfect button nose. "This feels like a much bigger deal than writing fake emails for advice."

Zoey takes her hand back and nods. "I'm hesitant too. Letting you share our personal stories? I'm not sure. Not that I don't love our house or your offer. It's very generous."

Sam steeples her fingers on the table, meeting each of our eyes in turn. "Ladies, are you in or are you out? I need you. I really do. This is big time. Ride or die. I can't mess this book up. And you all know I couldn't have done any of the Dr. Love stuff without you."

"Oh, we're well aware," Harper says. "I doubt you'll be getting a story from me, but I'll agree to it."

"You already know I'm in," I say.

"Me too. Assuming I can find a man," Delilah says.

"Finding men isn't your problem," I tell her. "There are two of them eyeing you at the bar right now."

I point, and Delilah giggles when two guys in suits lift their drinks her way. Her cheeks turn a rosy pink, making her look even more like a Disney princess. Any minute now, a bird is going to land on her shoulder and start tying ribbons in her hair.

"Okay, fine," Delilah says.

Zoey is the only one still silent. "Fine," she finally says. "But I'm only doing it because I like our house. And you guys. I won't make anything up, though."

Sam waves a hand. "No made-up stories for the book."

"But what if none of us can help? What if we stay single?" *And cursed*, I think.

Sam smiles. "Even if I don't get any material for the book, the deal stands. But I have hope for you all."

At least one of us does.

# two

*Abby*

ON THE WAY OUT, Zoey and I fall into step on the sidewalk since our buildings are near each other. Zoey is quiet and keeps smoothing back her ponytail, which is already perfect and totally sprayed into submission. This is how I know she's still uncomfortable with Sam's love cliché idea.

"It's going to be fine," I tell her. "If we find a guy and happen to fall into one of those tropes, great. You don't have to go chasing after a relationship. I mean, Sam pretty much promised that our lives can go on as normal, and then she'll keep paying rent after she gets married."

"It's not just that," Zoey says. "I hate change. It's getting real, you know? The idea of us all moving on at some point. It starts with one person getting engaged. Then all our friendships will change. It's the beginning of the end."

"Wow," I say. "You're totally doom and gloom about this. Stop worrying so much."

We reach her building and she lets out a long sigh. "Sorry. I'll work on it."

"Maybe something good will come out of it. Besides rent."

Zoey smiles. "Maybe you'll end up meeting someone amazing!"

"Doubtful. You see all this?" I wave my hands over my ripped skinny jeans and Hawkins Middle School AV Club graphic T-shirt. "Very few can handle it."

Her brow furrows. "What's the AV Club?"

I smile, making a mental note to force Zoey to watch *Stranger Things*. "Don't worry about it."

Zoey and I are like the odd couple. She has on a skirt and blazer, with her crisp white shirt buttoned all the way to the top. She even has on pantyhose, which I personally think is a crime in Texas.

"Oh, before I forget," Zoey says, "I gave Zane your number."

"Zane?! You're setting me up with Zane?!"

Though Zane is gorgeous with his dark blond hair and blue eyes I could drown in, he is exactly like Zoey. Except with the dial turned up to twenty.

I'm shocked, though I don't hate the idea. I might have a teensy crush on her brother, but there is no way he feels the same. Plus, it's a total party foul to harbor a secret crush on your best friend's twin. Which is why I've never mentioned it.

*Crush? What crush. I have no crush.*

Zoey looks at me like I've lost it, then starts to laugh so hard that she snorts. "No. Oh my gosh, *no*. I'm not setting you up with Zane. He's got some kind of bug with his Eck0 app. You know, his startup. I recommended you." She laughs again. "You and Zane going out? Wow. No."

I refuse to be offended, since I agree completely. Zane and I would be even more of an odd couple than me and Zoey. Still, a tiny part of me is hurt. Why couldn't Zane and I work? They say opposites attract, and we're basically from different continents. I stuff the hurt feelings down into the deep, dark hole where I hide my crush.

"I love bugs," I say. "The computer kind. Not the flying-cockroach-as-big-as-your-face kind."

"Ew. One thing we can agree on. He'll probably text you today. Be nice."

"I'm always nice," I say, itching to bust out my phone and check to see if he's sent me a message yet.

Still laughing, Zoey walks inside her building, and I head to the job I hate more than flying cockroaches. Today, I'm mostly removing viruses from people opening attachments and doing other mundane work that has me wanting to stick a flash drive in my eye. When my phone finally buzzes with a text from Zane, I practically fall out of my chair.

**Unknown number**: Abby, this is Zane, Zoey's brother. We've met a few times. She mentioned that you are someone we could hire on a freelance basis to help solve some tech issues we're finding in our app. Please advise if you're free and would be able to help. Thanks, Zane.

I'm already chuckling. I've never read a text that sounded like a formal letter before. Who texts like this? Zane actually makes Zoey look like a completely unbuttoned wild woman.

This is going to be too much fun. Because there is no way I can *not* mess with him.

**Abby**: Hey, Z. Whattup. I do tech like Kanye does bad tweets. Happy to help for a fee or your firstborn child.

While I'm waiting for a response, I plug his number into my phone. It vibrates in my palm a moment later.

**Zane**: Am I to understand that you would be available? Thanks, Zane.
**Abby**: I'm available. In all senses of the word.

*Oh my gosh.* I slap my hand over my mouth as soon as I hit send. Why did I type that? Sometimes my fingers move faster than my brain. I wanted to be funny, but it sounds like I'm flirting instead.

**Zane**: Wonderful. My assistant will be emailing with the details. It's somewhat urgent, so we'd like to get started as soon as possible. Tonight, if you are able. I understand you might need to work nights and weekends, due to your current job. We're at the office late most nights as well. Thanks, Zane.

I can't decide if Zane missed the flirtation in my previous text, or chose to ignore it and stick to business. I grin, unable to help myself as I start typing again. Zane is like a couch in a furniture showroom, perfectly pristine with throw pillows placed at exact right angles. I just want to jump up and down on it, or maybe kick off my shoes and take a nap.

**Abby**: Thanks! Can't wait to see you.

I finish with a kissy face emoji. It makes me laugh so hard that Micah, the other poor, unfortunate IT soul who works with me, swivels in his seat.
"What's so funny?"
Micah is basically the only person I can stand in my office.

Probably because we're equally overqualified and equally miserable. We're also both secretly trying to find other jobs and working side gigs, which I'm pretty sure is frowned upon.

"Oh, nothing. Just messing with my friend's brother."

"Which friend?" he asks, a little too eagerly. I made the mistake of inviting my friends to my office Christmas party once. Micah has been referring to them as the Hot Squad ever since.

I give him a look. "Reminder: never gonna happen," I tell him. His ears turn pink. "Not that you're not a nice guy. Just, no. I'm talking to Zoey's brother, Zane. Twins, hence the Z names."

I totally get it, because my brother, Jason, married a Jessa, then had two boys, Jace and Joey. Jessa is due with their third any day now. I'm waiting on a call from my mama so I can drive home. I can't wait to meet my new niece, and not just because her name is Addie. I don't know why they departed from their preferred naming convention, but I like that it's close to mine. I have big plans to spoil her rotten.

"So, why are you messing with him?"

"I'm doing some work for his startup, Eck0."

Micah shifts closer, trying to look at my computer screen. "Eck0? I think I've heard of them. So, Zane hired you to help them with an issue."

"Yep. And he's got a stick so far up his backside that he's got antlers," I say.

As if to prove my point, an email from Zane's assistant is already waiting in my inbox with an NDA to sign and a few other forms. We often have to fill out something, but the sheer amount of paperwork is overkill.

Micah snorts. "Have fun working with him. If he fires you, send him my way."

"Fired? Me? Yeah, right."

"I know, I know. We all know you're the best." Micah rolls his eyes and gets back to work. "Just don't forget about me if you hear of any potential jobs."

"I always remember the little people who make this possible," I tell him.

His phone rings, and as Micah answers, I go about adding my electronic signature to a few dozen forms. When I've sent them back, I shoot Zane a text.

**Abby**: Tag! Finished my paperwork. I'm not sure I read all the fine print, though. Hopefully I didn't sign away the deed to my car.
**Zane**: You should never sign contracts you haven't read. Please be advised to read them carefully, sign, and return.
**Abby**: Kidding. Of course, I read them.

I didn't. Somewhere in the second paragraph, I zoned out.

**Zane**: Just to be safe, I've had my assistant send fresh copies.

"Argh!"

Micah shushes me, pointing to the phone he's still got up to his ear. When I check my inbox again, there's another email with the same forms. Okay, so that backfired.

I can't handle doing that again, so I close out my email and start working on my actual job. If Zane wants to make sure I've read them, I'll give him plenty of time to know that I have. I put my phone on silent and stuff it in my bag.

Almost an hour later when I finally check, there are no less than five texts from Zane, asking about the paperwork. Each one sounds more irritated than the last. A final text comes through as I'm reading.

**Zane**: Abby, have you had a chance to read the forms? My assistant says she hasn't gotten them. Sincerely, Zane.

We've moved from "Thanks, Zane" to "Sincerely, Zane." My guess is that his irritation level has risen. I can imagine him pacing through the office, running his hand through his hair the way Zoey does when she's mad. I like the mental image of him flustered, with perfectly mussed hair. I bite my lip, trying to shake that thought.

*He's Zoey's brother. Off-limits. No matter how hot he might look with ruffled hair and a scowl.* Why is it that scowly guys are so hot? But I know why: Mr. Darcy. That Jane Austen created generations of women who want growly, grumpy men who are hiding a gooey, romantic center.

Instead of searching up Mr. Darcy gifs (which is where my brain wants to go), I send him a meme of the kitten clinging to a branch with the words "hang in there" emblazoned on it.

His response comes just seconds later.

**Zane**: Do you know when you might have them done? Appreciatively, Zane.
**Abby**: My lawyer should be done looking at them within the hour.

We both must have the same kind of phone because I can see the dots as he types, then they disappear. As I watch them reappear and disappear, I zip through the forms, adding my signature and sending it back to his assistant.

**Zane**: Abby, this is a serious matter. If you're unable to complete simple forms, please recommend someone else. I'm only using you as a favor to Zoey.

*Ouch.*

As usual, I pushed things a little too far. I enjoy messing with him. I guess he doesn't feel the same way. Apparently, I'm just annoying. I'm more hurt than I should be.

"You okay?" Micah is suddenly standing over my desk, frowning at me. "You look upset."

"Fine," I say.

"If this is about that job, I'm really happy to take it off your hands."

"I've got it," I say. "Thanks."

Micah wanders off, probably in search of the coffee that is the only decent part of this office. And it's not even good coffee.

I type out a plain, boring text to Zane with stiff fingers. Then I delete it and tap out a message somewhere between boring and over the top.

**Abby**: Your assistant should have received it a few minutes ago. Signed, sealed, delivered.

I considered typing "I'm yours" at the end to complete the song lines. But I can't bring myself to do it. And I hate that I'm censoring myself for Zane. For anyone else, I would have written it.

I'm about to put away my phone when it buzzes in my hand.

**Zane**: Guess that means you're mine? ;) We're working through dinner over here. Want to come by when you're done at your office? Ordering from The Wall. Text me your order. Gratefully, Zane.

I can't help the huge grin that takes over my face. Zane

responded to my message with a joke! As for the idea of being *his* ... I have to fan my face with one of the folders on my desk.

I almost text Zoey to ask if she knew her brother actually had a sense of humor underneath his impenetrable shell. And if she told him the name of my favorite Asian takeout. In the end, it feels weird to talk to her about Zane.

Instead, I send Zane a gif of Tom Cruise from *Top Gun* giving a thumbs-up, along with a request for orange chicken, extra spicy, and fried rice.

The rest of my day, I find myself humming the Temptations under my breath. Five o'clock can't come fast enough.

## three

Zane

"Is Abby good at her job?" I demand when my sister finally answers her phone.

"The best," Zoey says without pause. "Why? I already told you this when I recommended her."

"I know, it's just—is she always so ..."

I fight for and don't find the right word for how distracted I've been by Abby this afternoon. I don't want to admit to my sister that the distraction is two-fold. Abby has made me nervous about her professionalism and qualifications with her silly texts, and then by ignoring me for a few hours.

But also? I've *always* been distracted by Abby. My sister's best friend is unapologetically herself—quirky and outspoken. She's also gorgeous yet doesn't flaunt the fact with heavy makeup or skintight clothing. There's a sense that she finds or creates joy wherever she goes, like she's wringing out the most she can from her life. It's a quality that has always reminded me of my mom.

Abby's texts have kept my mind from work all afternoon. And it's been the highlight of the year. Not an exaggeration, which is definitely a sign I'm working too much.

Zoey laughs. "Is she messing with you already? Abby's amazing at her job. She also likes to push buttons. I love her. But she can be … infuriating."

She definitely is that. But if I'm being honest, Abby is also a lot of things I would never admit to my twin.

Intriguing. Captivating. Surprising. Oddly *addictive*.

All afternoon I sat through meetings about venture capitalists with my phone in hand, checking for texts. I barely registered whatever Jack was saying about the potential new VCs. Thankfully, that's mostly his arena. I show up for the dinners, but he's the one with all the charm to win them over.

"What's she doing?" Zoey asks. "I'll help you decode Abby if you need me to."

"I've been waiting a few hours for her to sign the NDA and other paperwork I sent over."

"That doesn't sound like Abby. She's incredibly serious when it comes down to work. Are you sure she got the forms? Maybe you should double-check. When my firm used her, she had everything back to us in twenty minutes."

I run a hand through my hair, feeling strangely guilty for my response to Abby earlier.

"Zane?" Zoey says. "What did you do?"

Maybe with her twinsense, Zoey seems to suspect I've done something stupid. Which I have.

I roll a pen back and forth across my desk. "She did send back the forms, actually. Rather quickly. Too quickly." I pause. "So, we sent them again."

"Zane! Stop being an idiot. That's completely your fault. She's probably busy working now. Let me guess. Have you been bothering her all afternoon?"

"Not all afternoon."

"I swear to you, Zane. Don't make me regret sending her your way. She's the best. And she's my best friend. I don't want you mucking things up."

"I have no intention of—"

"And another thing." Zoey's really on a roll now. I love it when she gets like this, even if it's directed at me, because she looks just like Mom used to when she got passionate about something. It makes me feel like a piece of her is still around, living on through Zoey.

"Make sure you keep it *professional*, Zane."

"As opposed to ..." I just want to make her say it. My dating life is a constant point of contention between Zoey and me.

We may be alike in many ways, but not in our love lives. Ever the ice queen, Zoey doesn't date. Period. At least she hasn't since we graduated college two years ago. Like me, she's professionally driven. Unlike me, she doesn't see casual dating as a fun way of forgetting about work. I also suspect she's in love with her boss.

"As opposed to getting up close and personal with Abby, then dumping her. Your usual MO."

"You make it sound like I'm some kind of heart-breaking Casanova. I'm not sleeping around or leaving a trail of broken hearts behind."

"Riiiiight. You've probably dated every girl in the city at least once."

"Maybe twice," I deadpan. "But just *dated*."

"Uh-huh. Anyway," Zoey says, and I can imagine her waving a dismissive hand, just like Mom used to. I swear I feel my heart constrict just a little bit. I don't know why Mom's on my mind so much today. Loss is like that though. Even all these years later, sometimes the pain of it is like a sudden slap in the face.

"This is all a moot point. Abby wouldn't want to date you anyway."

"Ouch."

It really does hurt, though I'm sure Zoey wouldn't believe me. I'm not sure why she has such a low opinion of me. Sure, I go on a lot of dates. But what I said was true: I'm not sleeping around. Not even close.

Being part of a startup means that I don't have time for a relationship. For the past two years, I've hardly had time to eat. Dating casually is legitimately a way to enjoy someone else's company, to blow off steam. I'm a perfect gentleman, opening doors, paying the bill, being open with my expectations. It keeps things light.

And yeah, maybe it's also a way to keep my heart guarded. After losing Mom, I'm really not sure I can think about getting close to someone again. So, I don't.

"Sorry, little brother. Not every woman falls for your unique brand of charm."

"Haven't met one yet who doesn't." I smirk, knowing she'll hear it in my voice.

"You're gross. I'm going to go. Just remember what I said —be good to Abby. Even if she's not into you, I'm sure you could make her miserable in other ways. Don't."

"Anything for you, Zoey."

She makes another disgusted sound. "Oh, and I took the liberty of sending over the menu from The Wall. It's her favorite. The way to Abby's heart is through food."

The Wall is my favorite Asian fusion place. Abby's got good taste.

"I thought you didn't want me going anywhere near her heart."

"I don't. A well-fed Abby is a better-working Abby. Trust me. Keep her in coffee and food and she'll make all your tech problems go away. Oh! And chocolate. Or Twizzlers. If you could install a steady drip of caffeine and sugar, she'll be good to go. I've got to run, baby bro."

"You only have two minutes on me!" I yell, but she's already hung up.

Meanwhile, the only thing running through my mind right now is what she said about Abby not being interested in me. It bugs me. Not that I think I'm all that, no matter what I said to Zoey. I just don't like the idea that my sister can be Abby's best friend but doesn't think that I'm a good enough guy to deserve her.

*We'll see.*

*From: MiseryLovesCompany@drlove.advice*
*To: DrLove@drlove.advice*

Dear Dr. Love,

I've been crushing on a guy in my workplace for the past year, and we've been secretly seeing each other for a month. Our policy says that dating is allowed, but I think he's nervous about starting anything because he's up for a promotion.

I'm tired of watching the office floozies flirting with him and am ready to steak my claim! I'm not sure how much longer I can take the waiting.

Sincerely, Misery Loves Company

———

*From: DrLove@drlove.advice*
*To: MiseryLovesCompany@drlove.advice*

Dear Misery,

Real talk: your guy isn't nervous. He's not interested.

And, because you're writing to me, I know you're a smart woman who deserves better. Much better.

He's hiding behind the excuse of the workplace, and if you don't believe me, push the issue. I'm not normally into ultimatums, but in cases like this, sometimes you need to set a hard line to find out where you both stand.

    I'm sorry. You deserve better. Solidarity, sister.

    Miserable on your behalf,

    —Dr. Love

PS—Just for future reference, it's *stake* your claim, unless we're talking about prime rib.

    PPS—As women, let's stop calling each other floozies. It only makes it okay for guys to think that they can call us floozies. Respond with the movie I stole that quote from and I'll give you a gift card to the coffee shop of your choice.

---

*From: MiseryLovesCompany@drlove.advice*
*To: DrLove@drlove.advice*

Dear Dr. Love,

    *Mean Girls.* Duh.

    Also, you were so right. He was apparently seeing several other of the office … women. Dating in the workplace is okay. Two- and three-timing isn't.

    Guess who got the promotion?

    Thank you!!!

    Sincerely, Single and Promoted

# four

*Abby*

I KNOW I shouldn't keep trying to ruffle Zane. But I just can't seem to help it. I've still got on my *Stranger Things* tee, but I trade my jeans for some men's tweed pants that hang low on my hips and put my hair in braids. The finishing touch is a lollipop.

Which immediately draws Zane's critical gaze as he lets me into the office, which is a very basic and boring space in a strip shopping mall. I do my best to keep a blank face while his eyes zero in on my lips. I was trying to get under his skin but watching him look at my mouth gets under mine in a totally different way.

I pull the lollipop from my mouth and toss it in the nearest trash can. "Hey, Zane! Long time no see. I'm ready to get up and personal with your system."

I waggle my eyebrows at him and feel like I've won an

award when his cheeks flush. Make Zane Blush could be a great new game.

"Come on back," he says tersely. I follow him, noting the way the tight line of his shoulders matches Zoey's when she's stressed. Only, Zane's shoulders are much broader than I remember, even in his suit jacket.

Do men wear shoulder pads? I make a mental note to find an excuse to pat him down later and check. For *research purposes.*

Despite the lack of character, this place immediately draws me in with its frenetic energy. I thrive in work environments like this, which makes me feel a tug in my gut. I have not felt this in my current job in a long time.

I realize that Zane has been talking to me while I was busy checking the place out. I give him an apologetic look. "Sorry. Got distracted. This place has energy! I love it."

His assessing eyes sweep the room, but more like they're finding fault than appreciating it. "Thanks. We've worked hard. It'll be better once you fix what's wrong." He starts walking again, leading me toward a series of cubicles and desks in the back. I swear I hear him mutter, *"If* you can fix what's wrong."

Oh, he did *not* just throw the gauntlet down like that. Forget Make Zane Blush. The name of the game is Prove Zane Wrong. Now I wish I'd worn my headband with the unicorn horn, just so I could gloat that much more when I shatter his low opinion of me.

"This is where we have you set up," he says, extending an arm out to a utilitarian desk in a corner that has Ikea written all over it. Not literally, of course, but it has that spartan Swedish look. I don't mind though, because he has several monitors set up just as I specified in an email to his assistant. I'll probably end up doing a lot of work on my laptop, but I wanted to take the first deep dive into their system directly on their servers.

"Come to papa," I say, trailing a hand over the giant monitors. "Hello, darlings. Ready to go to battle?"

Zane coughs, sounding like he's covering up a laugh. The idea that I could make him laugh thrills me more than making him blush. Not as much as earning his respect though. Doing all three would be like the perfect trifecta.

"All the login information is inside the folder, along with an example of the problem we're running into."

I flip open the folder and begin reading, eager to get started.

Zane keeps standing there until I look up at him. "Anything else?"

"I also have food, as promised. I'll go grab it."

The office chair squeaks and has no back support. This will have to go. If I need more than one night's work, that is. My hope is to knock out their issue tonight and make Zane's jaw drop. Half the time when people hire me, they think it's some massive thing that takes me like five minutes to figure out. From the start, this doesn't seem like a big deal. I boot up the computer and get to work.

I barely look up when Zane comes back in with my order. "You can just set that on the desk," I tell him.

"Do you need anything else?" he asks.

I wave him away, already waist deep in code. "Nah. Thanks for the food. I'll eat when I come up for air."

"Want me to refrigerate it?"

"No, it's fine." He hesitates, and I'm again forced to look up at him. "What's the problem?"

"I just don't want you to get food poisoning. Food left out for more than a half hour—"

"Zane. I got this. Now, shoo."

"My office is just over there if you need me."

Finally, Zane leaves me alone, and I put on my earphones, cranking up Vivaldi. Sometimes I like techno or rock, but when I'm starting a project, Vivaldi has a great energy that gets me going.

Minutes or hours later, I push back from the desk, my neck and my jaw tight. I stand up, stretching. It's definitely been hours. The office still has a slight buzz but has cleared out a lot.

This bug is much larger in scope than what Zane described. Either he was way too optimistic, or he just doesn't know squat about the development side of things. I'm guessing it's the latter. To someone on the outside, the issue with their code would look like a glitch. But on the back end, it almost looks ... intentional. Which has the programmer in me all kinds of excited. I love a good challenge. And if someone is hacking or sabotaging the app, nothing would bring me more joy than catching the rat.

Snagging my takeout containers and a pair of chopsticks, I head out in search of Zane's office.

"You lost?" A guy with a mess of blond hair and an untucked button-down shirt intercepts me, grinning as he eyes my chest. I'm about to say something I'll probably regret later, when he says, "I love that show."

Oh, good. Not a creeper. Just another *Stranger Things* fan. "Me too. It's amazing."

"You'll probably think I'm a total dork, but I have the LEGO set of the Upside Down."

"Seriously? I wanted that, but they stopped selling it."

He and I grin at each other for a minute until I remember where I'm headed. Away from this adorable guy, who seems like my type but does nothing for me, and toward the man who definitely isn't my type and yet has my heart jumping like my nephews after I've given them Pop Rocks.

"Can you point me in the direction of Zane's office?"

He immediately looks nervous. "Zane? He doesn't like being disturbed." Lowering his voice, he says, "Plus, I think his flavor of the week just stopped in."

*Gross.* Zoey has always griped about Zane's dating habits, but I never really witnessed it.

I have no reason to be bothered or feel the odd prickle of jealousy that's skating over my skin. Zane is my best friend's brother and my sort of boss for now. That's it.

"It's cool. He's expecting me."

"Oh! You're the tech genius." He looks suddenly a little less enthused.

I do a little bow and almost drop my orange chicken. "That's me. I'm Abby."

"Josh. I'm on the programming team here if you need anything. I'm happy to help if you get stuck. I helped design what you're poking around at."

And there it is. Subtle, but it's a classic example of the delicate male ego after being threatened by a smart woman. If I give him five more minutes, he'll be mansplaining something I taught myself in high school.

"So … Zane's office?"

"Right." Josh leads me toward the back of the big open space to an office door that's open. He stops a good ten feet away and points. "Good luck. Call if you need help." He smiles again, reverting back to the nice-guy persona he started with.

"If you hear screaming, that will be Zane, not me." With a wink, I saunter away, stopping outside the open door when I hear voices.

"Zane, why? Things were going so well!" The whine in

32

this chick's voice is like nails on a chalkboard. This is the kind of woman Zane dates? Triple yuck. That thing that isn't jealousy swells inside me, like a balloon with too much helium.

The icky feeling in my stomach intensifies when I catch a glimpse of the woman inside the office. She's a model type, waify and gorgeous, stuffed into a dress that shows off her tiny waist and not-so-tiny, um, other assets.

Essentially, she's the antithesis of me. Just like the kinds of girls who spent middle and high school terrorizing me. Calling me the nerd girl (not inaccurate) or worse, pretending to be my friend so they could play some stupid prank and humiliate me.

I feel my neck getting hot.

*Nope. You're not still that girl. You've owned who you are and are unapologetically awesome. We're past this, Abs.*

My pep talk totally works. Maybe that's because in my head, I hear it in the voice of Agent Gibbs from *NCIS*. He's very convincing.

*Got it, Gibbs. I'm awesome.*

"What about the weekend trip?" she whines. "I was looking forward to alone time with you. Lots of alone time."

*Ew.* I don't want to imagine Zane having alone time. Not with this kind of woman anyway. Would I mind being alone in a room with him? No.

Other than the obvious fact that I'm not his type. *And he's not yours*, Gibbs reminds me.

*Right.*

"That was a work trip anyway," he says. "I'm sorry."

Without being able to see Zane from my position out here, I can just focus on the deep rumble of his voice.

The deep timbre of his voice goes right to my belly, launching dozens of flapping wings. I try to imagine them as bats, not butterflies, but for some reason, that launches my brain into picturing Zane as Batman. With that square jaw and serious broody thing he has going on, he'd make a delicious Bruce Wayne.

Not helping.

"I'm sorry," Zane says. "Things are just crazy with the launch. It's not a good time."

A pause. "Maybe after your launch? I can wait." The hopefulness in her voice is almost worse than the whine. I can smell the desperation and decide to do us all a favor.

I take a breath and walk right into his office. "Zane, I've finished looking around. It's not good."

His face snaps up to me. The woman in the chair across from his desk eyes me from head to toe, finally turning back to Zane as though she's dismissed me as a non-threat.

*Oh, honey. If you only knew.*

I don't take my eyes off Zane. And there's the look of shock I hoped for. Only, it's not as satisfying now because I can see thinly hidden panic.

"What?" he asks.

"Bugs. You've got bugs. An infestation."

The woman jumps to her feet. "Bugs? What—"

I turn to face her. "Have you spent a lot of time around him? I only ask because these kinds of bugs tend to multiply. It's not safe until I can do a full scrub and get them out. But it's a big job."

Zane jumps to his feet. "Abby! What are you—I don't—"

"It's fine. I can handle it. You just need to know what you're dealing with."

The woman shoots Zane a horrified look and practically runs out the door with her purse. As she brushes by me, I notice that there is a tiny dog in there. Poor guy.

I sit down in her empty chair and put my feet up on

Zane's desk, digging into my takeout. I didn't realize how hungry I am.

Zane slumps into his seat, running a hand over his hair, reminding me of Zoey. I love that they have all the same tells. It gives me an insider's guide to how he works.

"You're welcome," I say.

"What?"

I point my chopsticks to the door. "For getting rid of your first pest problem. That kind is particularly hard to eradicate. You've just got to cut and run, or they'll burrow deep."

That blush, which I can't help but find adorable on Zane's otherwise chiseled face, appears once more. It shows me his human side. I can't tell if he's furious with me, impressed, or something else.

Slow clapping from the doorway grabs my attention. I tilt my head back, looking at the man standing there from upside down.

Even from a funny angle, the man is gorgeous. Tall, which is something I love as a vertically challenged person. Dark jeans that hang off narrow hips, highlighting the broad chest stuffed into a blue polo.

"That was quite the performance," he says, eyes fixed on me. They're a deep brown, like a perfectly brewed shot of blond espresso. Nice. But I prefer Zane's deep blue.

The blood is all going to my head, so I sit back up. Zane glares, his gaze ping-ponging between me and the man, who has stepped inside the office. He leans against the wall, looking like he should be on a movie poster or something. That wicked grin has bad boy hero written all over it. A little too cocky for my taste.

"You've definitely traded up," he says to Zane.

My brain is trying to process his words but keeps returning an error message.

"Huh? Who's trading what now?" I ask.

The man laughs, but the sound doesn't have the same effect on me that Zane's deep voice does. In fact, the longer this new guy stands here, the more it highlights how much I prefer the man across the desk. The one who is all wrong for me. And who, according to his sister, wouldn't ever be interested.

"I never thought Zane would date someone so smart and sassy. I saw you come in, and her come scurrying out and put two and two together."

So many words.

So many flattering words.

I only wish that they were coming out of Zane's mouth.

"You've misunderstood," Zane says, just as I blurt out, "Your math is wrong."

"What?" the guy asks.

Now both men are staring at me and, holy mama, it's hard to formulate complete sentences.

I clear my throat and sit up, pulling my feet off Zane's desk. "Your math. You said you put two and two together, but you got a five. Or maybe more like a five thousand. Zane and I? We're not a couple." I laugh, thinking again of the vapid but gorgeous woman I just chased off. I can't even compete with that. "Totally not a couple."

Zane looks offended. Probably because I'm insulting his choice of women.

"Abby is our tech specialist," he practically growls. "We hired her to fix the glitch."

"Oh." The other guy points between us. "So, you two aren't ... together?"

I expect Zane to say something about how ridiculous the idea is. Or to laugh like I'm doing now, though it's more of a giggle. Because even if the mental image of Zane as Batman seems stuck in my brain, there is no way he would see me as his Vicky Vale. Or Catwoman. Or Rachel Dawes. Take your pick of franchises, and I don't hold up to a single one.

But Zane doesn't say anything. Surprising.

"Zane is my best friend's brother," I explain, like that puts the final word on it.

"Great. I'm Jack, since my partner here is too rude to introduce me."

Jack leans closer to shake my hand. A waft of cologne hits me. Nice, but a little too much. I pull my hand away just in time to sneeze.

"Bless you," Jack says, going back to his position on the wall.

"Back to the task at hand," Zane says, his voice clearly irritated. His blue eyes pin me in place. "Do we have bugs or not?"

"Oh, you've got bugs. Big ones. Much worse than what you thought."

His irritation gives way to a look of panic. He and Jack exchange a glance. Jack peels himself off the wall and perches on the edge of the desk.

"Is this going to delay our launch? It's in a month. How big is the scope of the problem?"

"You'll be fine," I say. "But you'll be seeing a lot more of me. Paying me a lot more too."

Jack turns to look at Zane. "Should we cancel the trip?"

"No," Zane says. "We need extra VCs even more now. It's going to be fine. Abby will take care of us. Right?"

He looks slightly desperate, and it's the most I've seen his tough shell crack. It softens me even more toward him.

I smile. "I've got you. Didn't Zoey tell you how amazing I am?" I flutter my lashes at him, happy to see him squirm in his seat.

"She did," Zane says.

"Great."

Jack eyes me with a look I don't know how to interpret, like he's sizing me up. It makes my fingers start to twitch.

Jack looks at Zane. "If you just got rid of Charlotte—"

"Chelsea."

"Right. Charlotte was the one from last month, I guess?" Jack asks. Zane doesn't answer.

I snort, and Jack flashes me a wide smile.

"If you got rid of *Chelsea*, you need a date for the weekend. And mine just fell through."

Zane's eyebrows shoot up. "What happened to Anna?"

Jack waves a hand. "Don't worry about it. Anyway. Are you taking Abby?"

I'm sure the look of shock on my face mirrors the one on Zane's.

"Taking me where?" I ask.

"No." Zane shakes his head firmly.

Jack and Zane ignore me. Their eyes are locked, like they are two bulls about to fight.

I wave my hand between them. "Hey—guys. Where are we going?"

"We're taking some of our VCs—the potential venture capitalists—on a trip," Zane answers, though he doesn't take his eyes off Jack.

"So, Abby isn't your date?" Jack asks.

"Abby is still right here, guys," I say.

Still, the two fighting males ignore me. Zane's nostrils flare. I would find it comical except I feel like somehow, I've become the red flag. I'm choking on the testosterone in here.

"Abby isn't my date," Zane says.

"So, you won't mind if I ask her." Jack's statement is a challenge.

The last few minutes are like staring at a cipher without the key. I'm following, but barely. I understand that there's some work trip with investors and these two do—or don't?—want me to go.

What I haven't figured out is the context here. Give me code any day of the week. It has discernible patterns. The pieces fit together into a whole. People? Way too unpredictable.

"Fine," Zane says, not looking at me though I know he has to feel my eyes on him.

With a wide smile that I somehow don't trust, Jack turns to me. Weirdly, the longer he stays in this office and the more words come out of his mouth, the less attractive he becomes.

"Would you like to be my date on a corporate retreat? Purely professional, of course."

I think he added that last bit because I was so busy peeling my jaw up off the floor.

"You want me to do what now?"

"We have a weekend with some potential VCs. They're bringing their wives, and we're bringing dates to even things out." With no warning, Jack steps into my space and takes my hand. I fight the urge to yank it back. "Would you be willing to be my date for this investor weekend?"

I'm staring into Jack's eyes. But I keep sneaking glances at Zane. There's this thing Zoey does when she's really upset, and Zane is doing it now. He looks like he sucked in a big breath and is holding it. His cheeks are red, and his eyes are practically bugging out of his head.

I narrow my eyes at Jack. "I'm not going to sleep with you."

Why this is the first thing that comes out of my mouth, I don't know. I want to be able to rewind the last few seconds and say something, anything, other than that.

Jack's eyes go wide, and then he squeezes my hand, barking out a laugh. "Noted. I like a woman who speaks her mind. So, what do you think?"

I think I want to fall right through the floor. Especially when I glance up and see Zane staring at me with the kind of eyes you usually see in movies with laser beams coming out of them. I fully expect to see steam shooting out of his ears.

What I don't understand is why he's upset. He doesn't want me, so I don't know why he cares if Jack asks me to be his date. But Zane definitely cares.

Here's the thing: this isn't my life.

I am never the girl in the center of male attention. Especially between two men who look like Jack and Zane. I'm the nerdy girl at the beginning of the movie, before the makeover. The difference is that I don't *want* the makeover. I tried being someone else, letting other people tell me how I should look. That one time was enough to prove that changing for someone else is never the right move. I'm me. And though I still battle insecurities from time to time, overall, I've come a long way.

Jack is still holding my hand, laughing a little, probably still at my idiotic sex remark. "Come on, Abby," Jack says. "Be my date. It will mean a free weekend at a resort, good food, and probably boring conversation with strangers."

"Abby needs to fix the glitch. She's going to be too busy," Zane says.

I raise one eyebrow at Zane. His lack of faith in my abilities is really ticking me off.

"Not so busy that I can't take a few days away."

"You promised me that we could launch on time," Zane says.

"And you will. I can work from anywhere. Even from a resort."

Zane and I are still glaring at each other when Jack drops my hand, looking disappointed. But it's the pleased look on Zane's face that has me speaking up.

"I'll go," I tell Jack.

A grin breaks over his face. "You will?"

"Yep."

I'm going to regret this. I already know. Because the tension and testosterone in this room is at unsafe levels, like a nuclear reactor with an unstable core. I also have zero desire to spend time rubbing elbows with investors' wives at some resort. I can already imagine Zoey's face when I tell her. She won't believe it.

And I really do have a lot of work to do if I want to work out the issue with their code. I'll probably spend the whole time ordering room service while my face is buried in a laptop.

But something about the angry set of Zane's face just pushes those buttons I have. The ones that make me feel like I have to prove myself. I have to. And I will.

"So, we're good?" Jack asks. "Abby, you'll come with me, and Zane, you can get another date?"

"Oh, Zane never has a problem getting dates," I say.

When did my mouth spring a leak? I can be a little too honest, a little too outspoken. But I don't usually broadcast every thought as soon as it comes into my head.

"It's no problem," Zane practically growls.

The low sound sends a little shiver through me.

"I'm looking forward to our weekend, Abby," Jack says, winking at me before ducking out the door.

I realize the second he's gone that I'm alone with a version of Zane who looks like Zoey the time she found out her boyfriend was cheating on her junior year. Essentially, his eyes scream murder. And I'm not exactly sure why. Is he upset with me or with Jack?

"So, um. I'm going to get back to work," I say, grabbing my takeout container. "Thanks again for dinner."

Zane just grunts, doing something on his phone.

At the door, I turn back. "So, when is this trip?"

"This weekend. I've already texted you an itinerary."

Of course, he has. Feeling a mix of confusion, disappointment, and irritation, I leave Zane and make my way back to my workspace. I may not understand what just went on in the office or what kind of trouble I'll be in this weekend, but for now, I can lose myself in what I do understand: code.

# five

## Zane

"I AM GOING to poison her coffee."

Zoey sighs and the sound comes through loud and clear via the Bluetooth connection in my Lexus.

"Then you probably shouldn't have admitted it out loud. Now I'll have to testify to it when I'm called under oath."

I squeeze the wheel tighter. I need to calm down, so I don't crash. Not that we've been moving more than five miles an hour since I left the Eck0 office. You'd think there'd be no traffic at nine o'clock at night, but something is always under construction in Austin.

"Do you mind telling me what she did to get you so riled up? And what you did to provoke her?"

"Provoke her? I did absolutely everything she asked for. The setup she wanted down to the letter." Not that Abby had asked for much. I'd expected a long list, but all she wanted was an empty desk with double monitors.

"Uh-huh," Zoey says. "And the food? You ordered from The Wall?"

"Yes," I seethe. Though Abby didn't start eating until it was already cold. Who eats food that's been sitting out more than an hour? Abby, that's who. I shudder just thinking about it.

"So, you did *nothing* to her?"

"No. Well …"

"Well, what?"

I finally make it to my neighborhood. Once I'm in the driveway of the small home I purchased a year ago, I turn off the engine and just sit, looking at the dark windows. It's a house that screams settling down with a wife and kids. In fact, I'm the only single guy in the whole neighborhood. Every other house has swings or bicycles out front. And then there's me: the single guy who has barely furnished the place and is never home. I'm not sure what I was thinking, buying a place like this. It only highlights what I don't have. And what I'm not sure I really want.

"I didn't *do* anything, but Abby did walk in on me trying to break it off with Chelsea."

"Was she the redhead?"

"No. The blonde."

"Huh. I didn't know about a blonde."

"We only went on two dates," I say.

"Ah. So, your latest two-date girl stops by the office, and Abby did what?"

She actually did me a favor, if I'm being honest. I catch myself smiling as I think of Chelsea practically sprinting from my office with her purse-dog. If I had seen the dog first, I wouldn't have gone on even one date with Chelsea. Call me picky, but dogs in purses is a deal-breaker.

"Hello? Zane? You still there?"

"Sorry. I'm here. It's fine. I'll handle Abby. She isn't the problem. It's me."

I can almost hear the sound of Zoey's jaw dropping. "Hang on. Did you just admit that you're the problem?"

I groan. "I shouldn't have called you."

"Don't hang up. I'm sorry for giving you a hard time. Look, I knew it was risky recommending Abby. She likes getting under my skin, so I should have known she'd do the same to you. But she really and truly is the best."

This makes me feel a little better. Both about Abby's ability to fix whatever's going on with our app and website, and that it's not just me. If she does this to Zoey too, then I feel a little honored. Like I've made it past some kind of approval process.

"Any tips? Besides keeping her fed and full of caffeine?" I ask. "Don't keep her up past midnight? Or maybe it was don't feed her past midnight."

Zoey laughs. "Aren't you just full of surprises! Admitting something is your fault, asking for help, and now making jokes. If I didn't know any better, I'd say Abby is having a good influence on you."

Is she? I'm not sure any of those are good things. I know what Dad would say about all three.

"And if you're thinking about Dad—"

"How do you *do* that?"

"We're twins. And even if we were just regular brother and sister, we grew up in the same house. We have shared experiences. And I can almost hear Dad telling you to be strong, to be a man. Not to ask questions, not to ask for help, and not to show weakness."

I close my eyes. Dad isn't a bad guy. Truly. He's just a military man who had to deal with raising two kids alone when his wife died in a car accident while they were in high school. The only way he knew how to deal was with more rules. The laughter in our house was buried right next to Mom. He did his best, but it's like the scales tipped, forcing me and Zoey into being just as structured as Dad.

We've talked about this, after we were both in college, out of the house where it felt like we had a little breathing room. And even though we'd both like to loosen up a bit, it feels like an impossible task sometimes. How loose is too loose? What does balance look like? Structure and rules feel safe.

Right now, this whole conversation feels unsafe. I steer us right back into the shallow water. "Yes, Zo. I'm asking you for help. Mark this day on your planner."

"Already putting down a gold star. Okay, crash course in handling Abby. First, I gave up fighting the force that is Abby. She's Abby and she isn't changing. It took me the first two years of college to figure that out. Now, I appreciate her quirks. And I know she's usually looking for a reaction when she pushes my buttons, so I don't give her one."

"Okay. I can try that." Abby definitely pushed all my buttons today. She was like that kid who gets on the elevator and uses both hands to hit the button to stop on every floor. And I'm embarrassed at how effective it was.

"Second, realize that under her crunchy outside, she's got a soft center."

Zoey pauses, and somehow, I know what she's going to say next. There's one thing we always describe that way. I prepare myself by bracing my head against the steering wheel and squeezing my eyes shut.

"Just like Mom's chocolate crunch cookies."

My mouth practically waters at the memory, even as my chest burns. Mom never wrote down her secret recipe, something Zoey and I realized the first time we decided to make a batch after she died. We were sophomores in high school, and I remember finding Zoey crying on the kitchen floor, Mom's recipe cards spread all around her on the tile. The sight of my sister's tears and Mom's handwriting on the cards was like a knife to my gut.

"It's not here," she had said. "Mom's the only one who knew the recipe."

I had wrapped my arms around her, and we cried together. Not over the cookies. Okay, maybe one or two tears were because of the cookies. They were really *that* good. But more because we wouldn't walk into our house, smelling that delicious smell again. The scent that told us Mom was home, and she had been baking.

I lean back, blowing out a steady breath. "I miss her," I say, trying to wrangle the emotion that's rising up, threatening to cut off my airways.

"Me too, Z."

For a few minutes, we sit like this. The perfect kind of silence, one that says so much without either of us needing to speak.

Finally, Zoey clears her throat. "So, you've got a handle on Abby?"

"I've passed Abby 101."

"Passed?" Zoey laughs. "No. You just crammed before the final, which is apparently this weekend. How did she get roped into this VC thing anyway?"

I groan. Abby must have mentioned it to my sister already. *What else did she say? Specifically, what did she say about me?*

"Jack," I tell her. "That's how."

"Ohhh." Zoey's tone is the one she'd use if you told her that racoons tore up a bag of trash all over the back patio. "Say no more."

Zoey isn't Jack's biggest fan. And neither am I, if we're

being honest. On paper, he is the perfect partner for the startup in a lot of ways. But the more time I spend with him, the less I like him. And the more I regret being tethered to him. He's too slick, too smooth, and I'm not sure I really trust him.

Especially after the time he hit on Zoey, making the kinds of comments you never want to make to a girl's brother. If we hadn't already started Eck0, I never would have asked him to partner with me.

After today? I like him even less.

"Don't let Jack hurt Abby," Zoey warns.

Just the thought has my blood pressure rising. I don't even want to think about Jack and Abby. Even if this weekend is about wooing VCs, not women, I hate thinking of Abby as his date. I barely restrained myself from hopping across the desk, knocking Jack out of the way, and asking Abby myself.

*It's just because you feel protective*, I tell myself. *She's your sister's friend, so naturally, you want to take care of her like you do Zoey.*

That explanation is starting to feel really thin. The truth is that I liked the idea of Abby as my date for the weekend. But she's Zoey's best friend. I can't just date her casually, then move on. I'm not sure where that leaves things.

"This isn't even like a real date. It's a business thing," I tell Zoey and myself.

"Uh-huh. And you think Jack wasn't planning on more than business with whomever he brings?"

She's right. And that protective anger and weird feeling that can only be jealousy shoots right back up my spine. I'm ready to punch Jack again for asking Abby right in front of me.

*You could have asked her, coward.*

Why didn't I? I make a mental list of reasons. She's my twin's best friend, which could be complicated. She pushes my buttons. And she's got all the manners of a feral cat, putting her feet up on my desk, eating food that's been sitting out, scaring off the girl I had been dating. She wears T-shirts about TV shows and has pink hair.

The list really falls apart when I have to admit that I like Abby's pink hair. And her pink lips that match. I actually don't even mind whatever weird pants she was wearing today, because the confidence she wore drew all my attention.

And as much as Abby got under my skin today, it's the first real thing I've felt in a long time. I almost don't recognize what it's like to feel anything other than stress.

"I'll watch out for her. But since Jack asked her, I find myself in need of a date. Do you think—"

"No. I am not setting you up with one of my friends. Not a chance."

"But it really is just a business thing. Whoever comes will get to eat fancy food and go to the spa. For free. Am I really such bad company?"

"You're amazing. But I would never set you up with someone I like. I know how that would end."

"We've talked about this. I'm not ready to settle down, so I'm just dating casually."

"I know what dating casually means, Zane."

"I promise it's not like that."

"We are not going down this road. What happens in Zane's pants stays in Zane's pants."

I can't help but laugh. "Nothing is happening in my pants."

"Lalalala! Can't hear you! Byyyeee!"

"Okay, okay. I'm done now. Zoey?" I think for a second

she's hung up.

"Just stay out of Abby's pants."

"ZOEY!"

She's laughing again, and despite how much I'm hating our current topic of conversation, I love to hear her laugh. She doesn't do it enough. Neither do I.

"Are you ever going to settle down, little brother?"

"Are you?"

"Sure," Zoey says. "Sometime."

"Same. But I'm okay with casual. For now."

I look at my dark house, wondering how long "for now" is going to last. I'm not happy. I can recognize this. And yet, the idea of changing, of looking for something outside of the safe square I've drawn for myself feels like walking across one of those bridges with the glass bottoms.

"Fine. Just remember what I said. Abby seems tougher than she is. And she's dang good at her job, so trust her. I'd like for this to end with my two most important relationships still intact."

"Aw, I'm one of your most important relationships?" I tease, knowing full well that Zoey and I are still great friends. Even if we do have a few hard lines drawn about the things we don't talk about. As far as I'm concerned, Zoey comes fully equipped with some kind of protective garments that will be unlocked on her wedding night. She ends all her dates with handshakes or kisses on the cheek.

"Believe it, little bro. You and Abby are my two closest friends. Don't jack it up. Separate the work and the personal."

I laugh. "Yeah, like you do with your boss?"

Her voice goes shrill, the way it always does when she's lying. "I do not have—"

"Night, Zoey!"

I disconnect the call, shaking my head. My sister shares the same stubborn streak I do, so I'm not surprised on my way inside the house when she blows my phone up with texts. I don't need to read them to know she's denying that anything is going on with her and her boss.

I grab a glass of water, using one of the three glasses I own, and lean back against the counter. I text back one line: *methinks the lady doth protest too much.*

**Zoey**: Shakespeare is going to rise up out of the grave and et tu, Brute your flabby butt for poorly misusing his quote.
**Zane**: My butt isn't flabby anymore. Would you like me to send a pic of how it looks in my suit pants? You can share it with your friends when you ask if they'll go on my corporate trip. -Zane
**Zoey**: Blocked. You are blocked. Forget everything I said about you being important. You are dead to me.
**Zoey**: Also. Do you even know how to text pictures?

I'm standing in the dark kitchen, grinning down at my phone when another text pops up. One that makes my heart start revving like an engine at the starting line.

**Abby**: I had fun working for you today. Your office has a great vibe. Consider me impressed, Z.

I feel a warmth in my chest at her words and start to type out a thanks. It shouldn't make me so happy that she uses the same nickname that Zoey does. Before I can manage a nice reply, another one comes through.

**Abby**: Except for the stiff in the suit. That guy needs a vacation.

That warmth bleeds right into something more like irritation. I'm the only guy in the office who wears a suit. Even Jack dresses up only when we're doing important investor meetings or dinners. I've always heard the echo of the phrase "dress for the job you want, not the one you have." We may be a startup, but I see Eck0 going places. Topping Forbes and Fortune 500 lists.

Sue me if I dress the part. I love wearing a good suit. And if I'm not wrong, I saw Abby eyeing me today. I suspect that she liked the way it looked as well.

I try to think of an appropriate response. By the time I've changed and left my sparsely decorated house for the garage where I've set up a home gym, I've still got no smart reply.

And with Abby, I feel like I need to up my texting game. Be sarcastic and funny. Use gifs or memes appropriately. Stop signing my name like I'm a hundred years old.

Between sets, I send one line. It's lame, but maybe that's just me.

**Zane**: Thanks for all the hard work today, Abs. -Z

Or was that too personal? Why did I call her by the nickname I've heard Zoey use? I hate that I'm overthinking text messages.

I see the little dots as she types something, but I shut off my phone. Because even though I know better, everything Abby does draw a reaction from me. The kinds of reactions I'm starting to have are far from irritated. They're on the opposite end of the spectrum, and that can't be good.

When I'm going to bed, I break down and check my phone. And when there's not a message from Abby, I feel far more disappointed than I should.

# dear dr. love

*From: DisappointedinDenver@drlove.advice*
*To: DrLove@drlove.advice*

Dear Dr. Love,

I'm a newlywed and was expecting a life of bliss. Or, at least, that honeymoon period everyone talks about.

Instead, my husband leaves his clothes all over the house, dumps dirty dishes in the sink, and thinks passing gas at the dinner table is an athletic event, and he's going for gold.

How can I find the married life I was hoping for?

Sincerely,
Disappointed

---

*From: DrLove@drlove.advice*
*To: DisappointedinDenver@drlove.advice*

Dear Disappointed,

Lower your expectations.

Or get a dog. They're easier to train and usually pass gas under the table.

The best option, and the one the fewest people seem to

try, is sitting down together, talking through your expectations, and trying to see where you can each give a little.

Best of luck!

—Dr. Love

## six

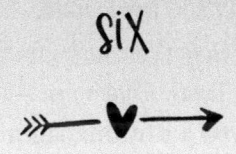

*Abby*

"I can't do it," I say, flopping back dramatically on my bed. "You'll have to go in my place."

"And spend the weekend on a double date with my brother? Pass."

I roll over and prop my head on my hand. "It's not like you'll be dating him."

"No. I'd be with Jack. And as gross as dating my brother would be, dating Jack would be worse."

"Is Jack really so bad?" I ask, the nerves in my belly feeling like a pit of vipers.

All week while working long days at my day job and longer nights at Zane's office, the dread has been growing. I've tried to really bury myself in work, which isn't hard, considering that there is definitely someone messing with the coding on the app. And they're good. Not as good as me but giving me a run for my money. It's no wonder Josh and the other tech people on his team can't figure it out. Josh has offered his help more than once, I'm sure not thrilled that I've been called in to clean up what he couldn't. He's still friendly, but I can sense the territorial feelings he tries to hide.

And speaking of hiding feelings, the sleepy little crush on Zane I've kept for years like a tiny ember, has grown into a fire you could probably see from space.

*There's the Atlantic Ocean, the lush green of North America, and that red pulsing thing in Texas? That's just Abby's crush on Zane.*

It would have stayed a tiny, manageable flame if he hadn't started being so *nice*. When I came in Tuesday, he'd put a container of Twizzlers on my desk. Wednesday, my squeaky chair had been replaced by an ergonomic version that I know wasn't cheap. It wasn't so much the expense of the chair, but the fact that he noticed my discomfort and fixed it without being asked. Last night he had dinner meetings and I didn't see him. I felt like a little kid whose lollipop was stolen. Pouty, sullen, and irrationally upset. That is, until he had a courier deliver me a flat white, my favorite coffee drink.

He was still stiff, too formal, and way too easily rattled by me in person. I don't know quite how to read the kind gestures, other than to assume Zoey has told him how to keep me happy. But a part of me gets totally giddy with every new thoughtful gesture. Now that we'll be getting out of the office for two days ... I don't know what to expect from him. I'm nervous enough about that. Zoey isn't making things better talking about Jack.

Zoey turns to me and, seeing the expression on my face, sits down next to me on the bed. "You'll be fine. I told Zane to watch out for you."

I blink at her for half a second. "You told Zane to watch

out for me? Like you told him to keep me supplied in food and caffeine this week?"

Her guilty look says it all. The coffee, the Twizzlers, the chair—he did it all as a favor to Zoey. Of course, he did. Why else would Zane be so nice to me? The disappointment in my belly eclipses the worry I had before about spending the weekend as Jack's date.

"I just gave Zane some pointers," Zoey says.

"Ugh. Do you know how embarrassing this is? It's like parents leaving specific notes for the babysitter on how to handle their problem child."

"You're not a problem child. You're doing Zane a big favor, Abby."

"Thanks, I guess?"

I scold whatever wayward part of me has gotten all worked up over my best friend's twin.

*Down, girl! Bad Abby! No crushing on Zane. NO.*

But whatever part of my subconscious starts feeling all fluttery when I hear his voice or see his face needs to go to obedience school. She's not listening, and still wants to jump up on the furniture and chase cars.

Hopefully I can keep Zoey from noticing. I can never admit my feelings to her. She would hold it over my head for the rest of our lives. Worse, she'd feel sorry for me. I mean, she already laughed at the idea of me and Zane dating. That should have been enough to warn me off.

Zoey makes a face. "I might have also asked Zane not to let Jack deflower you."

I stop breathing completely. I can feel the blush starting at the middle of my chest, zooming up to my cheeks and ears.

"Zoey. Did you tell your brother, the one I'm about to

spend the weekend with, the one who dates anything with a C-cup and legs, not to let his business partner *deflower me?*"

"Not in those exact words. But basically."

I fall back on the bed, groaning. Something stabs me in the temple, and I toss an underwire bra across the room. "Tell me again that I shouldn't feel like a child that you've asked your brother to babysit?"

Zoey stands up and begins going through my clothes again. "Stop wallowing. You're being dramatic. Now, I'm picking out your clothes, ironing, and helping you pack."

"Ironing?" I don't think I've looked at an iron in the last, oh, I don't know—ten years? "Is that something people still do?"

"Yes. Many of us iron."

I sit up, watching Zoey move the hangers around in my closet. "I don't even have the kinds of clothes that need ironing."

Though I'm not opposed to skirts and dresses, I tend to wear more funky, relaxed clothes. Nothing like the button-up white collared shirt Zoey put on *after* changing out of her suit today. This is Zoey's version of casual: khaki pants and a pressed white blouse. My casual is cutoffs I made myself from a pair of faded jeans and a ribbed black tank top.

"We can mix and match from Sam's closet if need be."

Sam is the only one in the house who's vertically challenged like me and somewhat close in size. Her style is a few steps down from Zoey's business and business casual, but still more Ann Taylor, where I'm more likely to shop in Forever 21. I feel like the *forever* in the name gives me the green light to shop there. I can forever pretend I'm still twenty-one, even if everyone else in the store is a teenager. Or a teenager's mom.

"Do you know anything about these VCs or their wives?"

Zoey's question drags me back to my present dilemma and my dread. Because not only am I spending the weekend with my flaming crush and his slimy partner, but two strangers and their wives. At a resort spa. There is not one thing about this weekend that feels comfortable to me.

I shake my head. "But I'm guessing that they have money, since Jack and Zane are courting them at a five-star resort. Which means they're likely older and a few degrees more fancy than yours truly."

Zoey hums a response, pulls a blue shirt from the closet, tossing it next to me. I play with the buttons, that nervous feeling squirming around in my stomach again.

"You're not going to make me pretend to be someone more ... normal, are you?"

Zoey stops what she's doing and spins to face me. Her eyes flash, and I know she knows exactly what I'm thinking about. She's the only one other than my parents or brother who knows exactly why this question matters to me. After so many years, I wish that my past didn't still surface every now and then, bringing all my self-consciousness up from the depths with it.

Touching my hand, Zoey says, "Normal isn't a thing. You're *you*. Don't change your style for anyone, Abs. You're perfect just the way you are."

I know this. I do.

Normally, I'm self-assured, full of swagger, not insecure and needy. But this weekend is so far out of my comfort zone that it throws me back a bit, back to the Past Abby who wasn't sure about anything. Most of all, herself.

I nod, giving Zoey a lopsided grin, and we both pretend like my eyes aren't wet.

The first sign that this weekend is going to be worse than I expected is Zane's date. And that's saying something, considering I had very low expectations to begin with.

"I get carsick," the leggy brunette says, cocking a hip and fluttering her eyelash extensions at Zane.

The only thing keeping me from becoming the regular kind of sick is that Zane doesn't seem impressed with her whole schtick. He hasn't even sneaked a peek at the impressive top half of her, which is shocking since she's been aiming those things at him since she stepped out of her car in cowboy boots, a short skirt, and a scrap of material posing as a top. Even Jack has had a hard time keeping his eyes away. Not surprising. Also not cool.

Two points for Zane.

My best friend's twin (always good to remind myself of that fact) looks downright irritated as he glances at me.

Oh. *Oh!* It's not that he isn't charmed by Charla's act. He's irritated because that means he has to sit in back with *me*. Not with his weekend date. Fantastic.

"Great. Hop up front, Charla," Jack says with a grin, opening the passenger door for her. He clearly doesn't mind the seat switch.

If I was waiting for either guy to open my door, they might have left me in the parking lot. Everyone already has their seat belts on by the time I climb into the tiny back seat of Jack's car. I don't know cars, but the engine purrs and it's all shiny outside, with soft leather inside.

"So many buttons!" Charla giggles, and I gag a little as Jack helps her with her seat belt.

*What kind of grown woman needs help buckling up?* My youngest nephew can strap himself into his booster seat, and he's six.

I look over at Zane, to see how he's taking the blatant

flirting in the front, but he's turned so far toward the window that I can only see the back of his head. I look at the small, white scar along his hairline. Zoey told me once it was from a car accident but never gave me the details. I'm one of those people who thinks scars give us character. They tell our stories. Maybe I can break up the awkward tension back here with swapping stories.

Without really thinking about it, I trace my finger along the line of Zane's scar. He practically jumps out of his seat, slapping my hand away.

"What?" he snaps.

"Whoa. Sorry. I was just wondering about your scar. Zoey said it was from a car accident?"

Zane's eyes go wide, but a moment later, he's fully under control again. Almost. There's a wildness to his gaze still that tells me this scar has to do with something really big. I wish Zoey had warned me. I like getting under his skin, but this isn't annoyance. It's pain. I recognize it well.

"Yes. It was a car accident."

He spins back to the window again, and I watch the tendons and muscles flexing in his neck. I shouldn't be thinking about how hot Zane's neck is when he's upset, but anything is better than thinking about the fact that I just brought up something painful from his past. People might think that I march to the beat of my own drumline and all that, not caring what people think, but the truth is I do care. A lot.

"What kind of music should we listen to?" Jack asks cheerfully, oblivious to the cloud of awkwardness hanging over the back seat. "Anything but—"

"Country!" Charla says, and I swear I hear three matching groans. Charla does not seem to hear them, or maybe she doesn't care, because moments later, the car is filled with someone crooning about love lost in a field and something about bottles of Bud.

Zane still has his head glued to the view outside the window as we make our way slowly out of Austin in the Friday afternoon traffic. I can't bear the thought that I upset him by casually bringing up something painful in his past. I've got a whole dungeon full of those memories, and I hate when one manages to escape.

"Zane?" I whisper. There's a slight movement in his shoulders, but he doesn't turn or answer.

Like I'm trying to tame a wild animal, I cautiously extend my arm and brush my fingers along his shoulder. He stiffens but doesn't pull away. I give his shoulder a little squeeze, trying not to think about how nice and firm his muscles are.

When I haven't let him go after a few beats, Zane turns slightly. Just enough for me to notice how the blue in his eyes is the same bright color of the endless sky outside.

"I'm sorry," I whisper. He nods, so I lick my lips and continue. "I didn't mean to pry. I didn't know."

Zane swallows, and I've never seen him so vulnerable. I've never seen him vulnerable, period. It turns something in my heart.

My hand is still on his shoulder, and I loosen my grip just slightly. The music—and Charla's singing—is loud, so I incline my head toward Zane.

"You see this one?" I point to a scar on my cheek, watching as his eyes track the motion. I know my face flushes. I can't help it; I hate the round, white scar.

Taking a breath, I continue, lowering my voice a little. "I had terrible acne as a teenager. My face looked like it had been put through a meat grinder. This was from a zit that got infected. Then it turned into staph. I ended up in the hospital for two days."

Zane's eyes are locked on mine, that deep blue gaze mesmerizing. They are an infinity pool, and I want to dive in.

"Do you know how embarrassing it is when someone asks about my scar, and I have to tell them it's from a pimple?" I swallow. Sometimes, truth-telling is hard work. "I used to wear heavy makeup to cover the acne, to cover this scar. I'm not hiding anymore."

With that, I let my hand drop. I don't want Zane to feel the way it's trembling. I've already exposed myself enough.

I didn't expect Zane to say anything. I wasn't asking for that. When his lips part to speak, the breath stills in my lungs.

Before he can say a word, Charla whips her head around between the two front seats.

"Don't worry. The scar is hardly noticeable."

Does the woman have bat ears to go along with her gravity-defying breasts? I had been whispering back here. *Whispering.*

"I've got some amazing concealer I'll let you try when we get to the resort," Charla says.

"Uh-huh." Nope. No way are we leveling up to the kinds of acquaintances who swap concealer. The joke will be on her when she realizes I don't have concealer to swap. Moisturizer, mascara and lip gloss, baby. That's my beauty routine.

But she's still going. "It's made from baby elephant bone marrow. Totally magical. As long as you don't think about the poor baby elephants."

Charla laughs, and I'm honestly wondering if she has a soul.

How could you *not* think about the baby elephants? Baby elephants are going to haunt my dreams.

Hannibal Lecter's creepy face invades my mind. *Can you hear the baby elephants screaming, Clarice?*

*It's Abby. But yes. Yes, I can.*

Charla has to be joking. *Dumbo.* She wants to rub Dumbo's bone marrow on my *face.*

She definitely has no soul. When she reaches back to grab my hand, I consider opening my door and doing a barrel roll right out onto the highway.

"We're going to be best friends by the end of this weekend. I can just tell. I'm so glad we're sharing a room!"

*Sharing a room?*

Charla squeals, then goes right back to butchering country songs, like she hadn't just confessed to murdering baby elephants for the sake of beauty and then dropped a very unpleasant bomb in my lap. One I hope to diffuse ASAP.

Slowly, so as not to pull the wrong wire, I turn back to Zane. Before I even speak, I know the answer to my question.

"Am I sharing a room with her?" I hiss.

Zane has a miserable look on his face. Forget the poor-Zane act, the whole I-have-painful-memories Zane. He is going to die.

"It was that or stay with Jack. We only booked two rooms."

And boom goes the dynamite.

## seven

*Abby*

I MANAGE NOT to murder Zane, though I do text Zoey to ask if she'd still be my friend if her brother mysteriously didn't make it home from this weekend.

So far, she hasn't responded.

The resort is nice enough to distract me from my homicidal thoughts, at least for a few minutes. As I wait in the lobby for Jack to straighten out some issues with our reservation, I'm reading about the amenities. It has two spas—because one isn't enough?—and a gorgeous outside with several pools, hot tubs, and a lazy river. There are also three restaurants and two coffee bars. Not to mention a handful of actual bars, which I may frequent, depending on how this weekend goes.

"Here." Zane nudges a coffee cup toward me. "It's a flat white."

Taking it doesn't mean I'm giving in. It just means I need

caffeine. I nod and take it from his hands, careful not to touch his fingers. I'm too on edge for that kind of contact right now.

"Thank you. A peace offering?"

"An apology," Zane says, smoothing his hand through his hair. "I'm sorry you got roped into this. Truly, I am."

I take a sip of my coffee, which is excellent. "You'll need to do more than this."

"I know. Spa treatments. Room service. Unlimited flat whites. Whatever."

"You think you can buy me off? I'm not that kind of girl." I give him the tiniest smile, my own version of a peace offering.

"I definitely don't think you're that kind of girl."

Zane slides his hands into his pockets, I suspect because he's trying not to run his hands through his hair again. Though I saw him in casual clothes plenty during college, I've gotten so used to seeing him in a suit this week that Zane in dark jeans and a polo shirt throws me off.

Charla and Jack join us, looking a little too cozy. Not that I'm mad about it. Honestly, imagining her with Zane makes me feel all squirmy and dirty. Even more than thinking about me and Jack. Yuck.

"You ready, roomie?" Charla links her arm through mine. "This is going to be so fun! But we only have an hour before dinner. I hope you'll let me do your makeup!"

Forget wanting to kill Zane for making me share a room with Charla. I need him to save me from what I'm sure will be an hour of torture, only to be followed by a painful dinner with the investors and their wives.

I'd much rather skip out on all of the festivities to geek out over the code. More specifically, trying to find out who is manipulating it. I feel like I'm playing chess, only whoever

I'm playing against doesn't know that another person has entered the game. I'm careful, biding my time, searching for clues and making my plan. That sounds like a whole heck of a lot more fun than a snooty dinner.

Even if dinner has the benefit of more time with Zane.

"Let's go!" Charla drags me by the arm and I barely manage to get my bags while juggling my flat white.

Zane shoots me another apologetic look, which I think will only be one of many this weekend.

He's going to owe me a lifetime of flat whites. And I rather like the idea of collecting.

---

"See? I told you this stuff was great," Charla says.

I've officially sold my soul. Because whatever Charla put on my face *is* amazing and just as magical as she said. I might even say that it's worth the deaths of however many baby elephants it took. (I'm still choosing to believe that's a lie.)

My skin looks radiant. Dewy. Glowing.

The rest of my makeup isn't so bad either. I refused to let Charla do my makeup for me, but I did allow her to stand over my shoulder, barking directions. She even talked me through doing winged liner using a random liquid eyeliner I found in the bottom of my travel makeup kit. Come to think of it, Zoey probably stuffed it in there.

Even my hair looks amazing in soft curls around my shoulders. I thought maybe Charla might suggest that I hide the pink ends, tucking them into an updo, but Charla said I should showcase them.

Anyway, the end result is that I feel like a Hollywood starlet, about to walk the red carpet on the arm of an A-list actor.

Except that actor tonight is supposed to be Jack. Blech.

Charla points to my cheek, where the round scar is just visible. "I heard what you said about not hiding anymore. I mean, I doubt anyone would notice if you didn't point it out. But still. I admire your confidence in yourself."

I could tell her how much work it took to get here. How hard I fought to have the confidence to walk into a room, without wondering if every single person was judging me for what I wore and who I was. Actually, I still wonder that sometimes. Overall, I *am* confident. I know who I am, and I feel safe being myself. But insecurities never fully disappear. Now, I'm just better at shutting them down. It's work, though.

But I'm not about to correct Charla and pry open the door to my past humiliations. Even though she's still going on.

"I love that you're not trying to impress anyone. You're so sure of yourself. And you're gorgeous, with a style that's all your own."

She's being so ... nice. I feel instantly guilty for all the not-so-nice thoughts I've had about her. My opinion of Charla has changed in the last hour. Maybe she loves country, can't sing worth squat, and has breasts that could double as weapons, but she's actually very kind.

"Thanks. You are a great beauty coach," I tell her. "Is this what you do for a living? Makeup and hair?" I'm asking out of curiosity and also so I can book an appointment for a trim when I get back.

Charla laughs, her nose crinkling adorably as she does. "I wish. I'm a CPA."

My mouth goes dry. "A CPA?"

"Surprised?"

"I, uh ..." There is no way to even hide my shock. I think I've set women back decades with my assumptions about Charla based on how she dresses and the fact that she

68

possesses the effervescent brightness of a middle school cheerleader. You know, before high school when they get jaded with life.

"I'm sorry. I shouldn't be surprised. I know better than to make assumptions about people. Truly. That was dumb of me. And shallow."

Waving a hand, Charla picks up a makeup brush and goes to work on her cheeks, leaning close to me as she does. Her hair tickles my shoulder. "Don't worry about it. Happens all the time. I work with numbers all day. Pays well but boring as all get-out. I let loose when I'm not on the clock. I'm bright and bubbly, which people tend to think means I'm stupid."

"You are anything but stupid. You're full of surprises," I tell her, standing so I can slip on my heels.

Another surprise is the tasteful, conservative black dress Charla is wearing. Her chest is modestly covered, and the hemline reaches her knees. She's wearing pearls. *Pearls.*

All of which makes my shorter black dress with a studded belt and matching choker seem slightly scandalous. We definitely don't seem like we're going to the same dinner.

Did a sinkhole just open up in the floor? Because I think my stomach just plunged into it.

Forget my confidence that Charla just admired. I've lost it completely.

I need to get away from the hot lights in front of the mirror. Fanning my face, I walk over to the bed and begin digging through my purse. Not like I'm going to find any bravery in there to combat the intense bout of nerves.

Room service delivers wine, right? Because I'm seriously considering locking myself in the bathroom for the rest of the night. Me and the giant jacuzzi tub can have our own date.

Actually, I'll change the wine order for champagne. Bubbles and bubbly. Perfect.

*Ab-by.* Agent Gibbs to the rescue. *This isn't you anymore.*

With a few deep breaths and some mental gymnastics, I agree with my inner Gibbs. This isn't me. My insecurities don't own me. The tightness in my chest loosens as Charla heads for the door.

"It's time." Giving me a last appraising glance, she says, "You're going to blow Jack away."

But I don't care about Jack. And it's not like I can tell Charla that I'm more concerned about what *her* date thinks about me. I grab my purse and flash her a smile that's a total lie.

"Let's go impress some investors' wives."

# dear dr. love

*From: JustaGuy@drlove.advice*
*To: DrLove@drlove.advice*

Dear Dr. Love,

My girlfriend keeps hinting about getting engaged. What she doesn't know is that I've been saving for her dream ring and am almost there.

The problem is that all the nagging is making me think twice. Is she going to bug me this much about everything if we get married? I'm feeling unsure if I should even propose now.

Sincerely,
Guy who can't think of a creative name

---

*From: DrLove@drlove.advice*
*To: JustaGuy@drlove.advice*

Dear Nicely Nagged,

Typically, people are on their best behavior while dating. The longer the relationship, the more of the real person you'll see.

If she's nagging now, you better bet she'll be nagging later.

As I see it, you've got two choices. The first is to run screaming for the hills. It's a valid, however cowardly, option.

The second is to talk about the issue head-on. The fact that you're writing to me rather than being direct with your girlfriend tells me that you've got some growing up and maturing to do yourself.

It's simple: walk or talk, dude.

Sincerely,

—Dr. Love

## eight

*Zane*

THIS ISN'T A DATE. It isn't.

*You would know,* Zoey's voice in my head says. *Considering you've been on a thousand of them.*

*Ha ha. Nice burn, Zo.*

If it's weird that I sometimes have mental conversations with my twin, then so be it. I've never heard of this being one of those twin things—and believe me, I looked it up when I started having arguments with her in my head—but I just consider the Zoey voice to be my conscience. My own personal Jiminy Cricket.

The thing is, I'm realizing as Jack and I wait by the elevators for Abby and Charla, I really haven't been nervous like this about a date. Maybe once or twice in high school, when I actually *liked* the girls I asked out, and when I cared if they said no.

Before Mom died.

For the past few years, dating has been like checking out library books. I'd pick one I liked, keep her for a week or two, and then return her. And while I know comparing women to library books might sound bad, it's not like I was ever *finishing the book*. Rarely did we make it past the first chapter. I didn't turn down the corners of pages or anything barbaric. No strings, nothing serious. I was always up front about that, and other than when women got clingy, like Chelsea, no one got hurt.

*That you know of.* I really wish I could get Zoey's voice out of my head sometimes. But maybe it's just what I need to hear tonight.

Because as much as I hate the feeling of sweaty palms and my stomach dropping out of the bottoms of my feet, it reminds me of how it used to feel. Of who I used to be. I think the nerves are a good thing.

Except that I'm not supposed to be feeling anything. Because *this isn't a date*.

I'm wearing a path in the carpet between the bank of elevators and the gift shop. Meanwhile, Jack is the picture of ease, leaning against the wall, reading something on his phone. Sometimes I wonder if he has a soul. Or if he sold it in exchange for the constant, cocky brand of confidence he wears.

"Nervous isn't a good look on you," Jack says, not looking up from his phone.

"Yeah, well, one of us has to care about this meeting."

Jack slides his phone into his pocket and smiles. "I care. But I'm too busy manifesting success over here to worry."

*Manifesting.* That's Jack's favorite word. He manifests success and wealth and all kinds of things daily. I prefer good, old-fashioned hard work. Which is why I'm always the last one to leave the office and the first one in.

I wish I could manifest myself right out of this situation. I'd rather be at home. Working out. Feeling the tension ease as I push my body to the limit. This place has to have a gym. Probably a nice one. As soon as we make it through this dinner, that's where I'll be.

Maybe it's just nerves because a lot is riding on these investors. We've got so many VCs already, but we need more to make it through the home stretch, to the launch in a month. The wining and dining has never been my favorite part. I'm the one who does things behind the scenes, where I'd prefer to stay. But Jack insists that we both need to be the face of the company. I know he's right, even if I hate it.

And tonight, added to the normal pressure, we have two wild cards: Charla and Abby.

Charla is a mistake. A desperate choice. Her number had been in my phone, listed under Charla From Bar, CPA. I'd had a vague memory of her in my head as a pretty, bubbly brunette I'd meant to ask out but forgotten. The CPA by her name made me think maybe she was professional. But the outfit she showed up in had me wondering if the CPA stood for something else, like Car Park Attendant.

And then there's Abby. I've only ever seen her in a skirt once, and it had been paired with motorcycle boots. She looked amazing, but if she wears something like that tonight, how will the VCs and their wives react? And how will I keep myself from being totally and utterly distracted by her? That's the real question.

At that moment, the elevator dings. And, as though Jack and I can both sense the occupants before it opened, we straighten up, watching as our dates step out.

I'm not sure what's more shocking: the way Charla has transformed so that she actually looks like a CPA, or the way my whole body reacts to Abby in a dress.

First my breath hitches, like the oxygen in the air has been replaced with some other kind of compound, much too dense for my lungs. Then my chest tightens, and my heart takes off like a racehorse released from the starting gate. It's gone, and I may never catch it.

Abby doesn't look like she stepped out of an office, but she also doesn't look like she was pulled out of a mosh pit somewhere. No. Abby looks ... gorgeous. Unique. Tantalizing. Tempting. And like the no-nonsense, smart-mouthed woman who's been haunting my office and my mind all week.

Her white blonde hair leads down to pink curls. She still doesn't have on a ton of makeup, but a little more than usual. Her eyes are dark-lined and gorgeous, the hazel color I've been trying to pin down looking more green than brown. But it's her lips I'm drawn to, full and bubble-gum pink.

I don't even realize that I'm walking toward her until Jack steps between us, wrapping his arms around Abby in a hug.

Because she's not my date. She's his.

Despite that fact, and despite the reality of Charla standing here, I have to fight the urge to toss Jack over my head and into the potted fiddle-leaf fig next to the elevator.

With all the discipline in my body, I turn to face Charla, copying Jack as I give her a quick hug. "You look perfect," I say, meaning it. She looks exactly like what I'd hoped when I told her that we hoped to make a good impression on the investors at dinner.

So, why am I terrifically disappointed?

Maybe because I feel suddenly sure of what I want. And it's not casual dating and then amicably parting ways. It's not careful distance so my heart isn't involved. It's not the kind of women I've been dating. Pretty. Boring. Safe.

I want Abby.

While I watch, Jack holds out his arm to her with a smile. "Shall we?"

Abby looks at me, as though waiting for something. I wonder if my realization is all over my face. Can she feel my longing to be next to her? Can she sense how much I want to tear Jack's arms off?

That day in my office, I should have fought Jack for her. I should have claimed Abby and asked her to be my date. Watching her with him is torture.

But I didn't ask her. I let Jack win. And I don't say anything now as Jack leads her away.

Charla takes my arm. "Everything okay?"

*Not even close.* "I'm fine," I tell her.

Our table is large and round, which is going to make conversations awkward. Jack seats himself between Abby and Charla, leaving me without a clear view of Abby. Because I can't see her face, I'm desperate for any little thing I do see. Her hand on her water glass. Her hair grazing the tablecloth. When she leans to the side, I see a tattoo peeking out of her dress near her collarbone. How have I not noticed it before?

And what's the tattoo look like?

As if she feels my eyes, seeking her out, Abby finally catches and holds my gaze, giving me a secret smile that I want to tuck in my wallet the way some men keep pictures of their kids. It's the kind of look I want to remember forever and see again and again. My eyes are drawn to the tiny white scar on her face, the one she told me about on the drive here.

It's barely noticeable, reminding me of a tiny piece of a constellation, a lone star winking out from her high cheekbone. Remembering the vulnerability in her voice when she told me about what I'm sure was humiliating at the time, I wish I had gotten a chance to do the same. To open myself up to her.

She caught me off-guard, asking about the scar on the back of my head. My hair almost covers it, and I don't have to see it since it's on the back of my head. People don't often ask about it, but I still wish I could easily cover it. Too bad I hate long hair, and mullets aren't ever going to be in style.

It came from the safety glass—you know, the stuff that isn't supposed to cut you—in the car accident that killed my mom.

I shake my head, realizing that Abby has leaned back again, hidden from my sight.

---

The dinner doesn't turn out as horribly as I thought. Jack does that schmoozing thing he does so well, and the VCs seem to be enjoying themselves. Eventually, we switched the seats around so that the women are on one side of the table and the men are on the other. It's more convenient for the business talk but feels very ... chauvinistic. Like we've relegated the women to the children's table at Thanksgiving.

And because Abby is now directly across from me, I'm subjected to the occasional looks she shoots my way, telling me she agrees.

From the brief snippets of the women's conversation, I've heard confounding phrases like capsule wardrobe (like, a time capsule?), blowouts (tires?), and microblading (which sounds like a slow death or maybe like inline skating for tiny people). Abby crosses her eyes at me when one of the investors' wives—Sara, I think—mentions making appointments tomorrow to have their nails dipped.

I can't help but grin back at Abby, then realize that I've missed out on some question that Rick, Sara's husband, just asked.

"I'm sorry—could you repeat that?" I ask.

"I was wondering about the specs for the app. Jack said you were the one to ask. Is it on track for completion?"

Of course, Rick would ask this question. My eyes go straight to Abby. I don't want to reveal that we're having issues, but I also don't want to feed him a line.

"It will be on track," Abby says, leaning forward in her seat.

A hush falls over the table for a moment as the two investors take her in and the women look slightly scandalized that Abby joined the men's conversation. I can't help but wonder how they see her: pink hair brushing the tablecloth, her hazel eyes bright, her voice confident. She's captivating. I have to force myself to look away so that I'm not staring.

"And you are?" Philip asks, touching the edge of his mustache. He's been doing that all night, as though he thinks it's going to crawl away like the caterpillar it resembles.

"Abby. I'm helping with the neural networks and sorting the data structures for maximum efficiency. That way, when millions of users download the app the first day, it's not going to crash."

I don't even know what all the words mean since I'm not the tech person, but there's something sexy about the way Abby's dropping lingo.

Rick smiles. "I'd like to think of myself as dabbling in development. Forgive me for asking, but are you handling the website as well? I'm curious about the adaptive development, and how you're balancing the UI versus the UX."

I get the impression that Rick is just dropping terms for things that are over his head. The back of my neck begins sweating, and Jack gives me a tiny panicked look that I might have missed if I didn't know him so well.

Abby scoots her chair back. "Would you like to take a

peek at the wireframe? If it's okay with Jack and Zane, of course."

She looks to me, not Jack, for approval, which makes pride spread through my chest. I'm not crazy about letting people see more than they need to see, but when Abby winks at me, I nod. She thinks it's safe, and I trust her.

Moments later, Abby has a small tablet in hand and has positioned herself between Rick and Philip, scrolling through the mockup of our website, and then what looks to be a whole lot of code. It's immediately obvious that Rick had no idea what he was talking about but is just agreeing with whatever Abby says.

When she says something about a gorilla hammock, I wonder if she's playing around with him too. Her face is dead serious, but there's a brightness in her eyes. Kind of like the one she had when she was messing with me that first day.

Jack meets my eyes, smiling and a few minutes later, Rick shakes his head, giving me a wry grin.

"Well, you had me pretty convinced until now."

*Until now?* I swear for a few seconds, it feels like every organ in my body vaporized. Poof. Gone.

"After hearing all that? I'm *sold*." He half stands and holds out his hand to shake mine, then Jack's.

I know I'm grinning like an idiot, but I'm so relieved that I don't even care. Philip follows suit, shaking our hands and giving Abby a gentle pat on the back.

"With someone as knowledgeable as Abby on your team, I feel much more secure."

Neither Jack nor I bother to correct him, explaining that she just started this week as a contractor. If they're on board because of her, better to let them think Abby is full time.

Abby meets my eyes, and I see the glow of pride in her smug grin and the pretty pink flush in her cheeks.

I swallow around a growing thickness in my throat.

Twice today, Abby has rescued me in some way. First, with the whole scar thing. I knew she told her story just to take the pressure off me when she struck a nerve. I hadn't been prepared for her to ask, and my emotions shot up to the surface before I could cage them.

It wasn't her fault, but I saw how badly she felt. Now, she just made the final move to seal the deal and secure these investors.

All without toning back her Abby-ness a single ounce. As evidenced when she turns to Philip and asks, "How many programmers does it take to screw in a lightbulb?"

Jokes? She's telling jokes now? I want to send her some kind of signal, one that says: *Abort! Abort! Abort!*

We've got things locked down. Now is when we should walk away from the table.

*Please don't let it be a dirty joke. Please don't let it be a dirty joke.*

Philip smiles—at least, I think he's smiling under that terrible mustache—and says, "How many?"

"None," Abby says. "That's a hardware problem."

Rick barks out a laugh, and both Philip and Jack join in. I sort of get the joke, but I'm still panicking slightly. Jack gives me a hard look, telling me to relax as Philip orders a round of after-dinner drinks.

And for the next forty-five minutes, I sip my port, watching Abby keep Rick, Philip, and Jack entertained with developer jokes and stories from coding nightmares. There's a tiny part of me that's still nervous, but a bigger part feels proud watching Abby work the table. Unlike Jack's slick and polished exterior, Abby is charming, but utterly herself.

Hilarious, a little irreverent, and completely alluring.

By the end of the night, I've all but forgotten Charla, who joins me as we all stand from the table. It's then that I notice

Jack has tucked Abby under his arm. A wave of jealousy hits me, as palpable and overwhelming as the heat when you walk out of an air-conditioned building in Texas during the summer.

I can't feel this way about my sister's best friend. I can't.

*And why not?* that annoying Zoey voice asks.

But as I'm watching Jack with Abby, still tucked under his stupid arm, all my reasons have flown straight out of my head.

Rick beams at Abby, then Jack. "You're a lucky man," he says. "Better keep this one close."

"I plan to," Jack says, looking down at Abby.

But she's staring right at me, not him. I swear she looks ready to bolt. That fuels my ego, and my drive.

*Plans change, buddy.* I think, looking at Jack. *Plans change.*

# nine

## Abby

"And then I told a coding joke, and they all pretended to get it. Oh my gosh, you should have seen them laughing," I say, trying but failing to keep my voice down.

I'm in a stairwell in the resort, the only quiet place I could find once Charla went to bed. I've got my laptop to work but had to call Zoey first and brag.

"Zane fake laughed at your coding joke?" Zoey's voice is full of disbelief.

"No. He was the only one who didn't."

He just stared at me, actually. With a look I couldn't quite read but that made me want to climb over into his lap and kiss him.

The look on his face when he was pleased with me made my whole body go hot. Tonight, when I had the investors eating out of my hand, his face had gone from shock to something like pride and admiration. And then shifted into something even more intense, like a raw longing, or a promise.

Now that I'm talking to Zoey, thinking about Zane like that makes me feel all kinds of awful. I mean, realistically, if I liked Zane and Zane liked me, Zoey wouldn't stand in our way. Would she?

It's just that she has warned me away from him so many times, talking about how he's never serious. How he doesn't do commitment, but instead has dated half of Austin.

*Zane dates women like Charla. Not women like you.*

That's a sobering thought. One that helps me banish my wayward Zane-chasing thoughts.

"I'm proud of you, Abs. But I knew you'd be amazing," Zoey says, yawning.

It's only nine thirty, but that's at least thirty minutes past her bedtime. And I need to work on the latest anomaly I've found in the code. I'm finally one hundred percent sure of two things: someone is absolutely sabotaging the code, and that person has on-site access to the servers. As in, they work at Eck0.

"I'll let you go, but I've got something to run by you first."

"Go ahead," Zoey says, yawning again.

"Say I found something while digging around that makes it look like someone is intentionally messing with the app."

Zoey gasps. "Are you serious? How sure are you?"

"Almost positive. I haven't told Zane yet because I wanted to be totally sure."

"I know he'd want to know if someone is hacking in. You should go tell him right now."

I bite my lip before answering. "That's the thing. It's not a hacker. It's someone on the inside, who works at Eck0."

One of those people is Jack, despite the fact that he

professes not to know much about programming or development. There's just something about him I don't trust.

But after seeing him tonight wooing the investors, I can't believe it's him. No one would work that hard at getting financial backing and then tank it.

"I can't believe it." Zoey sounds stunned. "I mean, I can. I've seen a whole world of corporate sabotage in the past two years. But still. I hate that it's happening to my brother. He's worked so hard."

"I know."

She sighs. "I would wait until you're one hundred percent sure. I know Zane. First, he'll freak out. Then, he'll want every shred of evidence to go over it himself."

"That's what I figured. Thanks, Zo."

"Anytime, Abs."

We say our good nights and I settle into my little nook at the top of the deserted stairwell to do a job that's less and less about the money and more and more about the man who hired me.

---

Somewhere, an alarm is going off. Not my phone alarm, I realize as sleep starts to scatter and fade. Normally, I wake up to The Black Keys, the volume starting low and then getting louder, coaxing me gently from sleep.

The beep-beep-beep I'm hearing yanks me from my sleep with a jolt. I stand and start walking, to where I'm not sure, but immediately trip over something and crash to the floor.

Why am I on a fake cowskin rug? Wait. That's not fake. Why am I on a real cowskin rug?

My eyes crack open finally as a semi-familiar voice reaches my ears.

"Ohmygosh, I am so so sorry! I forgot to hit snooze on my alarm."

It all rushes back to me like an instant download. The resort. Charla. The dinner. Checking code until well past three in the morning.

"Coffee," I groan, pulling myself up. Great. Now I have rug burn on both knees from this cowhide. It's probably payback for wearing the baby elephant concealer.

"You're bleeding!" Charla says, as I sink back onto my bed.

"Hazards of hotel living," I mutter. "What time is it?"

I blink up at Charla, realizing for the first time that she's wrapped in a tiny hotel towel, hair soaked and droplets of water glistening on her skin. I'm bleeding and have hair that I can tell is like a bird's nest and my eyes are so puffy I can hardly see. And she looks like the centerfold in a freaking swimsuit issue.

"I don't think we have a first aid kit, but we could probably call down for one?" Charla looks unsure.

I examine my knees. Typical rug burn. Just big, raw patches with some blood. "I'm not hemorrhaging or anything. It's cool."

"Um, your eyes," she says. "Are you okay?"

I sigh. Whenever I don't get enough sleep, my eyes blow up like puffer fish for the first few hours I'm awake. My roommates love these mornings and are always trying to sneak photos with me in them. Because I can't see all that well, what with the puffiness, I'm an easy target. Thank goodness Facebook lets you un-tag yourself from pictures.

"I just went to bed late. I'm okay. Did you say something about coffee?"

"I think you said something about coffee. I already had my green tea." She must notice the look of desperation on my face, because she snaps to it. "I think there's a machine in the bathroom."

Charla spins so quickly that her towel lifts, giving me an eyeful.

That's one way to wake me up. Did she mistakenly use a hand towel? Or a washcloth?

This is all too much. Even hotel coffee made in a bathroom with tap water will do, at least to wake me up enough that I can go downstairs for real coffee.

Someone knocks on the door. I really hope room service somehow heard my silent cry for help and has brought a plate of bacon and a double espresso. I stumble toward the door, but Charla has beaten me there. She opens the door, not seeming at all fazed that she's wearing a glorified washcloth.

Both Jack and Zane are standing there, wide-eyed.

I don't know which is worse. Charla in her barely there towel, or me, looking like a half-dead mole with a nest of blonde and pink hair around my head.

"Come on in," Charla says, swinging the door open wider.

Because, sure. They've already seen it all. Why not?

Zane hesitates, but Jack strides right in, giving Charla an appreciative sweep of his eyes that makes her giggle. She slaps his chest playfully before darting into the bathroom with a handful of clothes.

"Be right out!" she calls through the door. "Don't do anything I wouldn't do!"

I don't know what she would or wouldn't do, but I can categorically say that her warning is wholly unnecessary. Jack is now reclining in the office chair, smirking at me.

"Not a morning person?" he says.

"If by that you mean that I am not a person in the morning, then yes. At least not until I have coffee."

Zane, who has been hanging back in the doorway, clearly not sure if he wants to enter this circus, swoops in decisively and holds out a to-go cup that smells like life and joy.

"A flat white," he says.

"You are the perfect specimen of a man," I say.

I take a few swallows, thankful that it's not hot enough to scald me, before I realize what I just said to Zane. I shouldn't be held responsible for anything I say the first few hours of any day. Especially not when running on a few hours of sleep.

I clear my throat. "Thank you."

"Are you okay?" He looks truly concerned, which is adorable, especially compared to the smug amusement on Jack's face.

"I just take some time to wake up usually. And I was up late."

"No, you're bleeding," he says.

Right. My knees. I glance down, and they look a little worse now. There is actually a trail of blood almost down to my ankle on my right leg. Perfect.

"I fell out of bed."

Zane looks horrified, and as the coffee drags me into further consciousness, I am mortified. I look like something dragged out of a swamp. I have morning breath. I'm bleeding.

It's probably good that he sees me like this. I mean, might as well just help me get over my tiny (aka: growing by the minute) crush on my best friend's twin by making sure he would never, ever be interested in me. No matter what I thought I saw in his eyes last night.

"Up late watching movies? Having pillow fights?" Jack waggles his eyebrows suggestively, and if I didn't need this coffee to exist right now, I would throw it at him.

Did I really think he was cute when I first met him? Every minute I spend with him, he grows more and more ... gross.

"I was working on the glitch," I say, glaring. He probably can't tell though, since my eyes are so tiny right now.

"Did you fix it?" Zane asks, his voice sounding way too hopeful. I wish my news wasn't disappointing.

The thing about talking to anyone who isn't a programmer is that they don't get our language. I *say* glitch, because Jack and Zane will get that. Except that glitch implies that it's one singular thing, when the reality is much more complex. I simply can't explain it to them. At least, not without analogies.

"Unfortunately, it's not one issue I can just fix. Code is kind of like a spiderweb. And when a bug lands on it, it impacts the part of the web where it lands, but also the whole web. Think of it like this: I'm trying to figure out where all the bugs have landed by following the movement of the web."

Then I have to figure out who brought the bugs. But I'm not saying that, not yet. I remember Zoey's words, that Zane will want a whole trail of evidence. I'm close. Probably by the end of the weekend. Maybe Monday. Or mid-week. I should be able to tell where the code was introduced, which will give me either a signature or a login or IP address to narrow it down. If they're smart, which I suspect they are, it's probably bouncing around various IP addresses to mask the location. But I'm smart too. I haven't had a challenge like this in a while, and believe me, I am here for it.

I'll figure it out, then give Zane all the evidence he needs. Plus, fix the damage. I'll be the hero of the day and also get paid.

But then I won't be seeing Zane every day. The thought makes my hopes crumble a little, but I remind myself that I don't want Zane. Too complicated. Too straightlaced. Too much Zoey's brother.

As he eyes my knees again, I remember that I don't even need to worry about anything happening with Zane now that he's seen me in my disturbing natural state.

Charla pops out of the bathroom, her hair up in a messy knot, still looking like a sexy model in an off-the-shoulder shirt and yoga pants. I'm a little surprised at the outfit, though, considering our fancy resort.

"What's the plan for today?" I ask around a yawn.

"Golf," Jack says. I realize then, because my tiny mole eyes are starting to open thanks to caffeine, that the guys have on polo shirts, khaki shorts, and funny shoes. Golf. Okay. Which means ...

"Spa day!" Charla squeals.

"Spa day?" I read about all the amenities on the flyer downstairs, a few things I know of, like massages, but also things I don't understand and can't pronounce. I swear I read something about a vampire facial. Heck to the no.

"Cool. You have fun. I think I'll stay up here and work."

Charla laughs, grabbing my hand and waving it around. I'm concerned all the movement is going to jostle my flat white.

"No, silly," Charla says, still flapping my arm around.

I remind myself again that she is a CPA. A smart girl who crunches numbers and just happens to act like the stereotype of a sorority girl slash swimsuit model.

"You and I are *both* going. We're meeting Sara and Mel in twenty minutes. Better get ready!"

The horrors of this morning are unending. I have to go to a spa. With Charla and the investors' wives. It's why I'm here. I glance at Zane with pleading eyes. But again, my eyes may not be open enough at this point to convey emotion.

I would much rather carry clubs or ride around in a golf cart or even wade into a lake to find balls. Alligators are almost never this far northwest, despite that story I heard about one being found in Dallas recently.

"Don't worry," Jack says. Because clearly, enough emotion is leaking through my swollen face to convey my panic. "We'll meet up with you later for a couples massage."

Just like that, I am fully and terrifyingly awake, and as Jack gives first Charla and then me a predatory grin, I think about how lovely wrestling an alligator sounds.

# ten

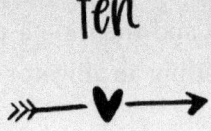

*Abby*

EVERY SINGLE ONE of my roommates would trade places with me right now. A free day at a high-end spa. I can't even complain to them about it because they'd be all, *Boohoo! Poor, pampered Abby and her first-world problems!*

And I get it. I do. This is a gift.

But the logic does nothing to erase the sheer panic I'm experiencing as I stand in a dressing room with just a robe covering me.

"Do I have to get naked?" I asked the woman who handed me the robe.

She only laughed, like she thought I was joking. I wasn't.

This day has felt like a fun house, where every room is worse than the last. Maybe if it hadn't started with me stripping down to nothing and getting hosed off in a room with a drain in the floor. This is what they do to prisoners. I half expected them to dump some kind of lice treatment on my hair or give me a flea dip.

After the hosing, which the woman administering it seemed to enjoy way too much, I was subjected to hours in a bathing suit with Charla, Sara, and Mel. Hours. Going through various pools and a steam room. That part wasn't terrible. I should not be complaining. Or miserable.

It's just ... this whole thing triggers a lot of memories for me. Spending so much time with women I don't know, women who seem so different and whose conversations hover around things I'm just not interested in: bags, shoes, and the spa treatments. The wrinkles on their foreheads, and the Botox to combat it. I've discovered that I'm the only one in the greater Austin area who doesn't have regular facials.

Tack on the fact that being in a bathing suit—or, like right now, *less than* a bathing suit—makes me feel so vulnerable. So *exposed*.

I don't hate my body but have the same self-consciousness that most women do. Maybe a bit more, just because of all the stuff that happened in middle and high school that I try to forget.

I don't love parading around wearing next to nothing. Especially when the women I'm with don't seem to have any qualms about it. Because then I'm not just self-conscious, I'm self-conscious about *being* self-conscious. There were even women who walked around totally in the nude without a care in the world. I mean, Go, ladies! You do you. But it only highlighted the insecurities I still need to kick to the curb.

I had to admire a group of women who had to be in their eighties, walking around with it all hanging out. Emphasis on *hanging*. I've resolved to start a fund for the breast lift I will most certainly need one day. So, I guess if I want to look on the bright side, I can say that today was educational.

"Abby! Are you coming?" Charla knocks on the door, making me jump.

I pull the knot on the robe tighter. "Just a sec!"

If the goal was to relax, it's been a total fail. Every muscle in my body is tense, and my fight-or-flight response is in high gear. I don't have any hope that the massage at the end of the day is going to help, because it's a *couples* massage. With Jack.

He hasn't done anything to make me think he's trying to cross any boundaries I set up, but then again, we're going to be lying naked in a room together. Covered with sheets or towels or something—I think?—and with massage therapists, but *still*. If I feel uncomfortably aware in a bathing suit with other women, there is no way I'll relax naked in a room with Jack.

When I don't think I can put it off any longer, I open the door.

"Hi!" Charla waves, like we haven't just seen each other and spent hours together.

"Hey."

"Could I talk to you for a minute?" Charla tugs at the sash on her robe.

Worry gathers in my gut. These kinds of talks are almost never good. "Sure. What's up?"

"It's about the massages today." She chews her lip, her brown eyes shooting me a look that's both pitying and pleading.

Whatever she's about to say, I think I'm going to hate it. "Okay. What about them?"

"I just wanted to double check that it's okay. About Zane."

*Oh no. Does she know I like him? Am I that obvious?*

Last night, I couldn't help but find my eyes drawn to him. A few times, I caught him looking at me, and he had this little smile, almost like he was proud of me. It made me feel pretty amazing.

Charla must have noticed me looking at him. She knows I'm into Zane, *her* date for the weekend. And now, she's doing that girl thing where she checks to make sure I'm okay if she and Zane *really* date.

Clearly, I can't blame her. Zane is amazing. It's sweet that Charla wants to talk with me about it. Sweet, but unnecessary. It's not like Zane asked *me* to be his date this weekend. He had the opportunity. But he didn't.

I can literally feel the heat of embarrassment crawling up my spine, vertebra by vertebra. The last thing I want is to talk about Charla and Zane. I don't want Charla to be a CPA *and* a nice girl. It was easier to focus on her inability to carry a tune.

I hold up a hand. "Say no more. It's fine."

Charla tries to hide her smile, but it does no good. She positively beams, then throws her arms around me. The embarrassment turns to dread and jealousy like the burning of a thousand suns.

"Are you sure? I don't want to step on your toes," she says, finally letting me out of the hug. I can see the wistfulness in her eyes. I can't blame her. Zane is amazing.

"You have my blessing," I manage to say, not prepared for the assault—I mean, second hug—that follows.

"I'm so glad you said that," she says, squeezing out a bit more of my soul with her bony arms. "I didn't want to move into your territory. You've been so nice. I have to honor girl code."

I barely restrain my snort. *Girl code.* I'd like to take girl code and show her exactly where she could stick it.

Sheesh. Even my insults are lame right now.

"Can we be done hugging?"

Charla laughs like I've just said the funniest thing, but thankfully, she lets me go. "You're the best," she says. "Thank you for being so awesome about this."

She practically skips away to the next part of the spa. If only she knew the thoughts in my head, which are vacillating between dismemberment and decapitation.

It's fine. Next week, I'll be done working for Zane. I'll see him occasionally with Zoey like I used to, and I'll be totally normal. Well. My brand of normal. I'll find some nice, cute, geeky guy who can speak code to me and we'll make super smart, nerdy babies. Zane will settle down eventually with someone like Charla.

Everything's going to be fine.

Even so, I'm dragging as I walk into the couples massage room, where a woman even shorter than me smiles and tells me to strip and cover myself with a sheet. And here I thought the robe was bad. At least there are no hoses in sight.

There's a partition between the two tables, but it's open. Jack isn't in here, so I rush to hang my robe on a hook and wrap myself in the sheet, burrito style, which makes me feel slightly more secure. I don't know how they'll get me out, but that's a problem to worry about in a few minutes.

My poor, rug-burned knees are stinging as I lie facedown on the table with a groan. I wiggle my way up like an inchworm until my face fits in the hole, allowing me to stare down at the dark teak floors. I thought the pain in my knees might subside, but I'm still groaning when the door opens.

"Abby?"

I turn my head as much as I can. Zane is in the doorway. Not Jack.

And it hurts. It shouldn't. But no matter how much I tell

myself that I shouldn't care about Zane, it doesn't make it hurt less.

"Wrong room," I say. "Charla's in the other one."

Looking everywhere but at my sheet-wrapped body, Zane closes the door and steps inside with a smile. "I asked Jack if we could switch."

It takes a moment for his words to register. But when they do, the elation hits my chest like a shot of helium, sending my heart shooting up through the top of my body. Oh. *Oh!* This is what Charla was asking me about—switching partners. I completely missed it.

Wait. It was *Zane*'s idea to switch?

"I don't mind," I say, trying to play it cool. But even as the words tumble out of my mouth, I'm suddenly very aware of the fact that I'm naked in a room with Zane.

Sure, there's a sheet l wrapped around me like I'm the mold for a paper-mache project, but suddenly all those parts of me that have never been gazed at with male eyes flare up.

If the CIA were watching outside with thermal heat imaging, I'd be the brightest red item in the whole building. Heat-seeking missiles would redirect their courses right toward me.

As Zane nods, stepping forward to toe off his shoes, I realize that he's about to also be naked, and I stuff my face back into its place, trying to breathe at a normal human rate.

I'm hyperaware of every sound. The rustling as Zane removes his shirt. The clink of his belt buckle. The shuffle as he removes his shorts. What I never heard was the sound of the partition moving. Which means if I just tilt my head, I'll get an eyeful of Zane undressing. Must not peek at Zane. Must not peek at Zane.

Closing my eyes makes it worse, because my other senses sharpen. I can *smell* him. There should really be a law regulating men's body products. They all have to be using pheromones of some kind. That's the only explanation I have for the strong compulsion I have to climb off this bed and plaster myself to Zane.

I've had crushes before. Little teensy, tiny pebbles, where this is a massive boulder rolling downhill, gathering speed as it goes.

I wish I had my phone. I need the phone-a-friend option. Some moral support or advice, most likely from Sam, definitely not Zoey, about how to get control of myself.

I'm thankful when I hear Zane settle down on the table. I silently count to sixty I tilt my head and peek over.

And what do you know? He's looking at me.

"Hi," I say. Abby Gates, brilliant conversationalist.

Zane grins, and I'm melting into a puddle on the floor.

"Hey."

"How was golf?" Nice, safe subject. One that's just as boring as baseball. Maybe *more* boring.

"I hate golf," Zane says, making a face. "I also hate schmoozing people. So, basically, it was horrible."

I'm laughing, and then he's grinning. Whatever tension and awkwardness I feel lifts like a morning fog, and we're back to being just me and Zane. The me and Zane we've become this week.

Friends ... *ish.*

"How was the spa?"

I smile, echoing his answer. "I hate spas. I also hate girl talk. So, basically, it was horrible."

Zane laughs, the sound filling up the room the same way it fills something inside of me. He doesn't laugh much, rarely smiles, and so this feels like winning one of those rigged contests at the fair, the ones with the giant stuffed dog as a prize.

"It was actually better than I expected," I tell him, totally skipping the part where they hosed me down like an inmate.

His brows shoot up. "What were you expecting?"

"I'm just not into all this pampering," I say. "I'm pretty simple. Plus, I really do hate all the girl talk. I'd rather stab myself with a fork than have to talk about what bags are hot this season."

"What would you rather talk about?"

Zane's voice is genuinely curious, and the question feels like new territory. It's innocent enough. But this week, Zane has mostly asked things like what I want to order from the takeout menu or if I've made progress on fixing their code.

This question is like Zane taking my hand and tugging me outside the fence surrounding the casual friendship we've built. It's exciting, but it's also new territory, and I'm not exactly sure what to do with it.

I blow out a breath. "I don't know. I guess I like talking about movies and TV shows. Books. Programmer stuff, but that's usually with co-workers, not friends."

"What do you and my sister talk about? I've always wondered."

He's wondered? *Always*? About me and Zoey?

About *me*?

My heart is an Olympic gymnast, doing some kind of complicated spinny-flip thing on the parallel bars.

"Zoey and I talk about everything, I guess. Work. Life." I pause. "Guys."

His facial expression doesn't change, but his voice seems lower when he asks, "Do you ever talk about me?"

I swallow hard. There are a few ways I could play this, and I don't know which is the right choice now. I'm not sure where the property lines are or if the top of the fences are electrified.

I'd like to say that we do talk about him, that I ask Zoey about him. I would love to drop hints about my interest in him, even in some small way.

But the truth is that I always tried not to think about Zane the way I'm thinking about him now. He was objectively attractive, a good guy aside from his whole playboy reputation. I didn't see him as a person of interest because he was off-limits. You don't date your BFF's brother. Definitely not her twin. Too many things to screw up there. So, no. I didn't talk to Zoey about Zane. But I don't want to say that.

I stick with humor, always my default and my shield.

With an exaggerated eye roll, I say, "All the time. I mean, we basically wouldn't have a friendship if we didn't have you to talk about."

He laughs again, and I think that I need to secretly record the sound. I could probably play it for plants and make flowers bloom, even on non-flowering varieties. It's that magical.

The massage therapists choose that moment to come in, and disappointment crashes over me like a rogue wave. There's a very tall man who looks like a Swedish assassin, and the petite woman who told me to strip when I walked in.

*Oh, please, let me have the tiny woman.* I think that the Swedish assassin might permanently damage my muscles with his giant hands.

And so of course, he walks over to me with a smile, cracking his massive, deadly assassin knuckles.

"Hello," he says, in a lilting, airy voice that doesn't seem to fit his hulking frame. No trace of an accent either. Not Swedish. Not an assassin. "I'm Nathan, and I'll be performing your deep tissue massage today."

I try to prop myself awkwardly up to shake his hand, realizing as I do so that I can't actually get my hand out. Nathan eyes the burrito-sheet thing I have going on.

"Let's get you situated," he says, and begins tugging at one end.

Nathan obviously didn't realize how tightly I'd wound myself up or else he's unaware of his own strength. Because when he tugs, two things happen.

First, it throws off my balance from the precarious position I was in.

Second, his strong tug doesn't just pull the sheet loose; it starts to unravel *me*.

Before I can react, the sheet is going one way, spinning me in the other.

It's like when you yank on a piece of paper towel, but instead of the perforated edge yielding, the whole thing unrolls, falling off the counter and leaving a trail of paper towels behind.

Only, in my case, there's not that much sheet, and I roll right off the edge of the table.

The cold air hits my skin just before I hit the floor, continuing to roll because of the strength in Nathan's tug.

I'm naked and rolling across the expensive wood floor, aware of all the air on my exposed skin and also the pain in my hip and ribs from my landing. I'm pretty sure my knees are bleeding again too. My elbow must have jammed into my side because I've managed to knock the wind out of myself, so I can't even get my breath to speak or to scream.

All thoughts of my bodily pain fade as I come to a stop just under Zane's face. His blue eyes are wide and fixed on mine.

*Oh, please, let them be fixed just on my eyes.*
*Just.*
*My.*

*Eyes.*

He blinks, and that's when enough air comes back into my lungs to scream.

I'm still screaming when Nathan throws the sheet over me, like he's tossing a blanket on a fire.

That's what I am: on fire.

I am burning with embarrassment, turning to ash. I stop screaming, trying to catch my breath. And then Zane's familiar voice is right next to me, his strong hand squeezing my shoulder through the sheet.

"Abs? Are you okay? Abby?"

I can't find words to answer him. He gives me a little shake, then gently pulls the sheet down from my face.

The two massage therapists have gone. It's just me and Zane. Wearing nothing but sheets. And I'm still lying on the floor like a crazy person.

"I'm sorry," I say. The concern in his face makes tears spring into my eyes.

"Hey," he says, that deep voice like velvet wrapping around my heart. "You don't need to be sorry. Are you okay? That was quite a fall."

"Did you ... see it?"

As if he knows I'm not just asking if he saw me fall, the tips of his ears turn pink. He shakes his head, giving me a tiny smile.

"No."

The breath I didn't realize I was holding whooshes from my chest. "Okay."

"Okay. Want me to help you up?"

"No! No. I'm fine."

Zane nods. "I'll settle in and close my eyes, so you can get back on the table." He pauses, and I can see him trying not to laugh. "It's probably easiest to lie down, then just *place* the sheet on top of your body. As opposed to wrapping yourself up like a mummy."

"Shut up."

Zane grins as he stands, revealing miles of tanned, muscled flesh. His abs have abs. And it's all topped by a broad chest with the finest dusting of pale blond hair.

It's a good thing that I'm not in any position to move, because I don't think I could keep myself from attaching to him like a vine.

"My eyes are closed," he says, once he's back up on the table.

Clutching the sheet tightly to my body, I make my way back up to the table, feeling all the places where I'm going to be bruised later. But deeper than the superficial injuries, I can feel the deep, deep impact of Zane colliding with my heart.

*dear dr. love*

*From: ParrotedinPoughkeepsie@drlove.advice*
*To: DrLove@drlove.advice*

Dear Dr. Love,

For our fiftieth wedding anniversary, I got my wife something she'd always wanted—a parrot.

I don't mind the bird, except for one quirk. There's no polite way to say this, so I'll just say it—the parrot stayed in our bedroom at first, and he has a habit of mimicking bedroom sounds. If you get my drift.

We've since moved the thing out of our bedroom, but now he's performing in the main area of the house. He seems to especially like doing so when we have guests.

It's really impacting our relationship. I'd like to get rid of our avian friend, but my wife thinks we can train him. So far, her efforts aren't working.

Any advice?

—Parroted in Poughkeepsie

---

*From: DrLove@drlove.advice*
*To: ParrotedinPoughkeepsie@drlove.advice*

Dear Parroted,

Honestly, while I'm sorry you're having this embarrassing problem and that it's causing conflict, good for you! I hope I'm still making bedroom sounds when I've been married fifty years. Congrats on a happy, healthy (and loud) relationship!

About the parrot ... I might suggest leaving him in a room with the television on one of those church channels. Maybe he'll pick up some hymns or Bible verses.

Or go in the opposite direction. Let him watch an R-rated movie on repeat for a while. Then you can just blame whatever comes out of his mouth on the previous owners, bedroom sounds included.

Best of luck!

—Dr. Love

# eleven

Zane

*MEDUSA.*

*Sodom and Gomorrah.*

*My father when he's disappointed with me or Zoey.*

Thinking about things that might turn me into stone or a pillar of salt or might simply vaporize me on contact was the only way I kept my eyes glued to Abby's when she rolled under my massage table a few minutes ago. Naked.

It was desperate thinking. Not my finest plan.

But it worked. As the tiny woman digs her skilled hands into my back, I congratulate myself on a successful display of discipline and self-control under immense pressure.

I did not peek, not even a little, despite all the creamy skin visible just out of my periphery. I might not have been turned to stone if I just glanced for a second, but I couldn't do that to Abby. No way would I exploit the moment. I could see just how panicked, how scared, how vulnerable she was as I locked my gaze on her eyes.

Her gorgeous, ever-changing hazel eyes had been more brown than green in that moment, with a little ring of gold around the pupil. That's what I was thinking about when she started to scream.

Now, things have calmed down and we're adequately covered while our massage therapists are getting started.

Except there is no way I can relax and unwind. My heart is still beating in my throat thinking about Abby.

I knew that switching was a bad idea when Jack proposed it. I didn't particularly want a couples date with Charla, but there was nothing tempting to me about her, so doing a couples massage or any other number of half-dressed activities wouldn't have been so difficult. Abby is a different story.

As I'm thinking this and trying to keep the rest of my thoughts in a respectful, gentlemanly place, Abby giggles.

"I'm sorry," she says immediately, still half laughing.

"Are you ticklish?" asks the big meathead with his hands on her back.

*I am not jealous. I am not jealous.*

"No," she says and then giggles again. "Sorry."

I find myself grinning. Her giggles are like uncorking a bottle loaded with happy. One that's been shaken up and is now fizzing and spilling out of the top. It's little things like this, things that would never make it on to a list of what you're looking for in a significant other, that have me so caught up in Abby.

Plenty of other things about her would make a more traditional list. She's beautiful, and not in the airbrushed, made-up kind of way. She's smart, definitely smarter than me. About some things, anyway. She's funny. I don't remember the last time I laughed with anyone like I have with her this week. After that first night at Eck0, she didn't seem to be trying to get a rise out of me anymore. Instead, we fell into an easy companionship. One I could really get used to.

Abby is also brave. Not a coward like me, who hides behind work and busyness. She lays all the cards on the table, challenging people to take her or leave her.

I know which choice I want to make.

Now she laughs, a loud burst of sound, and I hear the massage therapist sigh.

"You okay over there?" I ask, still smiling.

"It's just—" She breaks off, laughing again. "I can't ..." More giggles.

Her massage therapist is starting to sound irritated. "What areas are ticklish? I can try to avoid them."

*Do not think of areas. Do not think of areas.*

"Um, kind of everything."

"You're ticklish *everywhere*?"

She clears her throat. "Not usually. Just with you, right now."

"I'll try your legs."

*Do not think about her legs. Do not think about her legs.*

My mother would be proud of how hard I'm working to be the gentleman she always impressed upon me to be. I can still remember one conversation in particular, just before she died, when she said, "Women are a treasure. A gift. What do you do with treasure?"

"Hoard it?" I'd asked, being a snarky fifteen-year-old.

Mom had smacked me on the arm, but she was smiling. "No, Smaug. You protect it. You guard it. You always remember its value."

I don't know if Zoey got similar talks but for girls. Maybe Mom taught her to value herself or to watch out for greedy dragons trying to hoard women.

Abby is a treasure, and she grows more valuable in my eyes every moment I'm with her.

The room grows hotter as I do my very best not to think about how very naked we both are right now. This is torture.

"You're tense," my massage therapist murmurs, digging her elbows into my back.

*You have no idea.*

Abby laughs again, and the massage therapist groans. "Your calves too?" he asks.

She's laughing so hard that she can hardly speak. "I'm sorry." Giggle. "Ow." Gasp. "And my knees hurt. That's not funny. It's not funny," she says, and then loses it completely in laughter that doesn't stop.

I can't help laughing too, and I tilt my head toward the woman doing her best to loosen my stiff muscles.

"Maybe we'll just call it a day," I tell my masseuse. "Sound good, Abby?"

"Yes!" she practically shouts.

"Next is your private spa," the woman says. "Hot tub and shower are through that door."

Hot tub, okay. Shower? No.

"My bathing suit is in the changing room," Abby says, still breathing heavy after all the laughter.

"It's a private room," her massage therapist says. "Usually the bathing suits aren't necessary."

And after dropping that bomb, the door closes behind them both. I want to look at Abby, to read her face, but am so paranoid after the earlier incident that I have my head stuffed into the hole on the massage table.

"Abs? You decent?"

"Enough," she says.

We sit up at the same time, and I grin when I see how she's clutching the sheet to her body.

"What now? Clearly, the Adam and Eve-style hot tub and shower portion of the day is not on the table."

"Agreed." I pause. "What *is* on the table?"

She chews her lip for a moment. "I could go get our bathing suits? I never say no to a hot tub."

I nod, filing away the hot tub comment for later. "Great. Except I came straight from golf. No bathing suit."

"I'm sure your boxers or whatever cover about as much, right? Unless you're a tighty-whitey kind of guy."

"Not since I was seven."

"Good to know."

Abby has me close my eyes while she puts on her robe, then she disappears to find her things. I slip on my boxer briefs when she's gone, which are definitely much shorter and tighter than my normal swim trunks, but I hop in the hot tub that's in the adjoining room. The bubbling water does a great job covering things up.

As I wait for Abby to come back, I think about how much Mom would have loved her. There is not one woman I would have wanted to date seriously since Mom died, not one who would have been introduced at home if Mom were still around. I really hadn't thought about it.

But I'm thinking about it now. With Abby.

I go still sitting in the middle of the bubbling warm water, realizing that the reason I'm thinking about this now is because, for once, finally, I actually want something more.

And I want it with Abby.

# twelve

*Abby*

I FEEL like a battle-weary soldier when I stumble into the room at the end of spa day. It should really be Spa Day, capital letters to commemorate the struggle. The sheer battle of wills it took me to drag myself to the end. And the effort it took not to ogle Zane the whole time we were in the hot tub together. Maybe it was just me, but the tension in that room was thicker than the fog. I practically bolted after twenty minutes, claiming that I was too hot.

And I was. Just not because of the water temperature.

I need someone to talk to about today, and there is no way that could be Zoey. I dial Sam, groaning into the phone. "Is it possible for a spa day to make someone more stressed?"

"You should feel relaxed," Sam says.

"I know. I'd be the envy of like everyone in the house. So, don't tell them I'm complaining, okay?"

"Sure," Sam says, and I know what she means is that I'll probably have my horror story immortalized somewhere in her writing. Nothing is sacred, I've found. But she does at least change our names and fudge any descriptions.

"Well. Should I start with the part where they hosed me down naked like a prisoner, or when I fell off the massage table naked in front of Zane?"

Sam is already laughing before I finish the bit about the hose. "Definitely Zane," she says. "I can't believe you flashed Zoey's brother."

"What about flashing my brother?" Zoey's voice is suddenly right there.

I count to ten in my head, pinching the bridge of my nose. "Am I on speakerphone?"

"Hey, Abs!" a chorus of voices calls out.

"What happened with Zane?" Zoey demands.

"Nothing! I mean something. But not anything you need to freak out over."

With a sigh, I go into the whole day, from the hose to the endless girl talk to the embarrassing spectacle I made of myself during the massage not once, but twice.

"I didn't know you were that ticklish," Sam says.

"I'm not! I don't know. It was like one thing did tickle, and then I couldn't stop thinking about it or laughing. We had to stop early and get in the hot tub."

"You got in the hot tub with my brother naked?" Zoey sounds like a volcano erupting, as if the top just blew off her mountain and her words are the ash and lava pouring out.

"*No.* Bathing suits." I make sure not to say specifics, so I'm not lying but I'm also not saying that Zane was in his underwear.

Which was my suggestion, but I had no idea how *not* like a bathing suit his dark briefs were when I suggested it. Especially when they were wet and molding to his body. His totally amazing, muscular body.

Because he was so respectful of me, I did my best to keep my eyes glued to his face when we finally got out because our fingers were turning into prunes.

And I refuse to be ashamed about checking out his butt. It was like that kind of choice that really isn't a choice at all.

The downside is that there is no way any other man in the world could live up to Zane's backside. There aren't words. *That* stays out of the conversation too.

"Sounds like you two are really bonding," Sam says, and I can just hear the smirk in her voice, and the wheels turning. "Maybe I'll get my first love cliché: falling for your BFF's brother."

My mouth falls open, and I can't even make my tongue form sounds to protest.

Maybe because I'd be lying if I did?

"Aw, Zane and Abby would be so cute! I'd totally ship them," Delilah says in her Deep South drawl.

"I'll have to see this to believe it," Harper says.

But Zoey, like me, is silent.

"Do you like him?" Sam demands.

"I don't know—I mean, I'm not sure I, uh ..."

"You like him," Sam says, sounding smug.

"You *like* him like him," adds Delilah.

Zoey? Where is Zoey? I need to see her expression right now. Before I confess or deny anything.

"Can we switch to video chat?"

An instant later, I'm staring at Sam's deep brown eyes and her long, dark hair. Her eyes are soft, understanding, as she hands the phone to Zoey.

The moment I see her face, I'm reminded of Zane. Today, though, I don't see the similarities. I'm more struck by the differences. Her eyes are a little darker blue, her nose slimmer. Zane's lips are fuller, and when he smiles, the real kind when he's happy, not trying to impress investors, the left corner kicks up a bit more than the right. His hair is a dirtier blond, probably because Zoey gets regular highlights.

"Zo?"

"Abs." Her voice is like a spool of wire, rolled up tight.

I swallow and sit up straighter on my bed. "Zoey, I might have developed the smallest crush on your brother."

Crush is underselling it. Like when you buy jeans a size down, thinking maybe you can stuff yourself into them, or maybe they'll fit next month. Spoiler alert: you're going to donate them to the Goodwill a year later when you find them at the bottom of a drawer with the tags still on.

Zoey purses her lips and she runs a hand over her hair. "I wouldn't stop you from dating him, Abs. Did you think I would?"

I shrug. "I guess I never thought about it. I don't want things to be weird. Or bad. You're my best friend."

I sniff and realize too late to hide it that my all-over-the-map emotions from today have gone straight to my tear ducts. Zoey, who is a sympathetic crier, swipes a hand over her eyes.

"I don't want you to get hurt, Abs. Zane has never been able to commit. Not since …"

Not since they lost their mom. That was back in high school, before I knew either of them, so I only know the little bit that Zoey has shared. Their mom died in a car accident, one where Zane was the only passenger. Their dad is pretty gruff and no-nonsense, an ex-military guy who didn't do much nurturing. I met him once and felt like I should tuck in my shirt and stand at attention.

"I think that's why Zane is … the way he is about dating."

I nod. "Okay."

I feel all squirmy inside thinking about Zane losing his mom. I'd always thought it was icky how much he dated. But if it was a defense mechanism of some kind, that's dangerous. It activates that part of me that sees someone who's hurting. I want to deploy the search and rescue team.

"He might not even like me back. I mean he's so ..."

*Perfect.* That's the word I want to use. Not that I think he's without flaws. He needs to relax, though I've seen him loosen up a little this week. More than I thought he could. Then there's his playboy thing, which now seems less awful to me with what Zoey said about his mom.

Flaws and all, if you made a resume for the guy anyone would want to date, Zane would tick all the boxes. If we were back in school, he'd be the king of the cool kids' table. Meanwhile I'm ... me. Not the girl who gets *that* guy.

As though she can read my thoughts, Zoey levels me with the look she reserves for people who cut her off in traffic or don't leave at least a twenty-percent tip.

"Shut up. I know what you're thinking and stop. Now."

Zoey is the only one who knows everything that happened in high school, and why I might question someone like Zane being genuinely interested in me. I appreciate that she's vague enough that I don't have to explain with the rest of our roommates listening in. I bite my lip, giving her a little nod.

"My idiot brother would be lucky to even get a chance with you, Abs." Then her eyes harden. "If he hurts you, I don't even care why. I'll castrate him." Her eyes go wide. "*Chemically.* I'll drug him. Because I'm not going near his—I mean, I wouldn't—"

"We got it," Harper calls from the background. "Chemical castration. You're not going near—"

"Ahh! No more!"

The phone drops as Zoey throws her hands over her ears. I'm now seeing everyone from below. Sam reaches down for the phone.

She's grinning as her face fills the screen. "Well, now that we've got that settled, it looks like I might be getting my first story for my book. *And* I'm happy for you," she adds.

There's a knock at the door. Charla must have lost her key. Again. She's already on her second one. I wonder if there's a limit.

"Just a sec!" I call.

"Who is it?" Sam asks.

"Just my roommate," I say, but then a deep voice that is most definitely not Charla calls through the door.

"It's me," Zane says.

My eyes fly open. "It's Zane," I whisper into the phone. I forgot we were doing video chat and am holding the phone up to my face.

There are choruses of cheers and whistling over the phone.

"Don't do anything I wouldn't do!" I hear Zoey calling.

"Ew! You wouldn't do anything," Delilah says.

"Exactly," Zoey replies.

Zane knocks again. "Abby?"

"Hang on!"

"Keep me posted," Sam calls in a singsong voice.

I disconnect, hoping Zane didn't hear any of that.

I open the door, staring up at Zane's handsome face. I feel like what I just confessed to Zoey is evident in my eyes.

"Was that my sister?" he asks.

"What?"

Did he hear everything they said? I'm going to sink through the two floors below.

116

Zane tilts his head to the side. "I just thought I heard Zoey's voice. Are you okay?"

I nod, only now feeling like my lungs have released enough so that I can breathe. "Yep."

"I have a question. More of a favor," he says.

"Okay." I don't seem to be able to produce more than one-word answers. I can tell Zane notices, but he doesn't draw attention to it.

His hand goes up to his hair, that nervous tell he shares with Zoey. "I wanted to see if I could stay here tonight."

Forget one-word answers. No words. No air. Just me standing there with my jaw flapping.

"I think, uh, Charla and Jack are planning on staying in our room tonight."

Okay. Zane is here because he can't go into his room, not because he wants to stay with me. I'm relieved and disappointed in equal measure.

I swing the door open wide. "Come on in."

"Thanks." He shakes his head as he steps inside the room, brushing against my arm. "I didn't realize they were in there at first. I heard sounds I can't un-hear."

"Ew." I laugh, returning to my bed. Zane sits down on the very edge of Charla's bed, looking stiff. "If you're staying, might as well get comfortable. Want to order room service?"

"Now you're talking," Zane says, picking up the leather-bound menu book on the table between the two beds. "What sounds good to you?"

"Whatever. No sushi. I don't do raw fish."

Zane smiles. "I doubt they have sushi for room service."

"Hey, it's a fancy place. You never know."

He flips through the pages as I grab my laptop. I need a shield, a buffer between me and the man now stretched out on the other bed, shoes and socks off, hair mussed. I've never seen Zane so … unbuttoned. I love it.

My plan for tonight was to keep pushing to find the issues with the app. I really want something I can present to Zane. The sooner the better, because the truth that someone is intentionally messing things up weighs heavy on my mind. Working will now do double duty, keeping me from anything I might regret with Zane.

"Gourmet pizza?" he asks.

"That depends. Do you like weird toppings?"

"Only if bacon is weird."

"If bacon is weird, I don't want to be normal."

Zane laughs, because the thing is, I'm not really normal to begin with. Not like him, anyway. He could be used as the measuring stick when it comes to an upper-middle-class, white-collar man.

Maybe I should stop considering this. Because why would Mr. Poster Child for normal want to be with me, the nerd girl coloring outside the lines, even if I have his sister's blessing?

# thirteen

*Zane*

SHARING a room with Abby is a terrible idea, and I couldn't be more excited about it. Except that she has basically ignored me since I barged in here. Between her computer and her phone, she's been glued to electronics for the past hour. The upside is that I can pretty much stare at her.

I watch her fingers fly over the phone as she texts someone. The tiny smile on her face ignites a flicker of jealousy. I want to be the one making her smile like that.

"Who are you texting?"

She glances over at me, her smile growing wider. "My sister-in-law, Jessa. She's like one hundred months pregnant. Every time she texts or calls, I think it's her telling me she's in labor."

"You guys are close, then?"

She nods. "My brother is cool. He totally doesn't deserve

Jessa though. She's amazing. And their boys are total nuts, in the best way possible."

I see something in her face as she talks about her family. A warmth brightens her features, almost like the difference between being inside under all that fake light, and then stepping out into the sun.

"Do you want kids?"

The question seems to startle her, and the phone falls to her lap. Why did I ask that? It's a dating question. Not even a first- or second- date question. Have I ever asked a woman that? No. Definitely not. I haven't even asked my sister.

I try to keep my face neutral, like I'm not starting to sweat, like the question was just a friendly, getting-to-know-you kind of question.

"Actually, I ... yeah. I do want kids." She searches my face, her words gaining confidence as she nods. "I'd like a bunch."

My eyes widen. "Define a bunch? Like, a bunch of bananas? Or, like a bunch of grapes?"

Abby throws her head back and laughs. I watch the place where her pulse jumps, just beneath her jaw. Her skin there is pale and smooth. I want to drag my lips along it, to trace a path right up to her mouth. I swallow hard as she looks back at me, wiping a few tears from her eyes.

"I've never heard anyone make a fruit analogy with kids."

"And I've never heard someone say they want a *bunch* of kids. I'm just trying to get a ballpark here. Five? Fifty?"

Her lips twitch, a playful smile emerging slowly. "Why? What's your cutoff number? Don't think you could handle a bunch, Zane?"

I shrug. "I like a good challenge. Hit me with your number."

Abby regards me for a moment, and I feel slightly terrified because I swear it's like she's lasered right through to my brain. A scary thought. Because my brain is completely Abby-focused right now.

"Somewhere between three and five. Just depending on how hard it really is. Could you handle that?"

*With you? Yeah. I think I could.*

I'm sitting a few feet away from Abby, and though I just felt transparent and exposed under her gaze, I know she isn't reading my mind. If she could, she would know that a seismic shift took place a moment ago. Though I bought my house with the vague idea of a family and kids, it was foggy. Unreal. Way off in the future.

Now? It feels almost close enough to touch. Just across the space between the two beds.

I realize that Abby is still waiting for my response. Putting on a light smile that doesn't scream *have my babies!*, I say, "If you could handle it, I could handle it."

"You don't seem surprised that I want to have a big family," Abby says, her voice a little lower, a little softer than it was moments ago.

This feels like one of those iceberg questions, where there's a lot buried underneath. Some subtext I don't know. At least, not yet. A lot rests on my response, but I'm not sure what I need to say, so I go with the truth, hoping it's what she needs.

"Are you kidding? I could totally see you with a big, wild household. You'd be a great mom."

Though Abby turns away, ducking her head so I can't fully see her expression, I didn't miss her smile. *Ding! Ding! Ding! Right answer, Zane.*

Except it's got me thinking of my mom, and how happy she would be if she were a fly on the wall for this conversation. And then that ache rises up, the one that sometimes hibernates for days or weeks, and then takes me by surprise, as raw and real as when I lost her.

I'm thankful that the conversation dies out a bit. I need a moment to collect myself, to let the pain of missing my mom work its way through me. After a few minutes where Abby's typing is the only sound, I can breathe again.

"Has anyone ever mentioned that you're a workaholic?" I ask her.

Abby raises her head to look at me, slowly, like she's counting to ten in her head. Maybe she is, because I swear I see her lips moving as she finally meets my gaze, one eyebrow arched high. It's exactly the kind of look I was hoping to get, and I can't contain my smile.

"Have we met?" she asks. "I'm the pot. You must be … the kettle."

"Nice to meet you, pot."

"Likewise," Abby says, shutting her laptop with a satisfying click. She sets it on the chair she's dragged over next to the bed and turns her full attention to me. "You know it's your fault I'm working right now."

"It's also my fault you're *here* right now."

"Do you regret it yet?"

Abby's still got a saucy look on her face, one that I've come to appreciate in a whole new way this week. But I sense a little vulnerability there too, just underneath the surface. I remember what Zoey told me, that Abby's more sensitive than she lets on.

"No way I could regret it." I begin counting on my fingers. "First, you're fixing our tech problem. And I've been assured, mostly by you, that you're the best."

Her smile is goofy and wide, her hazel eyes bright. There's something about being the one to put that look on her face. I never did drugs, but the way my heart does a happy little kick, I feel like I get what all the fuss is about. Because I could easily become addicted to this feeling, to that look. To Abby.

"Second, you provided hours of countless entertainment today at the spa."

Her eyes fly wide, then narrow. She tosses one of her pillows at me and uses the other to hide behind. I catch the one she tosses, and only because she's not looking, hold it up to my face. It smells like her, warm sugar and coffee.

"I'm never going to live that down, am I?"

"Not a chance."

She mumbles something under the pillow that I can't quite understand. I consider throwing the pillow back to her but decide to keep it. I can fall asleep tonight smelling her.

Creepy? No. Probably not.

"Number three. You're letting me crash in your room to avoid … things which shall not be named. For that, I'm forever grateful."

Abby lets the pillow drop into her lap and tucks her wild hair behind her ears. It's still sticking up in a few places. Not that I would tell her. I know she thinks of me as someone who is buttoned up, smoothed down, and totally put together. And yeah, maybe I'm a bit particular about things being a certain way.

But being around Abby this week has done something to me. It's almost like her irreverence for those things, for decorum and rules and saying the right thing at the right time to the right people has softened me a bit. Not fully. I'm still a buttoned-up shirt, but now I'm half untucked.

It's surprising … and I like it.

She wrinkles her nose. "I was kind of kidding when I told Jack I wouldn't sleep with him on this trip. Not kidding that I wouldn't sleep with him—I wouldn't—but I didn't really think that would be on the table. Guess I was wrong."

I really hate thinking about Jack and Abby and *sleeping together* in the same sentence. Even if I'm the one lucky enough to be here with Abby right now.

"How well do you know Jack?"

*Why are we still talking about Jack?* That's what I really want to know.

"We've been friends since college."

"And how did you decide to go into business together?"

"Why so curious about me and Jack all of a sudden?"

Abby's tone is casual, the kind of casual that's not casual at all. I know she's not interested in Jack. She made that clear. So, what's she after?

"No real reason. Just curious. Since I'm looking into the business, I just wondered how things worked between you and Jack. You seem so … different."

"Glad you picked up on that. I might be offended otherwise." I grin. "Sometimes it takes that person who thinks in a wholly opposite way to round things out."

*You know who else is my opposite? You, Abs. You. Maybe we should round things out together.*

*Ew. File that under flirty lines that should never see the light of day.*

But it's something I've really been thinking about, more and more with each passing moment. Before Zoey suggested that I hire Abby, my sister's best friend was like a mirage. Alluring, but only from a distance. She wasn't a solid presence in my life that I could touch. I didn't hold out any hopes that something real might come from the nervous clenching of my stomach whenever I happened to see Abby. Plus, she's Zoey's friend. And Zoey has always told me that her friends are off-limits.

My sister and Abby have stuck together since freshman year of college. That kind of loyalty says a lot about Abby's character. And if she and Zoey could get along so well, doesn't it stand to reason that she and I could too?

"It does seem to be working well for you two." Abby pauses, picking at a loose thread on the pillow. When she looks up at me, it's almost shyly, through her lashes.

"Are you disappointed? That Jack upgraded, and you ended up with me?"

Hot rage works its way through my body in an instant. *Upgraded?* Abby thinks *Charla* is the upgrade? She thinks I'm *disappointed?*

Before I've thought it through, my bare feet hit the floor and I've breached the space between us. She's so petite, making me feel powerful as I lean over her. I'm overstepping all kinds of boundaries, showing too much of my hand, but something about the idea that she feels like the consolation prize has me all up in arms.

Abby's eyes are wide, her body frozen, like a rabbit in the gaze of a wolf. Maybe this makes me a terrible person, but I kind of like being the wolf.

"Abby," I say, my voice low and rough. "You are not a disappointment. *You* are the upgrade."

The words hang between us in the air. In a moment, the spell is going to break and I'm probably going to regret my honesty. And the fact that I'm essentially crowding into her space. While I'm watching, her throat bobs as she works to swallow.

"Okay," she whispers.

"Okay."

With a firm nod, I settle back on my bed right next to the pillow that smells like Abby and pick up the remote. "What should we watch?"

"Watch? Oh no. I've got something better in mind."

Abby rolls to face me, leaning on her elbow and propping her head up with her hand. The smile on her face is so wicked that my whole body goes hot. My hands are numb. And I feel my heart beating in the wrong parts of my body, like it's escaped the cage of my ribs and is taking a world tour.

"Like what?" The gravelly edge of my voice is embarrassing. And for the second time today, I feel like a teenage boy, way too affected by simple things that Abby says or does.

"It's time I get all the dirt on Zoey."

"Dirt?" Cold water couldn't have shocked me more. Thinking about my twin will do that to me. "On my sister?"

"Oh, come on. Please? You know she's been feeding me info on you for years."

*She has, has she?* My eyes narrow. Abby's widen suddenly.

"Not that I asked about you. She just needed to complain, and I was there."

"Uh-huh." Abby's cheeks are flushed, and it's a look I love on her. A look I'd like to be the cause of. And not because she's embarrassed. "What kinds of things has she told you?"

Abby stills, looking uncomfortable. Her gaze moves to the framed photographs of nature on the wall behind me. I glance back at the pictures, then at her.

"That cute bunny can't save you. What did you and Zoey talk about?"

I don't think she's going to answer at first, and I'm starting to get nervous. I've always been pretty straitlaced. Not a lot of dirt, no skeletons. My heart makes its way back to my torso but lands in my stomach, not my chest. I don't have a lot of dirt, except for …

"Your, uh, dating habits." Abby coughs, still not looking at me. "Mostly how she thinks you're a big, fat man slut."

I fall back with a groan and cover my face with the pillow. It's the one that smells like Abby. For a few seconds, I breathe in and out, letting her scent fill me, considering what to say that isn't too embarrassing or doesn't make me sound worse.

Why did it take me until this week to realize how stupid I've been? How selfish? Even if I wasn't sleeping with half of Austin, which I'm sure is what my sister and Abby think. Dating so flippantly was still stupid and immature and unfair. Mom would have had a lot to say about it. None of it good.

Finally, I roll over, mirroring Abby's pose and still clutching her pillow for support.

"Abs, I want you to know something." I make sure to keep my gaze firmly locked on hers.

"Okay." The expression on her face is sort of tortured, like she wishes she could have avoided this conversation altogether. But I pushed us right into it, didn't I? It's better this way. Get everything out into the open. If anything ever was to happen with Abby, we'll have to talk about our dating history at some point anyway. Now, at least she can decide before we even start if I'm worth giving a chance.

"I've dated a lot of women. That's true."

"Women like Charla and Chelsea," she says, and I realize how that must seem to someone like Abby, a woman who is completely the opposite of the women who work to put their worth all on the outside.

Abby keeps her beauty like a pearl, tucked away, tightly protected. Not that she isn't gorgeous on the outside, because she is. But the more time I spend with her, it's like she's opening bit by bit to reveal the true treasure.

It's one worth fighting for. One worth going after.

But I can't tell her all that. Not yet, when I haven't asked her on a proper date, or even flirted enough to give her the sense that I'm interested.

Interested? Ha. I'm smitten.

So, I hold back, for now, and simply give her the truth. "I haven't wanted to date anyone seriously. The past few years, since ... well, for a long time, I've just dated casually. *Dated.* I haven't been doing *more* than dating casually."

I pin her with a look, wanting her to know what I'm saying without having to spell it out. She gives me a brief nod, so I continue.

"I was always clear about my intentions. Casual. A few dates. That's it. Nothing more. There hasn't been anyone that I ever felt tempted to ask for more."

*Until now.*

*Until you.*

It's a good thing Abby can't hear the thoughts I'm projecting. I'm sure she would go running from the room if she knew how tempting she is. Not just physically, though I'd be lying if I said I didn't hate the space between us. That I wasn't battling thoughts of climbing over into her bed and showing her exactly how I'm feeling rather than saying it.

But more than ever, I know I need to hold back. Because I want more with Abby, and I want to do things differently. I can't risk scaring her off by confessing my attraction, physically and otherwise. It's too much. Too soon. It would be like tossing her into the deep end of the pool.

Then again, what do I know? I don't have serious relationship experience to draw from.

The air in the room has grown thick and hot, like it's a different atmosphere altogether. We're in a bubble, created by my words, by my feelings, and maybe—hopefully—by her feelings too.

Abby is hard to read. She speaks her mind most of the time, or what she speaks *is* her mind, but only a piece. The rest is under the surface, carefully guarded. I wonder if I can be the one to get past the barricades.

For now, I need to dispel the tension, to back us up a few steps, even if I'd like to do the opposite. I've been avoiding commitment for so long that it's hard to fathom I'm now wanting to race toward it. I feel a bit like a car heading down a steep hill, unsure if my brakes are going to work.

I forcibly relax my body and give Abby a brilliant smile. "So. Dirt on Zoey. Where do you want me to start?"

## dear dr. love

*From: TangledUp@drlove.advice*
*To: DrLove@drlove.advice*

Dear Dr. Love,
   I love my girlfriend, but I've gotten tangled up with another woman. My main concern is not to hurt either of their feelings.
   How can I come clean?
   —Tangled up

———

*From: DrLove@drlove.advice*
*To: TangledUp@drlove.advice*

Dear Tangled,
   If your main concern is not hurting them, I think I can help you out. Get them both together and tell them the truth. Then your main concern can shift to worry about both of them hurting you.
   Tip: I'd wear a cup.

   Hoping you get what you deserve,
   —Dr. Love

PS- If you forward me their phone numbers, I'll be happy to break the news and let them break your nose.

---

*From: TangledUp@drlove.advice*
*To: DrLove@drlove.advice*

Dr. Love,

You suck. I've complained to your manager and hope you get fired.

# fourteen

*Abby*

I'M NOT A MORNING PERSON. Just like I'm not ever going to be on time. But when the smell of coffee lifts me from my dream about playing polo while riding unicorns, I decide that I could rethink my stance on mornings. No big deal—just rewrite the code that makes me hate them.

At least, if I could wake every morning to find a shirtless Zane, smiling and holding out a cup of coffee.

"Morning, beautiful," he says, and just like that, I'm done for. Totally sunk.

"Hi," I manage to croak.

I know that in the morning, I truly am the furthest thing from beautiful. But Zane? He is a glorious sight.

Gone is Mr. Perfect, and in his stead is a softer, gentler version. One with sleep-mussed hair, delicious stubble, and a face that's somehow both bright and tired at the same time.

It's like trading in a stiff hardback book with the dust jacket on for a well-worn paperback that's been read through, its pages soft.

Did I mention his shirt is off?

He must have taken it off during the night, sleeping in just his shorts, or maybe his boxers, since he couldn't get into the room for his things. The last thing I remember is watching the movie *Up* with him and arguing about which of us was crying. Spoiler alert: both of us were crying. I'd seen the movie before, but I've never made it through the first five minutes without getting teary.

I realize I'm staring, but I can't be held responsible for my actions before coffee. Zane's grin widens, and I shake off the fog of sleep, pulling myself up a bit closer to sitting.

"I said that out loud, didn't I?"

"Yes. And I agree. You can't be held responsible for your actions right now. Hence, the coffee." He hands me the cup.

If I had any doubt that this was more than a crush, it vaporized the moment our fingers brush when he hands me the coffee. I might as well be wearing a sign that reads, *Abandon hope, all ye who enter here.*

"It's just from the coffee maker," Zane says with a boyish smile that turns the dial all the way up on my stuttering heart. "I haven't been down to the lobby to get you real coffee yet."

"Thank you," I say, taking a sip. It's not terrible and will do for getting me moving. "I've trained you well, young padawan."

My tone is light, but my inner voice is saying things like, *Marry me. How many children should we have? I prefer sapphires and emeralds to diamonds.*

Zane stretches his arms above his head, yawning, and

though I got to see a lot of him shirtless yesterday during the couples part of spa day, I don't mind getting another look at all that golden skin and the hard lines of his chest and abs.

How much working out does it take to get a body like that? When does he even have the time? Would it be weird to ask if he could bench press me?

"What are you thinking about so hard over there?"

Zane reaches out to smooth the furrow in my forehead I always get when I'm deep in thought. At his touch, everything in me shifts sideways, and I'm like a ship sinking in a movie, all the alarms blaring and lights flashing. People running amok on deck while the whole thing lists to port.

*What am I thinking about? Oh, not much. Like, how I'd love to toss the coffee to the side and tackle you, climbing your strong body like I'm a squirrel and you're my favorite tree.*

"Wondering what time it is, and what kind of breakfast they serve in this joint."

"A lovely one. With waffles."

"Belgian?"

Zane nods, looking pleased with himself.

"Let me guess: Zoey told you?"

"Yep. Part of the Abby handbook."

"What else is in that thing?"

"Mostly that to keep Abby running and happy, I have to keep her fully caffeinated and fed with her favorite foods."

"I'm not a car. Or a zoo animal," I grumble.

"Of course not," Zane says. "You're an Abby. One of a kind."

And then, as if he didn't just make my heart do a happy dance, he stands and says, "I call first shower!"

---

I'm more awake but no less twitterpated an hour later, strolling beside Zane as we head toward the elevator and, hopefully, better coffee and a big, fluffy Belgian waffle.

The carpets are so plush that the whole hallway has this hushed feeling to it, and I'm tempted to kick off my flip-flops and walk barefoot on it. So, I do.

"What are you doing?" Zane asks. His tone of voice is amused, not irritated like it might have been a few weeks ago.

"This carpet is amazing. You should try it."

"You want me to take off my shoes and socks and walk barefoot through the hotel?"

I make a face at him. "When you put it like that, it does sound crazy."

"Fine."

We stop so Zane can remove his socks and shoes. He's still got on his golf outfit from yesterday since all his clothes were stuck in the room with Charla and Jack. I would tease him about a walk of shame, but since he slept in my room, it doesn't have the same bite.

When his socks are tucked neatly into his shoes and he's standing on the carpet barefoot, he spreads his arms. "Happy now?"

"No, dummy. You've got to walk around. Shuffle a little. This is like the Taj Mahal for toes."

I move in a little circle, dragging my feet a bit so the plush fibers are practically massaging my toes. Zane just stares, and for a moment, I think that's all he's going to do: stare like I'm a loon.

But then he joins me, and it makes me ridiculously happy to see this tall, devastatingly handsome man shuffling around in circles barefoot in a fancy hotel. I start to giggle.

*"Now are you happy?"*

*More than I could say.* "Yep."

But then, familiar voices sound from around the corner where the bank of elevators is. Zane's eyes meet mine, and then next thing I know, he's opening a door next to us I hadn't even noticed and shoving me inside.

We're now standing flush, my back pressed against his chest, in a tiny housekeeping closet that smells of disinfectant and bleach.

"What are we doing?" I hiss, aware of every breath he takes, and how his chest pushes more firmly against mine.

"Hiding."

"Why are we hiding?"

"I don't know! I panicked!"

I giggle, and Zane shushes me, which makes me giggle more. His big hands land on my hips, and suddenly, there is no air in this closet. I'm a fire, and I've burned it all up.

The voices outside grow louder, even as the room seems to become hotter, smaller. I'm Alice, and I've drunk whatever potion makes me swell ten times my size. That's how it feels as I'm more and more aware of every inch of Zane's body, every place it's touching mine.

"Zane." My voice sounds choked. It's a warning. But for what? I don't know. Only that this moment feels too combustible. Too big.

His hands squeeze my hips, and I shudder as he leans closer, his lips brushing my ear. "Hush, Abs. They'll be gone in a minute."

Maybe I don't want them to be gone. Maybe I want to stay in this closet for the rest of my life.

And because this moment is so intense, like an overloaded system, my server crashes.

"This closet really should have been locked," I say. "Having access to all these chemicals is dangerous."

"Is it?" Zane's voice is low, making my toes curl. He sounds ... amused. But there is nothing funny about it.

"Do you know how many children a year die from ingesting simple cleaning supplies?"

"Can't say that I do."

Zane lifts one hand from my hip, and I'm disappointed until he brushes back my hair, tucking it over one shoulder. His fingers caress the sensitive skin there, barely grazing my clavicle before curling around bare side of my neck.

"Over one hundred thousand children a year are hospitalized."

*Stop talking, Abby.*

That's Gibbs in my head, and it's just the reminder I need to clamp my mouth shut.

I'm trembling, hopefully just on the inside, as two of Zane's fingertips find the pulse at my neck.

"Are you nervous, Abs?"

*Heck, yeah, I'm nervous. You're dismantling my world.*

I'm living in the Upside Down from *Stranger Things*, a world that looks very much like my own, except for the man behind me. The one who *looks* like the stick-in-the-mud twin brother of my best friend.

But in this world, Zane is sweet and kind and even funny. He makes my insides turn molten and has me twisted into a complicated knot that I fear may never come undone.

Without warning, his lips replace his fingertips on my neck in the most tender, electric kiss of my whole life.

Soft, yet firm, his mouth pauses there at my pulse, as though testing my reaction, and when I don't move—because I cannot move—he presses another tiny kiss to the side of my throat. Then another.

He's following the vein in my neck right on down, blazing a path of heat that I can feel everywhere. *Everywhere.* Even that place on my elbow where the body doesn't have a lot of nerve endings, even *that* place stands up and says, *HEL-lo.*

My eyelids flutter closed, and I'm still Alice, but falling right down the rabbit hole, tumbling head over feet into Wonderland.

In a move that I did not see coming, Zane spins me around, and then his lips are on mine. I completely freeze. My knees lock up. My elbows straighten. My spine is like a metal rod, holding me perfectly still.

Then, Zane's lips begin to move, coaxing me to do the same. It doesn't take much convincing. My hands slide around the back of his neck. I tilt my head, inviting him deeper, and Zane obliges.

The kiss is a beautifully choreographed dance, one I don't know, but that's okay, because Zane is completely in the lead. He has control over every part of me. If he told my pinky toe to wiggle right now, it would.

He kisses me and kisses me, until the danger of chemicals seems silly compared to the danger of Zane's mouth on mine.

A familiar voice sounds right outside the door. "Why are there shoes in the middle of the hallway?"

The landing is abrupt as Zane pulls back, our lips making a little noise as they separate. We stand there, listening.

Charla the CPA must be right outside this closet, looking at our shoes. Zane's mouth doesn't go far, hovering, his quick, panting breaths puffing out over my skin.

"I think those are Zane's shoes," Jack says.

There is a pause. And then the closet door flies open. Zane and I blink at Charla and Jack, who are standing just outside the doorway.

I don't know what to say, or how to move. We should move, right?

Zane still has both hands on my hips. I'm not sure if I look as thoroughly kissed as I feel, but based on their expressions, I suspect that I do.

Zane clears his throat, pats my hip, and urges me toward the doorway.

"Good morning," he says, stepping past me to grab our shoes.

"Why are you in a closet?" Charla asks, her head swinging between us.

"Yes, why?" Jack asks, looking so smug, so amused, that I want to shove him into the closet and leave him there. Instead, I walk into the hallway, closing the door.

Zane bends down in front of me, nudging my foot. I realize he's trying to put my flip-flops back on for me. I've never had a man put a shoe on my foot before. That seems like a weird thing to even want.

And yet, as Zane carefully slides one flip-flop into place and then the other, I think that this is an underrated gesture, the kind that could make a woman fall in love. He pats the top of my foot before working on his own shoes. I barely resist the urge to run my fingers through his hair, clasping my hands instead.

"We were just testing out all the amenities," Zane says. "Right, Abs?"

"Yeah," I say. "What he said."

Jack rocks back on his heels, his hands in his pockets. "Oh? And how were the *amenities?*"

Zane looks at me, his blue eyes practically searing a hole straight through me.

"Incredible. Perfect. But there's still a lot of testing to be done. A lot of amenities to explore."

Just when I think he's hypnotized me, dragging me into the blue of his eyes, Zane winks, and it's like someone has attached jumper cables to my heart.

# fifteen

*Abby*

PEOPLE ASSOCIATE HANGOVERS WITH ALCOHOL, but there are actually many kinds of hangovers. Too-much-ice-cream hangovers and junk-food hangovers. Once, Sam and I went to an all-you-can-eat salad bar, and we had salad hangovers. I wouldn't have thought it possible.

I discover a new kind of hangover Sunday when I return home from the resort, dragging my bags: a Zane hangover.

I drop my bags and sit cross-legged on my bed, wondering why the house is so quiet. I hold my phone in my palm, itching to text Zane. I said goodbye to him an hour ago, an awkward, pregnant goodbye where it felt like we should embrace or kiss or *something*, but instead just grinned awkwardly at each other like we were twelve-year-olds, until I climbed into my car.

One hour, and I miss him. I want to text him. Call him.

Drive to his house, wherever it is. I've totally passed the point of no return when it comes to Zane.

Maybe texting him is exactly what I need to do. People talk about the hair of the dog, drinking a bit of alcohol the next morning to ease the pain of the hangover. I can't imagine that actually works. Even so, I want—no, *need*—more of Zane to take the edge off. Just a tiny sip. One text. No biggie.

I mean, I wouldn't say *no* to a long drink of Zane.

The analogy is a little muddy, but the point is: one weekend was not enough.

And I'm really torn about where to go from here. There are two equally terrifying options, heading in opposite directions.

The first option is that I finish this job for Zane and go back to seeing him occasionally, casually. I'll go cold turkey on him. He reverts back to Zoey's brother. A casual acquaintance at best.

This choice is wholly disappointing, but *safe*. Easy. It takes no work. No guts. No risk. Zane would be like every other guy I've dated. Well. Without the date part, since we haven't been on a date. Just … had a partial couples massage, spent the night together in separate beds, and made out in a hotel closet.

The other option is the one where I dive right into what's been building between us. The amazing kisses. The flirting the rest of this morning over breakfast and as we checked out. The way he entwined our fingers for most of the car ride home.

Holding hands had never felt so … life-altering. They're just hands. Used for doing dishes and typing and opening car doors and a hundred other mundane things. But there was nothing mundane about Zane holding my hand, tracing patterns on the back of my hand with his thumb.

This option is clearly the winner. Even thinking about Zane has me feeling hot and cold, weak and woozy. It's like I have the flu. The love flu. Is that a thing?

The problem, though, with this, is the sheer terror of the unknown that comes along with it. I haven't had any serious relationships. I wasn't interested in more with the guys I dated. And strangely enough, guys don't seem to want to keep dating me when I'm not sleeping with them. And physical intimacy is in no way something I would enter into without knowing someone really well, being really committed.

Yeah, okay, maybe I even like the idea of waiting until I've married someone and have that whole safety net of trust before I leap. This creates a chicken-and-egg problem: I won't sleep with a guy I haven't committed to, and guys don't want to commit without sleeping with someone.

I'm realizing that this seems less like a chicken-and-egg problem, and more like a bad-egg problem.

Zane? He's a golden egg. But that makes it no less terrifying to consider what happens next.

I'm still holding the phone in my hands, biting my lip, trying to think of something clever, witty, flirty. But not too over the top. So much pressure! My fingers hover over the keys.

I could tell him how much I enjoyed staying up late with him, sharing stories. He gave me dirt on Zoey, and then we talked about ourselves. He told me how hard it is to please his dad, how disapproving his father is of the startup. I even told him about being bullied in high school, even if I didn't give him the details about what happened, and why I graduated from an online school. Maybe one day, depending on how things go between us.

As I'm staring at my phone, still debating, it buzzes with a text from Zane.

**Zane**: I have a question for you.
**Abby**: And I have an answer for you: seventeen.
**Zane**: Incorrect. Maybe you should wait for the question?
**Abby**: Maybe you should ask it instead of sending me other, random questions that aren't the one question you want to ask?
**Zane**: Fair point. My question is ...

I wait. And wait. And wait. The dots showing that he's typing come and go. I get the feeling that he's not unsure of what to ask but trying to make me suffer.

**Abby**: My offer to answer your question expires in three ...
**Abby**: Two ...
**Zane**: Would you like to come over for dinner tonight?

I'm thirteen years old, and my mom just bought me tickets to go see Finger Eleven in concert. That's what Zane's question makes me feel like. Or, what I imagine it would have been like, since my mom never approved of my taste in rock music.

*Zane wants to have dinner with me.* I drop the phone for a moment, put my pillow over my face and scream.

"Everything okay in here?"

I drop the pillow and scream for real, scaring Sam, who jerks a little, grabbing on to the doorframe.

"Sam! You scared me! I didn't think anyone was home."

Smiling, she walks in and sits down next to me on the

bed. I'm suddenly very aware of the open text thread on my phone and snatch it out of view. Her smile turns wicked.

"What's going on in here?"

"Nothing."

"Whose texts are you hiding?"

I don't answer, holding the phone to my chest. Sam scoots farther back on the bed, leaning against the wall and pretending to examine her nails, which are all bitten to the quick. That's one thing about Sam. She's usually totally put together, wearing some kind of cute, trendy outfit, but her nails are trashed. The more stressed she is, the shorter they are. I'm guessing the pressure of this book deal is really getting to her.

Which is probably why she's here: to get the details of my love cliché. I've fallen for my BFF's brother. Her twin, no less.

"Don't mind me. Just pretend I'm not here," she says.

"Ugh! Sam. I can't do this with you sitting there."

"Do what?" she asks, blinking her wide brown eyes at me. "What kinds of texts are you sending that you can't write them in front of one of your best friends?"

"Fine. Here." Because I know she's going to pester me until I tell her everything, I hand Sam my phone.

Greedily, she snatches it up and reads, her grin growing as she does. She shoves the phone back at me.

"Answer the man! He's probably going nuts over there since he just asked you out, and you stopped responding."

"Right." I shouldn't be nervous. I mean, I can't say anything but yes to his invitation. I want to ask if I can leave right this second. But I'm hesitating. I set the phone back in my lap, and Sam groans. "What if this is a mistake?"

"How can it be a mistake?" Sam asks. "Zane is a great guy, right?"

"Right."

"And Zoey would murder him if he ever hurt you, correct?"

"Yes. She would murder him with glee."

"So?" Sam lifts a shoulder. "What's the deal?"

I bite my lip. The deal is that this is all new territory for me. At least, that's how it feels. It's a blank computer screen when you're about to start writing a program. There is so much ahead you don't know yet, so many mistakes to make, so much blank space for error. We kissed, but made no promises or declarations. No commitments.

"It feels like a lot of pressure," I say. "I mean, what if we mess things up and then it's all awkward with Zoey forever?"

*And what if I get my heart broken?*

"What if you don't? What if it's awesome? What if you and Zane are the perfect match and then you get to marry him and have the best sister-in-law ever, with no drama because you're already friends?"

"I guess so ..."

"Worst case scenario: it doesn't work out. You and Zoey stay friends. Other than this job with him, how often did you see Zane?"

I think about this. Sadly, I have categorized each and every time I saw Zane for the past few years. I had dinner with Zoey and her dad around Christmas and Zane stopped by, wearing that charcoal gray suit I love. Last October I ran into him in a bar while he was on a date. He smiled from afar and lifted his glass to me.

"Probably once a year. Maybe twice?"

"No big deal," Sam says.

I'm quiet for a minute, thinking back over my last few miserable years of dating. "What about my first-date curse? I can count on my hand the number of guys who have asked for a second date. The last time I went on more than two dates with the same guy was in college."

Sam doesn't tell me I'm stupid even though I know how it sounds. There's no such thing as a curse. But I wish there were. Because saying I'm cursed is better than the alternative, which is that I crash and burn before I ever get to a third date.

With a soft smile, Sam scoots over to lean her head on my shoulder. "Permission to speak freely about your so-called first-date curse?"

"Is this Sam advice, or Dr. Love advice?"

She rolls her eyes. "Both. First, I think you didn't click with any of those guys. They weren't *the* guy. Or even *a* guy good enough for you. You dated some duds, Abs. Were you really disappointed about any of them?"

Most of their faces are a blur in my mind. "No."

"Second, I think that you have a tendency to self-sabotage. You're scared. While you are one of the bravest people I know on the one hand, on the other I think you have some deep-seated insecurities. Which is normal," she says quickly. "I think that it's safer for you to cut and run early. Or scare guys off."

Sam's words feel like a burr on my heart. Prickly. Uncomfortable. Painful, if I think about them too long. Which, of course, means that she's right.

I'm grateful when she continues, because I can't find my way around any words. "Love is terrifying. But if it wasn't, it wouldn't be so amazing when it works. I think you need to be brave with Zane, Abby. Don't make excuses. And don't sabotage it." She pokes me in the arm.

"Ow. You know I bruise easily."

Sam pokes me again. "Text the man. He's probably over there dying."

More than I've wanted anything in a long time, I want to believe Sam. I want to try things with Zane, despite the risks. Another poke. "Yes. Send the text. Three letters. Y-E-S."

"You're such a bully," I say, but I send the text. More than three letters.

**Abby**: I should stay home and work.

It's true. Zane staying with me last night kept me from doing a whole lot of the work I should have been doing for him.

"You foul temptress," Sam says, a note of awe in her voice. "I didn't know you had it in you."

**Zane**: I'm sure your boss will be accommodating.
**Abby**: You might not say that if you met him.
**Zane**: I'm sure he's an upstanding, respectable fellow.
**Abby**: He's kind of uptight.
**Zane**: Maybe he just needs someone to help him relax.

"Girl," Sam says. "Your text game is strong. You know this is how I won Matt over?"

I manage to hold back an eye roll. We have all, for at least a year now, been made aware of every detail of Sam's perfect relationship with her probably soon-to-be fiancé.

"Yes, yes. I know."

**Zane**: Abby.
**Abby**: Zane.
**Zane**: Come to dinner.
**Abby**: You're so bossy.
**Zane**: Your boss and I have that in common. Don't make me come get you. I know where you live.

**Abby:** I'll be there at 7.
**Zane:** See you at 7:15. -Z

That makes me grin. He knows I'll be late, and he doesn't care. At least, I'm assuming that means he doesn't care. He'll probably be like Zoey, where he knows I'll be late, but he'll still give me a hard time.

Sam squeals and practically mauls me with a hug when I set the phone down. "That, my friend, was some serious flirting. Now. Spill the details. *All* of them."

"Is this going in your book?"

"Probably. But I'm asking because I care," she says.

I shove her off. "Sure, you do." When she flutters her lashes at me, I continue. "Fine. I'll tell you everything. But move over so a girl can breathe her own air."

Though I roll my eyes, I'm secretly so excited to finally have a guy I like enough to talk about, even if I know Sam's going to put the whole thing in print.

# sixteen

Zane

A*BBY IS COMING FOR DINNER*. *Abby is coming for dinner.*

Which means I'm scrambling around like a remote-control car being driven by a four-year-old, all jerky and out of control, zooming around in circles. The only thing I haven't done is run into walls.

The door to the bathroom does not count.

My house is, like most things in my life, neat and orderly. But when it comes to my home, that tendency toward neatness translates to cold and uninviting.

That's a great metaphor for my life, really. At least, my life up until Abby. Things have their place and their purpose. But it's been pretty dull, and not somewhere you want to stay.

I don't even have a dining room table. Just a few barstools at the kitchen island. Two of the bedrooms have no furniture. What was I thinking, buying a house? And why am I working so hard at my job if what I really want is to build this life, the one within these walls?

Just before having the woman you really, really like over for dinner is not the time for an existential crisis. That's what I'm thinking as I hammer in a nail to hang the framed picture of me, Zoey, and my mom. It's been sitting on the table in my entryway for months, needing only a nail.

It took five minutes to actually hang it up, but months for me to make the time. Maybe right now is not the time for me to freak out, but it *is* the time to think about the priorities in my life. Because if I want to date Abby for real (which I do), there has to be time.

Not little slivers or an hour here or there. Real time that's prioritized, earmarked as the most important, even over a launch. The timing for this couldn't be worse. Or maybe this is exactly when I need to be considering my priorities and what I want for my future.

I stare at the photo. Mom's smile, which I'm reminded of every time Zoey smiles, is wide and bright, like she can't manage to hold it back. Zoey and I were maybe ten in the photo, which was taken by Dad in our backyard. I don't remember the moment, but I remember being that age. I was into video games and basketball and kept begging for a dog, even though Mom was allergic.

Around then, Zoey and I waged a secret war, one where we would punch each other on the arm or leg as hard as we could when our parents weren't looking. The goal was to not react when getting punched, so as not to alert our mom and dad. That, and land the biggest bruise.

I kind of miss those days. Not that I'd hit my sister now, but the simplicity of the game, the camaraderie of doing something all on our own—*that*, I miss.

I move back into cleaning mode so that the ache of

missing Mom doesn't grow, shoving me into some weird, dark mood before Abby gets here. Even the thought of seeing Abby lifts the worry and sadness. One thing I know for sure: Mom would have loved her.

My phone rings as I'm looking over takeout menus. I hesitate because it's Zoey, but then I figure she might be the best person to talk to before my first date with her best friend. Did Abby already tell her? Based on how close they are, I have to assume that's a yes.

"Hey, Zo."

"Hey, brother. What's cooking?" she asks.

"You know I don't cook. But I am having Abby over for dinner. Chinese, Thai, or pizza? Or Mexican? Indian? Italian? Oh, and by the way, I didn't listen to your advice about keeping things professional with Abby. I hope that's okay." My tone is casual, but I'm holding my breath waiting for her response.

Zoey laughs. "I never thought I'd see the day."

"What day is that?"

"The day where you've hopelessly fallen for someone. And that the someone is Abby."

I'm thankful she didn't use the L-word, because I think it might have sent me into a tailspin, even if a little part of me suspects that the strength and depth of my feelings for Abby are headed in that direction, if not well on their way.

"Me neither. Gloat or whatever you want to do later. Give me a hint on the food *now*."

"Why don't you ask her?"

I could. But I want to impress Abby. I have this idea in my head that she'll show up and I'll have the perfect meal by candlelight. We'll enjoy a leisurely, laugh-filled dinner, and then later maybe enjoy a replay of that epic kiss we had in the closet at the resort. My house—or maybe the swing in the backyard—is definitely a better option for romance than in a dark closet next to bottles of bleach and hotel towels.

Thinking of kissing helps me narrow things down. "Forget Mexican and Thai. Maybe American?"

It's important to consider what foods won't leave us both with dragon breath. Maybe I should have asked her to have frozen yogurt instead of dinner.

"Abby loves that burger place near your house. Avocados and muenster cheese with sweet potato fries."

Zoey sounds so amused by this, and any other time, I might be bothered or try to defend myself, but I simply do not care. I'm trying to write this down on a notepad I keep in the kitchen, just to be sure I don't mess up the order.

"You really like her, don't you?" Zoey asks.

I set down the pen and clear my throat. "I do. Is that ... okay?"

"I'm surprised but happy. I wouldn't have put you two together. I mean, I guess it makes sense. She's my opposite too, and she's my best friend. I've never heard you sound like this about anyone."

That's because I've never felt this way about anyone. It's like I've gone through a black hole and come out of the other side to find an entirely new system of planets and stars. I'm still mapping them out.

"You're a good guy, Z. *Mostly.*"

"Thanks?"

"Anytime." Zoey pauses. "Just know that if you hurt Abby, I'll be the one taking a tire iron to your car."

I can't help but smile. "Noted."

A few hours later, I realize that I'm in over my head. Way over my head.

I stare around the living room and run my hands through my hair, staring at all the bags from World Market.

What did I do?

The only thing I needed to buy was candles. I planned to walk into World Market, pick up a few candles, and then grab our burgers and head home. Instead, I pictured my empty house, wondering what Abby would think, and I kept piling items into my cart.

A few hundred dollars later and now I have throw pillows, art for the walls, and a three-foot-tall wooden giraffe that I can't quite explain. You know what I forgot? *Candles.* I also didn't have time to put anything away.

There's a knock at the door, and I panic. Should I hide the bags in one of the spare bedrooms? What if Abby wants a tour?

I take a deep breath and give the photo of me, Mom, and Zoey another look. I'm being idiotic and overthinking everything. The smile in my mom's eyes tells me to just let go—something that has never come easily for me—and enjoy.

I open the door, my pulse quickening at the sight of Abby in jeans and an electric blue top that really highlights the pink in her hair. I've seen her made up, in pajamas, and in casual attire. She's beautiful in them all.

Abby's brow furrows. "Who kicked your puppy?" she asks.

I sigh. "Come in. I'll show you."

When Abby sees the bags in the living room, she gives me a confused look. "You ... went shopping? Is this a case of buyer's remorse or something?"

"Or something." I sit down on the couch, pleased when

she sits down next to me. I don't pull her into my lap, even though I want to.

"No one ever comes over, and I'm never here. My house is empty, and ... I wanted to impress you."

"I share a house with four other women. It's like a glorified dorm room, or a small commune. I'm impressed that you own a house. And that you like World Market. Can I take a look?" she asks.

I nod, and Abby begins rummaging through the bags. "I like your taste," she says after a moment, sitting back on her heels and looking up at me with a smile.

"You do?"

"I do. And I have an idea. I smell something greasy and delicious. How about you feed me, and I help you find places to put all this stuff?"

The idea of Abby helping me decorate my house fills me with something I can't quite name. An emotion that feels both solid and also has things in my stomach jumping around.

"I'd love that," I tell her, standing and reaching my hand out for hers.

I pull her to her feet, not letting her go right away. For a few beats, we simply make eye contact, studying each other, until she smiles. It makes me smile right back.

"Come on," I say, finally tugging her into the kitchen, loving the feel of her small, cool hand in mine. "I know I need to feed the Abby if I want her to function properly."

"Ha ha," she says, then sniffs. "Is that a hamburger I smell?"

## dear dr. love

*From: Dongled_in_Detroit@drlove.advice*
*To: DrLove@drlove.advice*

Dear Dr. Love,
    I really love my boyfriend. Like, totally. The only problem? I'm a Mac girl and he uses PC.
    Every time we take a step forward, we take a double click back. I'm tired of his hands all over my touch screen, and don't get me started on the dongle problem.
    I think our software needs to be updated and we might be hardwired for failure.
    Any words of advice?
    Sincerely,
    —Dongled in Detroit

---

*From: DrLove@drlove.advice*
*To: AbbyGrabby@me.mail*

Dear Abby,
    Nice one. You owe me dinner since I sniffed out another one of your fake emails.
    —S

*From: AbbyGrabby@me.mail*
*To: DrLove@drlove.advice*

Ha! Great email. But not it.
—Abs

*From: Zoey.F.Abramson@me.mail*
*To: DrLove@drlove.advice*

Dear Dr. Love,
   Ha! This was Zoey, pretending to be Abby. You owe *me* dinner. I don't even know what a dongle is.
—Zoey

*From: DrLove@drlove.advice*
*To: Zoey.F.Abramson@me.mail*

Fine. But I'm not going to that crepes place again. Crepes are *not* a meal.
—S

# seventeen

*Abby*

I'VE GOT a case of the Mondays as I roll into my hated day job. Big-time.

"Long weekend?" Micah asks.

I groan and drop my head onto my desk. "Great weekend. Being here? Not so much."

I stayed at Zane's until almost eleven the night before. We ate burgers from my favorite place (thanks, Zoey), and then I helped him decorate his house. All but the wooden giraffe, which I couldn't stop laughing about, and he agreed to return. He didn't even seem sure why he'd bought it.

And after that, we made out like we were teenagers, about to be caught by our parents walking in any minute. Every kiss was as good or better than the first. I kept thinking Zane might push for more the way so many guys have, even on first dates, but instead, he seemed perfectly content to simply explore kissing. The man was like a kiss cartographer, intent on mapping out and claiming everything—at least everything above my collarbone.

When I got home, I couldn't sleep because I kept replaying it in my mind.

Micah drags me back from thinking about it again. "Are you feeling okay? You're flushed."

"I'm fine."

"How's the side gig going at Eck0? Figure out their issue?"

I haven't said much to Micah about it, considering the whole non-disclosure agreement I signed. "Working on it."

"Any chance for a full-time position? Maybe for two people?" Micah gives me prayer hands.

"I wish."

Honestly, I do. Sort of. I'd love to work with Zane. Seeing him daily has been great, and I already know I'll miss it when I finish up.

But the startup life? After the last week, I'm not sure. Zane is the last one to leave the office, many nights after ten. I'm not there in the mornings, but I'd wager that he's the first one there. Meetings, calls, emergencies—everything is high priority, all the time. And I know it won't slow down with the launch, at least not for a few months.

This weekend was an anomaly. Spending time with him at the resort, then having the leisurely dinner—I know that won't be reality with him. Not for a while. Startups are brutal. He seems to love it though, and since I know what it's like to hate your job, I'd never ask him to change.

Our boss appears suddenly in our doorway, reminding me so much of the boss from the movie *Office Space* that I have to stifle a giggle.

"Hey, my two favorite IT people."

"Your only two IT people," I say. He ignores me.

"We've got a fun one for you this morning."

"Define fun," Micah says.

"Someone opened an attachment"—Micah and I both groan—"and now there's a video playing of, uh, let's just say inappropriate content. We can't even shut the computer down. You two can fight over who gets to fix it."

"Not it!" Micah and I say at the same time as soon as our boss has gone.

We end up having to rock-paper-scissors for it, and as his paper covers my rock, Micah says, "May the odds be ever in your favor."

I think that train has already left the station.

---

I practically skip into Zane's office that night. Partly because I really hate my job. And attachments. And viruses.

But mostly because I want to see Zane.

As if he knew exactly when I arrived, Zane strides out of his office to greet me, looking practically edible in his dark blue suit.

*Abby, remember what we talked about. That's Gibbs again.* Usually that does the trick, but even Gibbs can't force the air in my lungs to not feel so thin and the blood in my veins to slow.

When Zane smiles, I freeze, right there in the middle of the still-busy office, like I'm a butterfly, pinned into place by his blue eyes.

"Abs," he says. "Why does it feel like so long since I've seen you?"

"Maybe I'm just that addictive," I say. *Hopefully*, I'm that addictive. To him, anyway.

Zane's smile widens. "Yes, you are," he murmurs. "Now

follow me. I have a few questions for you. And a fresh bag of Twizzlers."

When I get to the workspace I've been using, he not only has a new package of my favorite candy, but a piping hot flat white, a small framed photo of the *Stranger Things* season one poster, and a small potted succulent.

My eyes zero in on that. He got me a plant. A living thing. In a cute little ceramic pot painted turquoise and silver, two of my favorite colors.

"I'm going to kill that," I say, pointing. "I know succulents are the easiest plants to own, but I had this cactus once and—"

His warm fingers land on my shoulder, squeezing so that my voice trails off into a quiet squeak. Gently, he encourages me to sit down.

"It's plastic," Zane whispers, leaning so close to my ear that his breath skates over my skin.

*What's plastic?* My head is a carousel, spinning wildly out of control. Right. The succulent.

"Perfect," I say, trying to get the various systems in my body to behave.

*Hey, circulatory system: slow it down!*

*Respiratory system: in and out, nice and steady. That's it. There we go. Breathe.*

*Reproductive system: you have not been called to active duty. Stand down, soldier. I'm talking to you, ovaries.*

*Nervous system: stop being so ... nervous.*

*Skeletal system: way to be solid. Carry on.*

I realize that Zane is still standing close to my chair —*much* too close to my chair. And he's apparently asked me a question that I missed while trying to get myself under some semblance of control. I tip my head back, looking at him upside down.

"What? I'm sorry, I zoned out a bit."

Zane from a week ago—has so much really changed in a week?— would have gotten that furrowed brow and pinched look about his mouth. The new and improved Zane only chuckles.

"I just said that I have a few meetings tonight, so I'll be in the conference room. Feel free to use my office if you need more space."

"After you've made my space so feng shui? No way. I just need to water my succulent."

Zane touches my shoulder again, somewhere between a squeeze and a pat. This gets me all riled up again. Shoulders were never a part of my body I considered at any length. They're just there, being all shouldery, keeping my bra straps in place. I think that they've been vastly underrated.

"It's plastic," Zane calls as he saunters off to the conference room.

I watch him go, blushing when he turns to look back at me, like he knew I'd be watching him. And then he winks —*winks*!

I have to fan my hot cheeks with a piece of cardstock before I pull out my computer and start working.

"You're a pretty plant," I say, dragging the potted succulent over. I know it's fake, but if talking to real plants helps them grow, it certainly can't hurt a plastic one. "Good succulent. Sit. Stay."

The frenetic energy in the office gets me hyped, which is good. Launch is coming, but it can't if I don't figure out what's going on and who's trying to hijack the system.

A few hours later, I've installed a trap. A lovely, lovely trap that is practically invisible and definitely unavoidable. I can only hope that it's not Jack. He may not be my favorite person, but he's Zane's friend and partner. I don't know enough people around here to have any other guesses. In the next two days, I should know who.

I've got my earphones in, listening to DJ Marshmello and admiring my work when a tap on my arm makes me jump.

I immediately minimize my windows, spinning to face Josh, the only person other than Jack or Zane I know by name. Everyone else is too busy to do more than smile or wave, but Josh usually stops in once a night to say hi. And to offer his help, like I need it. I think he might have a baby crush on me, so I've done my best not to encourage it. Friendly, not flirty.

"You scared me!"

He pulls over a chair and straddles it backwards, grinning. "Sorry," he says with a sheepish grin. "I tend to disappear into my work too. How's it going?"

"Pretty well, which means I probably won't be seeing you after this week. Sad face emoji," I say.

He chuckles. "Well, congrats and I'm sorry. I know I'll miss having you around." He tips his chin toward the conference room. "And I'm not the only one. You know, I'm not sure I ever saw the boss smile before you showed up. I'm not entirely sure that you haven't replaced him with a twin."

This makes me laugh. Hard. "Zane actually does have a twin." Josh's eyebrows shoot up. "A twin *sister*."

"Oh. Right. So, no twin switches?"

"No parent traps either."

Jack emerges from the conference room, shutting the door behind him. He gives me a little wave, and the same knowing look he's been giving me since he and Charla caught me with Zane in the closet.

"Hey, how do you feel about Jack?" I ask Josh.

Josh makes a face. "He's not my favorite person."

"You like him less than Zane?"

"I never said I didn't like Zane. He's just intense. Jack is just so smooth. Like, he can talk his way into—or out of—anything. I don't like him, and I don't trust him. Anyway, better head back to the grind."

Josh heads back to his station, and I try to quell the queasy feeling I have. Finding out that someone has been sabotaging the company is going to blindside Zane. Even more so if it's Jack.

I try to remember how winsome Jack was with the investors, how serious he had been about securing the financing. I don't know how things are structured here, but I wonder if there's some other way he could access that money, even if the app fails. Or before it launches. Otherwise, I just can't see it. No matter how right Josh is about him being too smooth.

It's nearing eleven o'clock, and there's nothing more I can do tonight. Except watch and wait. An alarm will go off on my phone the moment someone steps into my trap. I'm both excited and nervous about finally figuring it out.

I hover outside the conference room for a moment, hearing voices, then shoot Zane a text telling him I'm leaving. I'm almost to the door when Zane calls my name. I turn to see him jogging toward me. His suit jacket is missing and so is his tie. The top few buttons of his white shirt are unbuttoned, and his smile is wide.

"Let me walk you out," he says.

I've got pepper spray and a taser in my bag, but I'm not going to argue with the man. "You're in a good mood," I say as he pushes open the front door, holding it for me.

"We just had a very productive meeting. And I've actually got a favor to ask you."

He could probably ask me for a kidney, and I'd say yes.

"We've got another dinner tomorrow night. Different

investors. Jack and I were wondering if you could come. Maybe spout a little of that tech mumbo jumbo and impress them like you did this weekend."

We reach the driver's side door of my car and I lean back against it, facing Zane. "Did you really just call it mumbo jumbo? I'm slightly offended on behalf of tech geeks everywhere."

"I did. That's about the extent of my knowledge of what you do. It's very impressive. I just don't know the words."

I pretend to think about it. "How about this—you give me three words that relate to what I do, and I'll go."

"Three words?"

Zane rubs a hand over his chin. It looks like he forgot to shave this morning, and the rasping sound his hand makes as it grazes over the coarse skin sends a little shiver through me.

"Three little words," I say.

"Code," he says confidently, counting on his fingers. "PHP."

"That's two. Good boy. One more and I'm yours."

His eyes narrow on me, and his nostrils flare slightly. I didn't mean for that to sound so flirty, but I don't mind his response. It's still a wonder that I'm the one who can get a reaction out of him.

Zane takes a step toward me. The dark look in his eyes makes me want to retreat, but the car is at my back. I tilt my head up to hold his gaze as he steps even closer.

When he puts one hand on the car next to my head, I forget to breathe.

He leans closer, closer, then closer still. My eyelids flutter, wanting to close, but I can't take my eyes off this man. We're cheek to cheek, millimeters away. I want to rub against him like a cat, feeling his stubble burn my cheek.

I feel his breath on my ear just before he whispers, "Algorithm."

The word has never sounded sexy before. I didn't know that it could. But Zane drags it out, so that the four syllables are more like ten, the word rolling off his tongue like it's in a language only meant to be spoken by him, to me.

It's all I can do not to grab him by his shirt collar and drag his lips to mine. Instead, I wait, counting my heartbeats, eager to see what Zane will do next. It's not like I couldn't kiss him if I wanted to. But I don't mind this game we're playing. The back and forth. The unknown and excitement of it. If I'd had to imagine, I would have pictured Zane delivering me some kind of NDA to sign or maybe a dating contract.

To my disappointment, he gives me a quick kiss, then steps away before things get interesting. He stuffs his hands in his pockets, looking pleased with himself.

"You win," I tell him, doing my best to seem unfazed, my voice level.

I'm a cucumber. An icebox. A woman in complete control.

"I'll go to your fancy dinner," I tell him. "I'll impress your investors and save the day. Again. But I'm counting this as *over*-overtime."

Zane only grins. "Send me the bill."

## eighteen

*Zane*

Tuesday morning, I catch myself humming in the shower. I nick my jaw shaving because I'm *smiling*. When I walk into work, a few people stop to stare. I realize that I'm whistling a cheerful tune.

Is it really so unusual for me to be happy?

Yes. Yes, it is.

I have always been more on the serious side, but after Mom died, there was only Dad with his regimented thinking and business-minded influence. Zoey and I both missed out on the softness, the human side that Mom offered, more than we even realized at the time.

There's one person responsible for this. For shaking me out of my slumber, making me realize that I've been living my life half asleep. The woman who reminds me more and more of Mom. Not in the looks or style department, because Mom definitely matched Dad in that way—classic, conservative, and neat. But Abby is like Mom in her humor, her honesty, and her relish for life.

This is all new, and I have no idea what I'm doing. Normally that would scare me. I'm the guy who uses the GPS on his car and his phone, just in case. I used to print out directions as well and only stopped because my printer broke.

With Abby, it's like I've hit one of those unknown areas on the map, where the blue dot showing your location hovers over a blank green space instead of showing you the road you're on. This would make me panic in any other situation, but I feel only a growing certainty about her. About us.

Especially after seeing her in my house the other night. The pictures on the wall and the throw pillows weren't what was missing in the spartan space. It was Abby. She's what was missing.

My last official girlfriend was in, like, tenth grade. I don't know the rules of serious relationships as an adult. I also don't know how I'll have time for it, making me again question the sanity of the life I've built for myself. Not for the first time in the past year, I wonder if I really want to keep running on this hamster wheel.

*No. I don't.*

The answer is so clear that it's shocking. I don't want to keep this up. I don't want to stay with Eck0, this thing that I helped build. I'm proud of it, but I don't want this life. I find myself pulling up the contract Jack and I set up, looking at the clause we set up in case either of us wanted to walk away. I could do it.

The idea, which I'd casually tossed around, has solidly planted itself in my brain. It feels like hope. A relief.

I just need to get through this launch with Jack. The man

in question corners me in my office, a sly smile on his face as he leans against the closed door.

"I see I'm not the only one who got lucky this weekend. Is Keep Austin Weird as freaky in the sheets as out of them?"

And just like that, my cheerful mood is gone, replaced by a mounting rage that has me standing, palms flat on the desk, ready to pounce across it. But if anything, it only confirms my resolve. I will leave. As soon as I can.

Jack holds up both hands and quickly changes tactics. "Hey, now. Sorry! Just trying to make conversation. I like Abby. She's a good girl."

*Right*. That's why he continually refers to Abby as Keep Austin Weird, the city's slogan that I'm pretty sure Austin stole from Portland. And why he thinks it would be okay to talk to me about how she was in bed. I'd never been one to spill details, not that there were many to spill.

I feel sick looking at Jack. Suddenly, I want nothing more than to launch this app and walk away. Walk away from my partner, whom I can hardly stand to be around. I want to leave this startup life that keeps me here until midnight most nights. The job that makes a typical life unlikely, a real relationship impossible. I've been saying for months that it will calm down at launch, but that isn't really true. We'll have to manage the launch tightly, staying on top of every detail for months. We might even be busier after. More work. More Jack.

"I like Abby," I say, my voice low and dangerous. "I respect her. And if you respected her, you wouldn't call her that or degrade her that way. I don't want to hear it again."

Jack looks like he wants to argue, but instead, closes his mouth and gives me a curt nod. I sink back in my seat, loosening my tie a little. Jack sits down in the chair across from my desk, smoothing the front of his collared shirt.

"So, the dinner tonight. Is Abby coming?"

"Yes."

"Good." Jack rubs a hand over his jaw. "Look—I'm sorry for what I said. I really didn't mean to be disrespectful. Abby is great. She really came through with the investors this weekend. You think she can do the same tonight?"

Despite his apology, every word Jack says about Abby makes me want to connect my fist with his mouth. Somehow, I manage to keep myself in my seat, hands clenched in my lap.

"I don't see why she wouldn't. She's brilliant. And knows way more about the tech side than you or I do."

He stands, smiling again, though it's tighter and more forced than it was when he walked in. He managed to ruin both our moods. *Well done, buddy.*

"One more thing," Jack says, turning back to face me as he opens the door. "In light of the awkwardness just now, I hesitate to say anything."

"Spit it out." *And then get out.*

Jack shuffles a little, running a hand through his hair. "It's just that the guys tonight are … older. Not just in age. They're old school. Old money. Old Texas."

"Okayyyy. I've read the files on them too. And?"

He meets my gaze for a moment, as though he expects whatever he's hinting at to make itself clear to me.

Blowing out a breath, Jack finally says, "It's just that Abby doesn't exactly have the sort of look that will reassure investors."

It's like he's dumped cold water on my head. I'm frozen in my seat, stunned by something so obvious that I might have thought of it myself a few weeks ago.

"I don't think …" I trail off, unsure how to finish that sentence. Because I don't know what to think.

In a way, Jack's right. I know the kind of guys we're meeting with tonight. Guys like my dad. Narrow minds. Rigid thoughts. They'll take one look at Abby's pink-tipped hair or whatever funky outfit she chooses, and it will be an uphill battle for them to hear anything else. Of course, that wasn't an issue this weekend. She had the investors totally wrapped around her finger.

"No." I shake my head, convincing myself even as I speak. "Abby is brilliant. All she needs to do is talk. You heard her—it's convincing. What she wears or the color of her hair won't matter."

Jack nods as I'm speaking, then waves a hand. "Right. No, you're right. Sorry for bringing it up."

And with a final smile, he's gone. But his words eat at me the rest of the day.

Abby doesn't need to change who she is, and how she looks doesn't impact her expertise in her field. But I know guys like the VCs we're meeting tonight. I remember the first time Dad met Abby, and how he raised one brow, dismissively, giving her a not-so-subtle once-over in her ripped fishnets, boots, and purple hair she had at the time. He's had years to adjust, and now loves Abby.

But the VCs tonight … we don't have the luxury of time to show them how awesome Abby is, how great our app is. We have one dinner. Two hours at most. A bad impression from the start could tank the whole conversation. Worry needles its way underneath my skin, attaching itself to my thoughts like a virus.

I pace my office, playing with the end of my tie. Is it really such a big deal to ask Abby to dress a little differently or tuck her hair into a bun? It's one dinner. It's just hair. It's not because *I* don't like it.

*This is just business.*

*She'll understand.*

*No, this is stupid. Don't ask her to compromise.*

*It's only clothes and hair. And it doesn't mean that I don't like them.*

For the rest of the afternoon, I debate. Back and forth, back and forth. I feel like the business part of my life is ganging up on the personal part of my life, tangling them up into a knot I'm going to have to cut free somehow.

What it really comes down to is that I don't want any reason, no matter how small or superficial, to stop these VCs from investing. Walking away from Eck0 would be much easier with this money secured, with our launch going off without a hitch, fully funded.

Then I'll have more time to spend with Abby. I won't be yoked with Jack. So, really, this all comes down to asking her to do something small now that will be huge for both of us down the road. It's a small thing that will make our future better.

Feeling resolved, I slide my phone out of my pocket to send Abby a message. She's planning to meet us at the restaurant rather than coming to the office. It takes me four attempts to word the text correctly.

**Zane**: Abby, for the dinner tonight, would it be possible for you to be a bit more on the conservative side? Maybe tuck your hair up and borrow a suit? Zoey could probably help with this. We just need to make the right impression with the VCs. Thanks, Z.

I wait, the phone in my palm, until I see the dots indicating that she's typing. They come, and they go. Come and go.

"Come on, Abs," I mutter, not sure why I feel so nervous about this.

It's not a big deal, I remind myself. Setting the phone down on my desk, I wipe my palms on my thighs.

A moment later a text pops up.

**Abby**: NP.

I'm not into text lingo, so I have to google her response. I refuse to be embarrassed that I find the answer in an article entitled, "Secret Text Codes All Parents Must Know to Understand Their Teens." I now know more than I ever wanted to about how teens are using emojis and I want to scrub my eyes and delete most of the fruit or food emojis from my phone. But I do find the answer.

*No problem.* The boulder on my chest lifts, and I toss my tie over one shoulder before I reply with some lingo of my own, pulled from the same article.

**Zane**: TY. VBG.
**Abby**: Wow. I really opened a door, didn't I?
**Zane**: YWSYLS.
**Abby**: I don't know what that means.
**Zane**: You win some, you lose some.
**Abby**: Okay, Tiger. Step away from the computer. You had to google this, didn't you? And you've still got the browser open?

I shut my laptop, grinning and feeling so much lighter about, well ... *everything*. The dinner, my day, and the future.

**Zane**: I do not know of what you speak. I shall see you at the dinner this evening. Sincerely, Zane Abramson the First

Abby replies with a laughing face emoji. I've never really enjoyed texting before. It always felt like the cheapest form of communication. But with Abby, texting is fun. Flirty. Addictive.

Despite my busy afternoon, putting out fires and setting things up before the dinner, I find myself repeatedly glancing down at my phone, smiling as I think of Abby.

# nineteen

*Abby*

IT'S NO BIG DEAL. *It's just hair. A change of clothes.*

*Zane doesn't know. This isn't like before.*

These are the kinds of lines I'm still repeating to myself when I get back to the house. I ducked out of my office a little early. I need to get ready for the dinner, but my stomach is in knots. The kind used in rope climbing or sailing, way too secure for me to undo.

"Hey, Abs!" Delilah greets me with a hug as I set my laptop bag on the kitchen table. "Aw, why so glum, sugarplum?"

I shake my head, managing a small smile. "Just work stuff. Hey, um." I clear my throat, which seems suddenly tight. "Is Zoey here?"

"Nope. She's at some work thing with her boss. Just you and me. Why? Do you need her?"

Zoey is the last person I need right now. "Nope. I need

*you*, actually. Could you do me a huge favor? If you're busy, it's no big deal."

She gestures to her blonde hair, piled into a messy topknot, then to her face which is devoid of makeup. "Do I look like I'm busy?"

Delilah never goes anywhere without a full face of makeup and totally done hair. She says it's a by-product of her pageant days, and that we should have seen her back then. This is exactly why I need her.

"I have to go to this dinner tonight. I'm supposed to look a bit more …" I search for the right word. What did Zane say in his text? "Conservative."

Delilah tilts her head, her button nose wrinkling in a way that could only look cute on her. "Like, in what way?"

I swallow. *It's no big deal.* "In all the ways. Hair, makeup, clothes. The works."

"Why?"

I repeat some version of what Zane said about the old-school VCs and making a good impression.

"I guess that makes sense. Are you giving me free rein?"

Delilah looks way too excited. Like a rabid and very hungry cat. I'm the easy food source in this situation. A bird. Or a chipmunk. Totally about to be devoured. But I need her help. And I trust her.

"With some limits. I think it needs to be tasteful. I don't want to feel like makeup is clogging my pores or like my eyelashes are too heavy. Nothing glued on that I have to peel off at the end of the night."

"I can do tasteful," she swears, holding up her fingers in what I think is some kind of Girl Scout promise. Not that either of us ever joined. She was busy winning pageants and I had my nose in a book or computer.

With a sigh, I resign myself to this fate. It's for one night. It's just my looks.

It's for Zane.

That last one is the hardest to swallow. Because not so deep down, a part of me wonders if this isn't actually for *him*. Am I enough for Zane?

"I'm all yours."

Delilah squeals and claps her hands, bouncing up on her toes. "You won't regret this."

The problem is that I already do.

―――

Almost two hours later, it's done. I've been transformed into some alternate version of myself, and it isn't horrible. At least, it doesn't look horrible.

"What do you think?" Delilah is standing behind me, holding my shoulders and beaming like a mom sending her baby girl off to the first day of kindergarten.

I stare into the full-length mirror hanging on the back of her door, trying to gather words for a response. I have on a black, knee-length skirt and a black blazer with a light pink shirt underneath. Black heels we pilfered from Sam's closet. My makeup is understated—natural but whatever she did with the eyeliner and all those brushes really highlights my cheekbones and my eyes. And my hair is in a sleek updo, all the pink safely hidden away, just like Zane asked.

"You did a great job," I finally say. That's true. "I look … perfect."

The twisting, knotting sensation in my stomach continues. I blink back tears, the same ones that threatened the whole time I sat in the chair, reminding myself that I trust

Delilah, that she's just doing what I asked. She won't hurt me.

"So, why do you look so sad?" Delilah whispers. She wraps her arms around my waist and gives me a hug from behind, not letting go. I consider fighting her but instead place my arms over hers.

"I'm fine."

She squeezes me tighter. "Are you? I can change the hair, or we can look through my closet again—"

"No. Like I said, it's perfect."

"You know that you looked perfect before all this too, right?"

Did I though? And perfect for whom?

"Right. Thank you. I better get to dinner."

Careful not to meet her eyes in the mirror, I extricate myself from her grip, grabbing the black Kate Spade purse she's letting me borrow. I've already put my phone, keys, and wallet inside. In my rush I smack right into the last person I want to see in the hallway.

"Abs?" Zoey grips me by the arms, looking shocked. "What are you wearing? And where are you going?"

"Just a dinner. Delilah helped me get ready." I try to shove my way by her, using Delilah's big bag as a mini battering ram. Unfortunately, Harper is right behind Zoey. We're crammed into the narrow hallway, and I'm going exactly nowhere.

Harper peers around Zoey's side. Her reaction is a mixture of shock and confusion. "What happened to you?"

I groan, looking down at my feet. With a last burst of energy, I shake off Zoey's grip and try to push past again. "I'm going to be late."

"Harper, a little backup," Zoey says, and Harper squeezes

in next to Zoey. Now they're a literal lady wall, blocking my passage.

"Not so fast, short stuff." Zoey looks over my shoulder at Delilah. "You did this?"

"Yeah?" Delilah sounds unsure.

"And you." Zoey has her fierce gaze locked on me, so much like Zane's that it makes my stomach sink a little lower. "You asked for this?"

I nod. "It's for a business dinner. I have to impress investors."

"Did my idiot brother ask you to do this?"

I nod again, and Zoey mutters something under her breath, the kinds of words I rarely hear spilling from her lips. She, like Zane, is usually the pinnacle of control. Right now, though, she looks like a train car that's come unhinged and is barreling off the tracks.

She spins me around and shoves me back into Delilah's room. "We're fixing this," she says, while pushing me down into the makeover chair I've been keeping warm for the last few hours. "Now. You!" She jabs a finger in Delilah's direction. "Grab the straightening iron. And there's a midnight blue dress in Sam's closet. Get it."

"Yes, ma'am."

"You better fix her," Harper says, shaking her head. "I love you, Abs."

Her unexpected—and unusual—sentiment warms me. "Thanks, Harpy." She snorts at my favorite nickname and disappears into her room.

Delilah scurries off, leaving me facing off with Zoey in the mirror. Which is a good thing. I have the distinct feeling that if I looked directly into her eyes, I might vanish in a puff of smoke.

"Zane said I need to look professional," I protest. "*Conservative*."

"Shut up about him. I'll deal with him later. You're going to look just fine."

"I'm going to be late," I say.

"You're always late."

"It's just clothes. And hair," I whine.

But this is the wrong thing to say to my best friend, the one who knows why this particular situation matters so much more. Why I avoid makeovers, and the reason the mere idea shakes loose all the insecurities that I usually have tied down tight.

Zoey leans close, her cheek next to mine, our eyes locked in the mirror. "Yes. It is. But it's more than that, and you know it. You aren't changing for my brother. Or his investors. You're going to look great when we're done with you. But you're going to look like *you*. You don't need to pretend to be someone else just to impress some uptight moneybags. Got it?"

"Okay."

I must not have sounded convincing, because Zoey grabs my chin and turns me so we're eyeball to eyeball. "Do. You. Under. Stand?"

Delilah walks in, glances at the two of us, and starts to back away slowly. It's a solid plan.

"No, you don't," Zoey says, pointing at Delilah without breaking eye contact with me. "Get in here so we can fix this."

Giggling nervously, Delilah says, "Do y'all need to take this outside?"

Zoey pins me with her gaze. "Do *you* want to take this outside?"

I consider. Like Zane, she's taller than me by at least six

inches. She doesn't have his muscles though. *His muscles, mmm ...*

I stand. "Yes. Let's go."

Zoey throws her arms around me. "There you are. There's my girl."

"Get off me! Cage match in the backyard. Now."

Laughing, she squeezes me harder. I realize it's futile. Especially when Delilah hugs me from the back, squishing me between them.

"I feel like a sandwich in a panini press," I manage to groan. "A little air, please?"

They both laugh, loosening up, but only slightly. Zoey pulls back, studying me.

"What?" I ask.

"How do you feel dressed like this?"

I fidget, tugging at the bottom of the blazer. "Like I'm going to a Halloween party dressed as you. And I don't want to go. No offense."

She grins. "None taken. You said you're supposed to be impressing investors. Do you *feel* impressive?"

"No," I say in a soft voice. "Sorry, Delilah. You did a great job."

"Thank you. But you did look weird. Like when people dress up animals in people clothes or like other animals." She shudders, and since she's still gripping me, it shakes me too. "I sometimes have nightmares about the bulldog dressed as a bumblebee."

The two of them manhandle me back down into the chair and Zoey starts undoing my hair.

"Look, Abs. It was thoughtful of you to want to impress my brother by changing your style."

"I was trying to impress the investors!" I protest.

"Right. It was a good thought. But your big, beautiful

brain is going to do that. Your confidence. And you looked totally defeated when you were walking out of here. Not like the warrior princess you are."

"It's just clothes. I'm still me underneath," I say, feeling more exposed than I have in a long time.

"Have you told Zane yet?"

"Not specifically. He knows I was bullied."

Delilah makes a small sound but doesn't say anything. I really should sit all my roommates down and tell them everything. I really should just be over it by now. It's been years.

"Maybe you should," Zoey says softly.

"I think you're right," I say. "But not tonight. Okay?"

Zoey nods, finally releasing my hair from the tight updo. She finger-combs it, then leans over to show Delilah something on her phone. "Like this, but a little toned down."

"Right-o, boss." Delilah gets to work on my hair. "I sprayed it within an inch of its life, so we're going to have to do some work."

"I'm highly flammable right now," I say, remembering the amount of hairspray Delilah used.

"It's only going to get worse," Delilah mutters, grabbing a tube of something that smells like mint and smoothing it on my hair. "Just keep away from open flames."

I wait for her to laugh, but when she doesn't, I nod. "Right. No Baked Alaska for me."

Zoey steps in front of me, leaning back against the dressing table, careful not to spill any of Delilah's expensive—and extensive—array of powders and creams and brushes.

"What we wear is just that—something superficial, on the outside. A mask, in some cases." She looks pointedly at me. "Or sometimes a shield."

I hold up a finger, tilting my head. "Hang on?"

182

"What?" Zoey looks irritated that I've interrupted her monologue.

"I'm just listening for the music that tells me this is the important emotional moment on the after-school special."

She goes to smack my shoulder, but I block her, feeling the heat of the straightening iron by my ear.

"Hey! Keep it civil, you two. Unless you want to rock a Van Gogh look tonight."

"Tempting," I say.

"As I was saying," Zoey says, rolling her eyes dramatically. "Clothes are superficial. But they can also be an expression of who we are. We shouldn't use them as a crutch or something to hide behind. But it should be *our* choice. You looked amazing like this. But you also looked defeated. Zane took away your choice. He took away your agency. He was asking you to use clothes as a mask. And it stripped you of your agency. Your confidence."

I can't cry, because I'll totally mess up the makeup. It definitely wasn't waterproof. As if realizing this, Delilah sets down the flat iron and begins fanning my eyes with her hands, until the three of us are laughing.

A warmth has been expanding in my chest, like a tiny sun is just rising over the horizon of my heart.

"Zane should never have asked you to change. I don't care who the investors are."

"What if I mess it all up?"

"Do either Zane or Jack know as much about the programming and development as you?"

"No."

"Are you going to walk into that restaurant like you know more than everyone else in the room?"

"Yes!"

"Exactly. And you're also going to show my fool of a twin

that you can do that without changing a single thing about you."

I want to defend Zane, and I know he didn't mean anything by it. At least, I don't think he did. I want to hope that it was for the investors. He seems to like me as is. And if he doesn't, then he's not the man I thought he was, and definitely not a man I want.

# twenty

*Zane*

ABBY IS LATE. I'm doing my best not to worry, but my best isn't very good.

I'm drumming my fingers on the table, watching the door every thirty seconds for her to sweep inside with the two tons of confidence she always manages to stuff inside her tiny frame.

"We're on track for a mid-April launch," Jack is saying. He gives my shoulder a crushing squeeze, his way of telling me to get in the conversation. But I've always hated this game. Especially now that my mind is elsewhere.

And the two investors have finished off a bottle of wine between them already somehow, which is bad considering the appetizers haven't even arrived yet. Jack gives me a less subtle look, and I clear my throat, turning my attention to the table.

"That's right. We're in the final stages now."

Davis—the one with the unfortunate hairpiece that looks like a beaver pelt perched on his round head—bangs his hand down on the table and begins humming notes that sound vaguely familiar. When no one joins in, he says, "Come on! *The Final Countdown?*"

He's humming again, only louder. Christopher, the one in the cowboy hat, joins him this time, and then they're both looking at us. Jack eyes me, shrugging, before he joins in.

So, it's going to be *that* kind of dinner.

The song is vaguely familiar, but I can't bring myself to join them. We're not in that kind of restaurant, the kind where loud humming—which is quickly morphing into singing—goes unnoticed. It's a steakhouse. Low lights, quiet laughter, and highly rated food. We honestly might get booted before having any serious talks.

Who am I kidding? Serious talks? These guys are starting their second bottle of wine.

I'm just about to use the restroom as an excuse to apologize to our server when I see her.

"Abby," I say, even though she's still across the room.

Jack and the investors turn to see what I'm staring at. One of them makes a low whistle that has the territorial side of me getting all hot and bothered.

Jack leans over to me. "I don't know what you said to her, but wow."

"Shut up," I tell him, my eyes glued to the woman who doesn't know that she holds my heart in the palm of her small hand.

Abby hasn't toned anything down. If anything, it's like she turned the dial up, and she looks incredible. Her blonde and pink hair is shiny under the mood lighting, hanging down in soft curls that I just want to touch.

Her dark blue dress hangs off one shoulder, exposing the

tattoo I had wondered about, a chameleon that goes from simple black to an array of colors, starting around her clavicle and curling around her shoulder. The heels she's wearing are sky-high stilettos, the kind I could see her joking about using as weapons.

And the smile on her face ... it's confident but full of challenge, like she's daring anyone to stop her. She ignores the hostess, who's buzzing around her like a gnat, and strides across the room, her eyes locked on mine. I'm instantly ashamed that I ever let Jack's concerns get to me. I would never have asked Abby to change a thing. This self-assuredness is all she needs. She could be wearing a trash bag and convince me to give over all my passwords.

We've all gotten to our feet, and I'm so thrown by her that Dan is the one who pulls her chair out for her.

"Hello, boys," she says. "Sorry I'm late."

Smiling at Dan and Christopher, she holds out her hand, showing off a black studded cuff bracelet wrapped around her wrist. They both practically jump to shake it.

"I'm Abby and I speak fluent geek. Please direct any questions about the tech side of things to me. Have we ordered?"

"Just the appetizers," I tell her, and she turns her gaze on me as Christopher snaps his fingers for our waitress. Normally, I'd be flinching with embarrassment, but I can't focus on anything but the flecks of green in Abby's hazel eyes.

"Sorry for being late," she says quietly. "And not sorry I didn't listen to you about the dress code."

I'm already shaking my head. "I'm sorry I asked. Truly. You look ... there aren't words. Honestly."

Abby nods, then turns back to the table where the waitress is writing down additional appetizers. This is going to be a long—and expensive—meal.

But when Abby lets me grab her hand under the table a few minutes later, I could care less.

What VCs? What bug? What app?

All that matters is the woman beside me, whose hand I won't let out of my grip.

---

Ordinarily, dinner would have dragged. The VCs are three sheets to the wind, as my father would say, and Jack is hardly any better. Neither Abby nor I drank, but it's almost like babysitting a table full of overgrown toddlers who ate a whole basket of Halloween candy.

I'm horribly embarrassed, but all I can do is grit my teeth, secretly tell the waitress to ignore any requests for more alcohol. I hope we can walk out rather than be thrown out. It's no accident that the tables surrounding ours have cleared out. I haven't missed the glares being thrown our way, especially from a nearby group celebrating their matriarch's eightieth birthday.

Jack, Dan, and Christopher sing along, just as loudly as her family, clapping and raising their empty wineglasses in a toast as the birthday song finishes. Jack pulls the waitress aside, whispering in her ear. She nods and heads back to the kitchen.

"I do hope he asked for the check," Abby mutters. "Otherwise, we might be rolling these guys out of here."

"It's like you read my mind."

Despite being the only two sober ones at the table, Abby and I haven't been able to talk. The VCs asked her question after question, Dan pretending to understand Abby-speak, while Christopher just looked impressed. I filed away more vocab words I can whisper in her ear later, since she seemed to enjoy that so much yesterday. Throughout dinner, I've clutched her hand like it's the only thing keeping me from tumbling over the edge of a cliff.

Except, I think as I squeeze her fingers, Abby *is* the cliff. And I'm falling, hard and fast.

I lean closer to her, smelling something minty as my lips graze her hair.

"Abs, I'm sorry again for asking you to put your hair up and wear other clothes. Jack gave me the idea, but I shouldn't have gone along with it. You're impressive on your own. Period."

"Thank you," she says. Tugging her hand out of mine, she grabs her napkin, balling it up in her hand before dabbing at her lips, which look plump and pink and far too tempting for our current location.

"I need to tell you something," Abby says, leaning closer, still clutching her napkin.

"Anything."

"When I was in high school—"

A shout at our table goes up, and suddenly the waitress is there with a half circle of other staff, singing and holding out a slice of cake with what looks like twenty sparklers toward Abby. Jack joins in the happy birthday song, but for some reason Dan and Christopher are belting out, "For He's a Jolly Good Fellow," arms around each other, swaying back and forth. Any minute, one of them is going to go down.

"It's not my birthday," Abby says, holding out her hands as if to push the flaming cake back.

The waitress just shakes her head, pushing it toward Abby again, looking desperate, as though her life—and tips—depend on Abby taking this cake.

Three things happen almost at once. Abby jumps back into my lap, muttering something about being flammable.

Dan loses his balance and topples in slow motion, grabbing onto the waitress like she's a handrail, not a one-hundred-and-twenty-pound woman.

And the beaver pelt covering his head goes up in flames.

There are shouts, but all I can see are the flames shooting up from Dan's toupee. Everyone's frozen, staring like he's the campfire we've gathered around and we're just waiting for someone to pass out the marshmallows.

Until Abby jumps from my lap, grabs the pitcher of ice water, and dumps the whole thing over his head.

There's a sizzle and loud hiss as steam rises from the scorched black remnants on his head. The whole restaurant has gone silent. While I'm still standing slack-jawed in shock, Abby gives him a hand up, as the serving staff rescues the waitress from where she was pinned underneath him.

Somehow, the cake ended up smashed into the side of Dan's face. While he's still staring in shock, Abby drags a finger through the thickest smear of icing, then pops her finger into her mouth.

"Mm," she says. "Buttercream." And then, with a pat on what's left of his still steaming hairpiece, Abby says, "Thank goodness it's just hair."

# twenty-one

*Abby*

"And then Zane pops up and goes, 'Check, please!'"

My roommates (minus Harper, who's been MIA lately) are all dying laughing as I've got my head tipped under the bathroom sink so Delilah can wash all the product out of my hair. After that close call with the flaming cake, I'm not taking any chances.

"And the VCs?" Zoey asks.

"All in," I say. "They made the commitment before they were so soaked in alcohol. And I did my part very well. Thank you."

Zoey gives me a secret smile that I know means she'll be seeing me later to ask more details, then exits the cramped bathroom.

"Done!" Delilah says, wrapping my hair up in a towel.

I give her a hug. "Thanks! And thank you for both my

makeovers today. You should start a YouTube channel or something."

Delilah wrinkles her nose. "Really? You think people would watch me put makeup on?"

"Are you kidding?" Sam asks. "You'd be an instant hit. Do it."

"Think about it," I tell her. "I can help with a website and whatever else you need."

"Speaking of websites," Sam asks as we exit the bathroom. "I suggested to my publishers that we hire you to help with mine. Before you say no, they're footing the bill. Which means good money."

"Maybe between that gig and the one with Zane, you can quit your day job finally and go out on your own," Delilah says.

"We'll see," I tell them, not wanting to talk about the fact that my job with Zane is going to be over in a blink. Until I find a steady way to get freelance work or find a new job, I'm stuck with Micah in the fourth circle of IT purgatory.

I'm not surprised to see Zoey in my bed when I make it to my room. She pats the space in front of her. "I'll French braid your hair?"

This is code for Girl Talk. Somewhere in the fall semester of sophomore year, Zoey cracked the code I didn't even know existed to get me to spill all my secrets: French braiding. Something about the soothing feeling of her hands in my hair, coupled with the fact that I can talk without making eye contact creates the perfect environment to get me to spill.

"Did you talk to Zane?"

I close my eyes as her hands begin to work through the hair at my scalp, dividing it into sections. "No. But he did apologize."

"I bet he did."

"Zo, it wasn't that big of a deal. I get it. These guys, alcohol aside, were pretty typical big oil men. Anyway, he said Jack suggested it."

Zoey makes an irritated sound. "Not surprising. You're going to talk to him though?"

"I hate talking about it."

She's silent for a moment, and I could almost fall asleep with her hands working their magic. Almost. Anytime I have to remember, I get anxious. I'd love to think that one day, I'll look back on my high school days without feeling the sting. Or feeling anything. I've made progress, but I'm not there. Yet.

"I know. I think it would help Zane understand. If you're really going to do this with him, you'll need to open up. To trust."

I know Zoey's right. Zane couldn't know why it bothered me so much that he asked me to change my look. Not without me telling him about the last thing that happened before I left public school to finish high school at home through online classes.

I just feel so stupid talking about it. Like, I should have known that when two popular girls suddenly started being nice to me and offered to give me a makeover, it was a trap. I guess I was thinking more about classic movies like *She's All That* and not *Mean Girls*. They dangled the promise of Jacob Taylor in front of me.

"He thinks you're really pretty," Becky had said. "We'll help you become irresistible."

What idiot buys that line?

This one. The one right here.

Though I like to think of myself back then as almost a different Abby. The naïve one, who didn't realize that you shouldn't ever change yourself for a guy.

The humiliation coming home that day to explain to my parents what happened hurt worse than the chemical burns on my scalp from the bleach and whatever else they poured on me.

I didn't even go back to school to clean out my locker. Mom and Dad refused to let me, going up instead to rail at the principal, who hadn't done anything the months prior about the teasing and bullying, and refused to do anything then because it happened off school grounds. I didn't want to go back, but I'm realizing now that a part of me always felt like a coward. I never faced down my bullies. I just ... left.

Suddenly moved by the memory, I reach back and grab one of Zoey's hands. She pauses mid-braid.

"Thank you," I tell her.

"It's nothing," she says.

"No, I mean for helping me be brave tonight. I needed that. In a weird way, walking into that restaurant felt almost like facing down the people I couldn't back in high school. I needed that, and I didn't even know how much."

"Psh. I barely did anything. You're the brave one," Zoey says.

I let go of her hand as she continues to braid, this time in a comfortable silence. She's tying a ponytail holder around the end of my braid when an alarm broke up the quiet.

"Is that your phone?" Zoey asks. "I thought your ringtone was that dumb pop song."

"*Call Me Maybe*. And it's ironic, since people are definitely calling when it rings. Oh! That's my alarm!"

I scramble off the bed and dig my phone out of the bag I borrowed from Delilah. I swipe it open. "I finally caught the rat," I say.

"The what? We have rats?"

I wave off Zoey's panic as I'm waiting for the app to load

on my phone. "The person jacking up the code at Zane's company. I set up a trap. I can track the full thing on my laptop, but this should be enough to show me ... huh."

I set the phone down and go for my laptop. The trap worked, but the data is confusing. Or, at least, it isn't what I had expected.

"Is it Jack? *Please* say it's Jack."

"I don't think so, but I can't really tell until I get on the actual program and follow the digital trail."

Zoey pats me on the head and then calls out from the doorway. "I'll make a coffee and Twizzler delivery before I go to bed if the light's still on, okay?"

"Yep." I barely notice when the door closes behind her. I'm fully immersed in the information on my screen. Though I was expecting to be able to run a simple trace, ending in a user login or IP, I do love a challenge. This guy—or girl?—is good.

But not good enough. By morning, I'll be able to walk into Zane's office with a name.

## dear dr. love

*From: ScornedinSacramento@drlove.advice*
*To: DrLove@drlove.advice*

Dear Dr. Love,

My ex-fiancé cheated on me, and now he wants me back. All my friends say once a cheater, always a cheater, but is that the case?

The problem is … I still love him. I don't want to move on. I want to forgive and believe him. Am I being naïve to think we could work through this?

Sincerely,
Scorned

---

*From: DrLove@drlove.advice*
*To: ScornedinSacramento@drlove.advice*

Dear Scorned,

I am so sorry for what you've been through. No one deserves to have their trust betrayed and their heart broken like this.

On the surface, I tend to agree with your friends. Cheating is a big red flag and an indicator of future behavior. But it's not always that simple. My own parents worked through infidelity. I was old enough that I knew what was going on, and it was hard on the entire family, but I got a front-row seat to how wonderful reconciliation can be.

If it were me, I would want to see massive evidence of his remorse. I would want to see real changes. I would absolutely go to counseling, maybe even before you decide what to do.

Circumstances can also weigh in. Was he fully in a relationship with another person? Was it a one-time thing? Did he break it off? Did you catch him, or did he confess?

I'd prefer to think that you are hopeful, not naïve to want to work through it. But there are very few cases where I'd recommend doing so. Loving him isn't enough reason to give him another chance. If you're tempted to get back together, don't compromise on the terms.

And then comes the hard part—if you say you forgive him, you have to mean it. No bringing this up every time you're upset. No passive aggressive comments. Do you think YOU can ever forgive him? Can you trust him again?

Best of luck on this hard choice,

—Dr. Love

# twenty-two

*Zane*

WHEN I ANSWER Zoey's call the morning after the flaming VC dinner (which is how I'm going to think of it from now on), I'm just walking into the office. Late for me, which means eight o'clock. Everything has felt a little off since last night. I had to stick around to get the investors rides home, which meant not getting any time alone with Abby. I didn't hear from her last night or this morning.

"Hey, Zo."

"Zane."

She sounds ticked, and my alarms start going off. Her voice has this chill when she's angry that's positively arctic. I don't think I've done anything, so I choose my default method when it comes to Zoey's anger. Ignorance.

"What's up?"

"Anything you want to share?"

It's a trap. One I know well. Zoey invented this one. The one where you crack open a door and see what walks through. And no matter what you say, she's waiting with a baseball bat.

"Anything you want to ask?" I've finally reached my office and close the door a little too hard, sinking into my chair.

"Oh, I've got a *lot* of questions," Zoey says. "Starting with why you asked Abby to dress differently last night."

I groan, running a hand through my hair before I catch myself and grab the edge of the desk instead. "That was stupid."

"You have no idea. You really don't."

"Honestly, it was Jack's suggestion, and I never should have listened to him. I apologized to her last night."

"I heard."

I frown, wondering why she still sounds so mad. "Okay, so what's with the whole frosty interrogation?"

Zoey gives a heavy sigh. "Look, you need to talk to Abby. But you should know that she—"

Whatever she's about to tell me is cut off when Jack storms into my office, looking as bad as I've ever seen him, which is saying something considering all the partying he did in college.

"We need to talk," Jack says. He begins to pace.

"Zo, I'm going to have to call you back."

"Zane, this is important."

"I know. But there's a situation here. I'll call you as soon as I can." I hang up even as she starts to say something else. I can't worry about it now, though her words leave me with an uneasy feeling. I set my phone down, steepling my fingers on the desk. "Well?"

Jack flops down in the chair across from me and rubs a

hand through his hair. "So," he says with a deep sigh, "about last night."

I wait, expecting him to say more. After all, there's a lot of things to say about the previous night. The drunk investors, Abby completely blowing away my expectations in her natural Abby glory, the flaming toupee.

The corners of my lips twitch just thinking about Abby dumping water on the thing. I'm certain it looked better after the fire than before.

"It was pretty—"

"Terrible," he says.

"Hilarious," I finish. I blink at him. "What? How was it terrible? We got them to sign off before everything went down in flames. Literally."

Jack leans forward, elbows on his knees, dropping his head into his hands. "I'm not so sure it's a done deal."

Panic is immediate, one of those emotions that railroads you. Zero to sixty in exactly no seconds. I wanted this. Not just for Eck0. "What do you mean?"

"Dan left me a message this morning. I have to call him back, but it didn't sound good."

My brain is already crunching the numbers, with and without Dan and Christopher's backing. I don't really like the options without. Not at all.

I tug at my collar, feeling a tightness that isn't there. "Why? I mean, the part at the end with the fire wasn't the best. But it also has nothing to do with us, and everything to do with the wine."

Jack starts pacing the room again. "I thought you were going to talk to Abby about a dress code."

"Don't blame any of this on Abby. She did a great job last night—and probably saved Dan from getting second-degree burns."

Jack looks like he's about to argue, which means we're really going to have words, when there's a knock at my door.

"Come in," Jack and I say at the same time.

Josh sticks his head in the door, looks between me and Jack, and tries to duck back out. Jack swings the door open and gestures for him to come in and sit down.

"It's fine. Come on in."

Josh perched on the edge of the chair. "Are you sure? I can come back."

"Really, it's okay," I tell him. "What do you need?"

Josh is one of the few full-time tech people. Obviously, he's not good enough to do what Abby has been doing, but he's the most competent person we have. He and Jack don't seem to get along, though Jack was the one who suggested we hire Josh.

Right now, Josh looks fidgety. And the unease that started with Zoey's phone call is growing.

"Spit it out," Jack snaps when Josh still hasn't said anything.

"Right," Josh says. "So, I didn't want to say anything until I knew for sure. And I wasn't sure. Not until last night."

Jack motions for him to hurry it up. "Skip the saga. What is it?"

"Someone's been intentionally messing with the program. Hacking in and planting bugs and traps. Things to shut us down completely."

Jack narrows his eyes at me. "What has Abby said about this?"

I shrug. "She's still working on it. I don't get updates because I don't know what she's talking about most of the time."

The look Jack's giving me makes me feel like a rubber

band stretched to the limit. "Shouldn't you know something by now?" he asks. "Something more specific?"

I really don't like that Abby has been under fire this morning. Twice. I open my mouth to fire back an answer, but I've wondered the same thing. Why hasn't she given me something? Why is it taking so long?

"She said I would know as soon as she fixed it."

"That's just it," Josh says, tugging at the watch on his wrist. "I don't think she's fixed anything."

"She's still working on it." And now I do snap. "Can we just all give Abby a break?"

"Maybe you're just blinded by your feelings for her, so you haven't realized that she's screwing this whole thing up for us," Jack says.

I get to my feet. "No. That's not what's happening here."

Jack looks at Josh. "Explain. What's happening?"

If he looked nervous before, Josh is sweating now. "I like Abby. I do But I don't think she's trying to fix things. She intentionally introduced new code. Loops. Traps. And information is going to an outside source."

No. I don't believe it. Not for a second. Even though Jack rocks back on his heels before glaring at me. I need to get him to understand before he does something stupid.

I remember the laptop she used at the resort. "She's been working on her laptop. I told her it was okay."

Josh shakes his head. "The IP address is for her office. Not her laptop. She's been funneling data there."

Jack leans against the wall, one hand buried in his hair and the other at his jaw. His eyes meet mine. I know that look.

Doubts rise like an inky cloud, impossible to ignore or dispel. I know and believe in Abby. I trust her. And not just because of my feelings. I trusted her before, because Zoey trusts her.

But I don't understand what Josh has found, or how to reconcile that with the Abby I know. Or how to explain any of this. I just don't know tech.

"I trust her," I say, but the words sound like I'm trying to convince myself.

Jack yanks his phone out of his pocket. "I'm calling her boss."

"What? Why?" This has gotten out of hand, much too quickly. Abby hates her job, but I'm not sure she'd want to get in trouble. Then again, I don't believe anything could possibly be on her computer.

I glance at Josh. He's staring down at the floor, as though disappointed in Abby. Or maybe in me. I'm sure the whole office knows that we're together.

Aren't we? I haven't made anything official. What happens now? Could she really have done this? And if she did, can we move past it?

Everything feels like it's spinning out of control. I want to stop it, but I'm not sure how or what to do.

"There has to be a reason," I say, not sure anyone is even listening to me. Jack is talking in low tones on the phone.

"Maybe she hates her boss," Josh says.

I frown, unsure if he means me or Jack. Neither of us is really her boss. Not technically. Her boss at the other job? That makes no sense. Josh watches Jack with narrowed eyes.

Jack finishes the call and turns to me. I hate the look on his face. I want to remove it with my fist.

"Abby didn't come into work this morning. Her coworker logged on to her computer. She has our whole program there. She's stolen everything. That's corporate espionage, Zane. We're talking jail time. Not just fines and losing a job."

"Jail time?" Josh looks like he's ready to bolt. We both ignore him.

"Do you know where Abby is?" Jack asks.

"No. But we'll figure this out."

My hand shakes as I pull out my phone. There's a text I must have missed when I was talking to Zoey.

**Abby:** I've figured out your bug problem.

I would feel relieved, but now that Jack has called her boss and said things like "corporate espionage," relief isn't possible. Not until all the information is lined up in front of me and Abby is totally cleared. Until there's an explanation for why she has any of our information on her work computer.

**Zane:** Where are you?
**Abby:** Headed your way.

"She's almost here," I say. "We'll figure this out."

"I think we have it figured out. But, sure, we'll wait for your girlfriend." Jack snorts and covers his eyes with the heels of his hands.

"There's got to be a reason," I say, feeling like a CD skipping over the same line again and again. "Don't make assumptions until we let Abby explain."

Jack drops his hands from his face and stares at me. There's a sharkish look about him, one I don't like at all. "You still think she didn't do this? After what Josh and her boss found on her computer? What other explanation could there possibly be?"

"It looks bad. But I know Abby."

*I love her.* But that thought feels fuzzy, a little unsure.

Jack tilts his head. "Do you? She's worked here for just over a week."

"I've known her for years through my sister."

Shaking his head, Jack crosses his arms over his chest. "You're not thinking with your head," he says. "Your judgment is clouded."

Josh, who has been sitting silently with his head down this whole time, looks up at me. He looks ... betrayed. "I really liked Abby too."

*Liked.* Past tense. For some reason, it's this one word that really fills me with dread about the whole situation. If I'm being fully honest, there is a tiny sliver of doubt. I hate that sliver.

With hands that feel unsteady, I turn my back on them both and text my sister. My office feels suddenly like a pressure chamber. I feel the need to pop my ears, and a headache is forming at my temples and at the very back of my head.

**Zane**: You trust Abby, right?
**Zoey**: With my life.
**Zoey**: Why?
**Zane**: This is sensitive info. Please keep it between us.
**Zoey**: Okay ...
**Zoey**: I'm worried.
**Zoey**: Type faster.
**Zane**: One of our tech guys found evidence that Abby was messing with our code. Looks like she also leaked it to her office computer, which is a big deal. A felony kind of deal. Did she say anything to you about anything?
**Zoey**: Abby? No. That's ridiculous. You know that.
**Zoey**: She found evidence that someone inside the company was creating the problems intentionally. I told her to wait to

tell you until she had evidence. Last night, I think she figured it out. She was up all night.

My breath catches in my throat. *This.* This is the truth. Not whatever Jack seems convinced of or Josh thinks he found. There's a reason we didn't put Josh on this task. He's simply not good enough. Abby found out, and someone's trying to cover their tracks, blaming her.

But how to convince Jack?

For a moment, all the blood seems to run straight to my head and my headache dials it up a few notches.

If it isn't Abby, and someone is messing with our system, who is it? And how did our information get on her work computer?

I don't have time to really consider that thought because Abby walks right into my office without knocking. Her eyes are tired, makeup smudged. I recognize Zoey's handiwork, a French braid in her hair. Zoey would have braided my hair if it had been longer. Something is off, and I can tell even from just a look that Abby isn't okay.

I resist the urge to wrap her up in my arms, to shield her from all this. I think she might fight me off.

She doesn't look at me. Why hasn't she looked at me?

Abby stops on her heel, glancing quickly at Jack. Her gaze lands on Josh. "You," she says, practically a sneer.

"I'm sorry, Abby. I had to tell them," Josh says, holding out his hands. "It's not personal."

"Please," she scoffs. "Save it for Judge Judy."

"Abby, we need to talk," Jack tells her in a careful voice, taking a step closer to her. I notice that he positions himself between her and the door.

The look in her eyes freezes Jack in place. She points a

finger at the center of his chest, not touching him, but he jerks as if she did.

"I expected this from you."

Then she turns to me, and her anger is a flaming arrow, shooting straight through me. I swallow hard, trying to find words, trying to catch up. This whole situation escalated so quickly. It's over my head, and I know I'm not doing what I need to do to protect Abby.

I can see through the anger flashing in her eyes to the sense of betrayal that I've let her down. Again. I've screwed up by not doing more, not doing enough. But what could I have done?

Tears fill her eyes, and I swear my heart has turned into something hard and brittle, because it shatters at the sight.

Abby points to Jack, but her eyes don't leave mine. "I'm not surprised that he thought the worst of me. But I expected more from you. I *deserved* more."

"I believe you, Abby." But my voice doesn't hold the conviction it needs, and if anything, her disappointment deepens. "Just tell us why our stuff is on your work computer. Explain what Josh says he found."

Abby holds up a flash drive. "This has everything you need to show that this bozo"—she points at Josh—"has been working with my traitor of a coworker to sink your launch. I don't know why, but I could make a few guesses. You can have the information on the drive verified by a third party since you *clearly* don't trust me. It's all there."

Abby tosses the drive at me, and I manage to catch it. And then she storms out, but not before kicking the back leg out of Josh's chair, sending him toppling to the floor.

It's an *Exit*.

One I would appreciate and maybe even applaud if she didn't also walk out on me. I pass the flash drive to Jack.

"Don't let Josh go anywhere until we look at what's on there."

That predatory look is still on Jack's face. "I don't plan to," he says.

Josh stands. "Guys, look—"

I slam the door, not interested in the rest. I need Abby. I have to make this right. I didn't do anything, but that's kind of the point. I didn't *do* anything. I believed her, but I doubted. I let Jack call her boss before asking Abby directly.

I jog through the building. She's almost to the door. "Abs, wait!"

She slams through the front doors, a bright slice of sun blinding me before the tinted glass blocks it again when the door closes. I push through, following her to her car. "Abby!"

Finally, she stops. I slow to a walk. The tenseness in her shoulders and back keep me from reaching out to touch her. I walk around to face her. She's playing with her keys, refusing to look at me.

"Abby, I'm sorry. Everything happened so fast. I was trying to—"

"I got fired. Did you know that?" She glances up, probably seeing the shock and sorrow on my face.

"What? No. You said that it was your coworker."

"Yeah. They'll fire Micah too, once they figure out I wasn't lying. Until then?" She shrugs. "He called me like five minutes ago, right after he got a call from Eck0."

"That was Jack."

"Yes. Your partner. And if you'd just asked him to wait a few minutes, I'd still have a job."

Swallowing feels like I've just taken a spoonful of cinnamon. My tongue is too thick, my mouth too dry. "I thought you hated your job?"

Her eyes narrow. "I do. Or—did. But it paid the bills. I

was trying to get enough jobs on the side to get out, but I'm not there yet. Now? I have no choice. And no job. Thanks for that."

"I'm so sorry. Josh came in with this story, and I didn't have any updates from you. I didn't believe that you could have done it. Jack called your boss to confirm. I should have stopped him."

Her anger dissipates like fog as she wraps her arms around herself. "Some of this is my fault. I know I kept you in the dark. In hindsight, that was really stupid. I wanted to come through for you with a big reveal. To be the Velma to your Fred, solving the big mystery with all the answers."

It takes me a minute. Is she speaking about Scooby Doo right now?

"But Fred always ends up with Daphne," she says. "There's a reason for that."

"Wait, Abby. What are you talking about? This isn't a cartoon. This is actual life. I'm not a Fred. You're Abby. And I lo—"

The word catches in my throat. Abby's eyes fly open, looking clear and green, with just the faintest hint of brown. She is so beautiful. So amazing. This should make it easier to complete that sentence, but instead, I back up like the big coward I am.

"I really like you. I trust you. And I'm so sorry how things went down this morning. Josh just walked in, spewing some story, and then Jack—"

Abby's shaking her head, and when she holds up both hands, I stop talking. My shoulders slump. I already know what's coming, but I don't want to believe I've lost her.

"I'm sure Josh was convincing. You had no explanation from me. And I know Jack is … Jack. But *you*."

The hurt in her voice is like a saw, grinding through me.

"You should have trusted me, Zane. If you had respected me, you could have held on for a few minutes. Asked me for my side before you called my boss. You can't pawn this off on Jack. When it comes down to it, you have to take responsibility. I deserve at least that."

I can't even argue as she gets in her car and drives off.

Because she's completely right. She deserves so much more than my inaction and passive trust. She deserves a better man than me.

# twenty-three

*Abby*

I HAVEN'T BEEN BACK HOME to Katy since Christmas. Way too many months. It's only a two-and-a-half-hour drive, more because I stop for kolaches at one of the bakeries inside a gas station in the tiny town of La Grange. Today I buy a whole dozen of the fruit-flavored ones and a few pigs in blankets. As if coming back with baked goods will distract my family from the reason why I'm coming home, my tail between my legs.

The smell of sweet bread and spicy sausage fills the car for the last hour of the drive. The rolling hills give way to the flat prairies. Boring scenery, giving me too much time to think about everything. Or, the one thing. Zane. I know that I overreacted. I could have told him my suspicions at any time. And Jack was the one who called my boss.

What could Zane have done, really? Still, it all felt so huge in the moment, like such a betrayal.

Speaking of betrayal, the actual punks deserving this treatment are getting theirs. I managed to squeeze a few details out of my former boss when he called begging me to come back. Aside from getting fired from their respective jobs, both Josh and Micah will likely face charges related to corporate espionage. Apparently, they took a payout from a competitor of Eck0 to derail the launch and "borrow" some of the software.

For Micah, the motivation stemmed from straight greed, but based on the weird vibe I saw with Jack, I'd bet Josh had a more personal stake. It's easy to believe Jack could have ticked him off by stealing a girlfriend, sleeping with his sister, or any number of other jerky Jack-like things.

It was a nice feeling, having my ex-boss grovel. It was even nicer telling him no. With Micah gone, there is no IT department. Too dang bad! Not my problem. I've got enough other problems, namely my busted-up heart.

As I finally exit the highway in Katy, I wonder if maybe I wouldn't have been so hurt had Zane not asked me to wear different clothes to the dinner. It's like that unlocked the door to my insecurities and let them all out to play. I haven't let them rule me in so long that I almost forgot what it's like and how powerful they can be.

Now they need to be banished back to the dungeon where they belong. Home seems like the best place for that, where I can draw on the strength of my family.

I already texted Jason, and he's coming over to Mama and Daddy's with my nephews. Jessa is staying home to rest. I'm really hoping that she'll go into labor while I'm here and save me another trip to Katy. Once she has Baby Addie, I told her I'd help wrangle the boys for a bit. I like thinking about Addie. About my nephews.

Even that reminds me of Zane, and our conversation

about having kids when we were at the resort. The night we both pretended we weren't crying over the movie *Up*, and the man attaching balloons to his house, flying to the honeymoon location he never got to see with his wife. Kind of like I've been pretending for the last two days that Zane hasn't been blowing up my phone with calls and texts.

I think whenever I manage to lock my insecurities in the dungeon, my feelings for Zane need to go there too.

Sam's words keep bobbing up to the surface, making me wonder if I just sabotaged my relationship with Zane. I can't think about that. Even if I suspect that maybe, just maybe, I overreacted and did exactly that.

This time though, I crashed and burned a relationship I actually wanted.

I pull into the gravel drive at Mom and Dad's, shaking my head at all the development. Growing up, there were farms on all sides of us. Our house is just a little old farmhouse on half an acre, loosely incorporated into the planned community built up around us. A guy rides a big, black horse along the fence of our property. He tips his hat to me, and it's such a stereotypical Texas thing that I smile.

He's one of the twins that lives on the property behind ours, the only other holdout against the development. I'm not sure if it's Elton or Easton—I can't remember which was the quiet one who loved horses, and which one recently got busted for hosting fight nights in their barn. They were always nice to me, even when I left school to finish at home.

Ugh, twins. It feels like reminders of Zane are everywhere. It's one more reason I had to get out of the house. I couldn't stand looking at Zoey, and I definitely didn't want to talk to her about Zane.

"Hey, sweet potato," Dad says, rounding the hood of my

car. He's got on his boots, as usual, but his jeans almost look new.

He gives me a hug that I feel all the way down in my bones. "Daddy."

When he pulls me back to examine me, I wave him off. "Blue this time?"

I tug a strand of my hair in front of me, still surprised to see the almost teal color. "I needed a change."

A lot of changes.

"And you! Look at those jeans. Very fancy."

Dad shakes out his legs, making a face. "Your mama burned my old ones."

I can't help but laugh at that. "Hopefully not while you were wearing them."

"Naw," he says. "She waited 'til I was in the shower. Came out when the fire alarms started going off."

"She burned them in the house?" I'm surprised but not shocked.

"Sure did. When you see the char marks in her nice farmhouse sink, you'll know where they came from."

I wince. "Oooh. Is she upset?"

Mom and Dad waited until I was out of college to redo their kitchen, and it's only a few years old. I'm pretty sure she likes it more than me most days.

Dad rolls his eyes, puts an arm around me, and directs me to the back porch. "She can't be upset with anyone but herself. I thought it might teach her a lesson. Those firemen gave her quite the lecture. But you know your mama. She's angling for a new sink."

"I bet she is. And, for the record, the jeans look nice."

"They chafe something awful, but there's coconut oil for that. Learned that trick on something called Pin-Interest."

I snort. "Pinterest, Dad."

"That's what I said. And anyway," he says, leaning close and chuckling near my ear. "Your mama says these really showcase my butt."

I shove him off, jogging up the steps to the porch. "Gross! TMI, Dad!"

He's laughing and waves me off. "I'll get your bag from the car and change your oil. Don't let anyone tell you that the empty nest years aren't full of fun!" he calls, still laughing.

*Ew.*

Before I make it through the screen door, it flies open and my nephews do their best to tackle me.

"Whoa there, beasts! Easy on your aunt."

"Why are you referring to yourself in the third person?" Jace asks. I ruffle his blond hair, realizing as I do that he's gotten taller.

"When did you learn what the third person is?" I ask him.

"From Tiktok," he says.

It's one thing for my dad to be on Pinterest, but my eight-year-old nephew and Tiktok? Nope.

"I'll have to talk to your daddy about that. It's a security risk."

It's also a risk for him to learn about things like twerking.

He shrugs, running off toward the direction my dad disappeared to. Both my nephews have my brother's big brain, but Jace's interests run toward all things mechanical. If Dad doesn't watch him, he'll probably rewire my car, switching the cruise control with the turn signals or something.

Meanwhile, Joey, the younger, sweeter, quieter one, is still clinging to my knees. I bend down until I can look up into his sweet cheeks, still plump even though he's now six.

"Hey, bud! What's happening?"

He blinks at me with lashes most women would stab someone with a stiletto to have.

"My new sister's coming soon."

"I know. Baby Addie." The one lucky child to escape the curse of J names. "Are you going to take good care of your sister?"

He nods, all serious. "I already promised Dad I'd plug his nose when he changes her poops."

I laugh. "You know what? Your daddy probably needs to get used to the smell, work up a tolerance. Maybe when he's changing poops, you could help by fetching him a throw-up bowl instead?"

"Very funny, squirt." Jason glares as he joins us on the porch. "I can't help my gag reflex. It's a physiological response."

"And I can't help finding it amusing." I give Joey another look. "You'll remember what I said?"

"Barf bucket."

I wink. "Good boy. Now, go make sure your big brother isn't hot-wiring my car."

When I stand again, Jason wraps me up in a hug, lifting me right off my feet. I could get used to all this hugging. I hadn't realized how much I've missed my family. Maybe it's time to consider moving home. My heart constricts at the thought of leaving Austin, leaving my friends.

I try not to think about Zane, but my brain keeps looping right back to him like one of those annoying pop-up windows you can't close. I'm hoping this trip home can be my factory reset. I need some unconditional support and some space to think.

Oh, and a job. I need one of those too.

"What's this I hear about you falling in love with a guy who got you fired?"

"Mama's got a big mouth. That's not …" I start to say, then stop. "Actually, that's pretty accurate. And, for the record, it sucks. I wouldn't recommend it."

Jason sets me gently back down and ushers me inside the house. "I could have told you that."

"I could have told myself that," I mutter.

"Does this mean you're moving to Katy and coming to work for me?"

The offer sounds more tempting now than it ever has. And yet, it still doesn't feel right. This isn't where I'm supposed to be.

I should be with Zane.

*Abby.* Thankfully, my internal Agent Gibbs shows up with a warning tone. *We've been over this. No Zane.*

"Abs?" Jason gives me a little shake.

"Sorry. Uh … I'm still considering my options."

Mom comes tearing out from the direction of the laundry room with arms outstretched, wrapping me in her comfort and warmth. "Baby girl!"

"Mama! Go easy on the ribs. I'd like to keep them all intact, please."

She eases up, then pulls back to inspect me, just like Daddy did. "Blue hair, huh? I prefer pink."

"You should try pink. I think it would look great on you."

Mom scoffs. "I've missed the window. Colorful hair either needs to come with youth or old age."

"Just be sure to let me know when I'm close to the cutoff age. I've got to follow all those conventions of society and all that."

Jason laughs and we both sit down at stools along the kitchen island. He pulls out his laptop, probably working on one of his new games. I try to check the sink for scorch marks but can't see them from this angle. When she sees me

217

looking and smiling, Mom gives me what she likes to call the hairy eyeball.

"I like Daddy's new jeans," I say. "Heard a funny story about how you convinced him to wear them."

"That's part of marriage. Learning how to get things done." She winks. "Now, come help me shuck this corn."

There's something about standing hip to hip with my mama in the kitchen where I grew up, pulling the husks off corn that warms me from the inside out. But then it warms me too much as I remember the night I spent with Zane in his house, helping him decorate.

I imagined nights like this, a future where he and I would cook dinner, maybe having a food fight or two. Years down the road, maybe I'd be lighting his suit on fire in the kitchen sink.

Except I'm not going to get that chance.

When Mama's arms come around me, the sobs really hit. I barely register the sound of the door closing as Jason leaves us.

"That boy has an aversion to tears," Mama says.

"And dirty diapers."

Mama laughs, squeezing me tighter and resting her head on my shoulder. "You really fell hard this time, didn't you?"

"I did. I can't stop thinking about him."

I place my hands on the edge of the sink, looking down at all the corn husks, and the silky strands that are caught under my nails.

"Maybe you shouldn't be trying to stop."

I'm pondering her words, still staring down at the corn husks and finally seeing some of the burn marks when Dad joins us in the kitchen.

"Sorry to interrupt your Hallmark moment," he says, making me laugh.

I pat Mama's hands and she releases me with a smile.

"We're all good," I say. It's not true, but for the first time since yesterday morning, I don't want to punch someone in the throat or bury myself in a carton of Blue Bell ice cream.

Dad holds up a crumpled-up white paper bag. "Hope no one intended to eat those kolaches you brought," he says. "Those boys are like piranhas."

# twenty-four

*Zane*

It's my luck that the monthly dinner with Dad and Zoey falls on a week where I'd like to hide out and avoid my sister. She's probably already got a hit out on me. Especially since I've been avoiding her calls and not reading her texts. She's waiting for me when I pull up to Dad's house, hands already in the lecture position on her hips.

"So, you're not dead?" Zoey asks in a bratty voice.

"Clearly not."

"Just ignoring me."

"I'd like to think of it as avoiding you," I tell her, walking right on past toward the house.

"Is there a difference?"

"Not really. Avoiding just sounds a little more mature than ignoring."

"Both of them not only sound immature but *are* immature."

I don't bother ringing the bell but use my key to walk right inside. I can smell garlic and onions. Dad became quite the cook recently, taking classes and watching on YouTube. I'm pretty sure that in the few years after Mom died, he existed on beef jerky and mixed nuts.

"Hey, Dad." I pat him on the shoulder, because he's not big on hugs.

He nods, meeting my eyes with his matching blues. "Zane. Glad you could make it."

That's his standard greeting, though I always make it. I haven't missed a family dinner since we started having them, even with all the startup craziness.

Zoey goes up on tiptoes to kiss his cheek. "Hey, Daddy. Smells good."

"Me or the stir-fry?" he deadpans.

"Are you making jokes now?" I ask. "Cooking and making jokes might indicate a midlife crisis."

"What's next?" Zoey asks, plucking a mushroom right out of the pan. "Long hair and a tattoo?"

Dad shoos her away with the spoon. "You'll burn your fingers. I'm much past midlife, in case you haven't noticed."

Picturing Dad with anything but close-cropped brown hair is laughable. He looks ready to go back into the service at a moment's notice, other than the grays taking over. I grab the plates and Zoey gets the silverware. We haven't changed up our chores since we were kids, and there's a comfort in it.

Until Zoey has to open her mouth, that is.

"Have you talked to Abby?"

"I've left her voicemails. I've texted. She's closing me out."

Zoey looks at me with half-lowered lids. "That's all? I expected you to show up at the house."

"If she doesn't want to answer her phone, why would I

think she wants to see me? She clearly doesn't want to talk to me."

"What did you do to Abby?" Dad asks, frowning.

I throw my hands up. "Is this how it's going to be? Both of you ganging up on me?"

"Usually it's both of *you* ganging up on *me*," Zoey says. "You're way overdue, little brother."

I turn to Dad, considering my answer. What did I do to Abby? On paper, not much. I didn't cheat on her or insult her or take her for granted. But in many ways, what I did was worse.

I didn't trust her enough. I didn't respect her enough. I didn't show her how much I value her.

I failed her.

"I'll take this one, since Zane's pleading the fifth," Zoey says, holding up a hand when I start to protest. "First, he tried to get her to change her looks to impress clients. Then, he accused her of some kind of bad tech practices that I don't understand and got her fired."

"I didn't—" I start to say, but Zoey cuts me off again.

"Oh, and all this while he was also dating her."

Dad's eyebrows shoot up. "You and Abby?"

I sigh, sitting down at the table. "Not now, I guess. It's a moot point since she won't talk to me."

Zoey smacks me on the back of the head. "Idiot," she mutters. I shove her hand away, and suddenly, we're ten, arguing over the remote control or who gets to sit in the most comfortable chair.

"I didn't raise you to give up so easily," Dad says. "Go get your girl."

Now it's my turn to be surprised. "You'd approve of me and Abby?"

"What's not to approve of?" he asks, one eyebrow lifted.

Long before The Rock, Dad had been giving us this look. "She's your sister's best friend and a great girl. Smart. Fiery."

"Like I said," Zoey says, poking me, "you're an idiot."

I manage to steer the conversation away from me or Abby during dinner, but my thoughts are definitely distracted, thinking about her. Wondering where she is, if she's found a job, how she's feeling. If she would ever consider forgiving me.

While Zoey and I wash dishes, Dad retires to the TV room with his crossword and whatever true crime documentary he's watching now. Zoey's uncharacteristic silence is like the ocean pulling back before a tsunami. It's unnatural and should serve as a warning to run for high ground.

Maybe I'm a sucker, or maybe I think that I deserve whatever she's going to dish out, because I'm not running or trying to climb one of the oak trees out back. When we've only got one sauce pan left to wash and dry, I nudge her shoulder with mine.

"Well?"

"Well, what?"

"When am I getting the lecture or whatever?"

Zoey takes the pan from me and dries. I can almost hear her thoughts banging around in her head. She sets the pan down and glances toward the TV room.

"Let's go out back," she says in a quieter voice.

I follow her out to the backyard, where Zoey set up strings of lights over Dad's small patio last year at Christmas. We sit down in the two Adirondack chairs, which were my gift.

"Think he ever sits out here?" Zoey asks.

"Doubtful."

It's a nice night, somehow with no mosquitos. After a few minutes with just us and the night sounds, Zoey says,

"I know Abby mentioned that she was bullied in high school."

"Yep." The thought of that gets me just as hot as it did when she told me. I feel like a pan of boiling water with the lid on, all the steam trapped inside with nowhere to go.

"This is her story to tell, and ordinarily, I wouldn't be butting in. But there are some things you need to know, and I'm pretty sure she didn't get to tell you."

"Well, spit it out, then."

"Calm down, cowboy."

Zoey shifts, swinging her legs over the side of the chair so she can face me. I angle my chair toward her, wishing she'd hurry it up.

"Abby was bullied off and on throughout middle and high school. Typical jock-versus-nerd type stuff. Her parents complained, but the school didn't do anything. In high school a few of the popular girls told Abby that some guy was interested in her. They said they wanted to give her a makeover to help her win him over, promising that she just needed to make a few changes."

I don't like where this is going, and not just because there's another guy being mentioned. Dread coils in my stomach.

"As I'm sure you've surmised, they didn't give her a makeover. What they gave her was chemical burns on her scalp. They plucked off her eyebrows completely."

I squeeze my eyes closed. Just hearing this, imagining it, makes me want to punch something. Or someone.

Zoey touches my arm briefly, then continues. "She was humiliated. Thankfully, not permanently injured, though they did have to cut off most of her hair because it was so damaged. She finished up high school virtually, doing online classes."

"That's horrible."

"It is." Zoey pauses. "In case you didn't connect the dots, genius, Abby tends to be a little touchy on the idea of makeovers. And of people not accepting her as is. Which is exactly what you did when you asked her to change for the investors."

I hadn't connected the dots. But I do now, and the realization is swift and painful. I lean forward in my chair, letting my head hang between my knees. I feel like I'm trying to breathe underwater. My lungs burn and there's no air.

I'm playing back over my texts to Abby, my apology at the restaurant, which seems so small now. If I thought I'd messed up before, the gravity of it hits me fully. I'm ashamed, and I hurt for Abby.

"In case you weren't sure how much you messed up, I wanted you to know. We're talking big-time, brother. If that weren't bad enough, then you go and make assumptions based on Jack and some random guy who works for you rather than trusting Abby, someone we've both known and trusted for years."

"I didn't mean for that to happen," I say, lifting my head to look at my sister. She seems thoroughly unimpressed with my excuse. Which is exactly what it is. I want to go back in time and kick myself. Then kick Jack and Josh. But me first.

"Good intentions really aren't worth much, are they?"

They aren't. Which is exactly why I stopped calling Abby two days ago. That was before I knew exactly how badly I screwed up.

Zoey kicks me in the shin.

"Ow." I glance at her. "Aim higher. I deserve it."

"Oh, boo hoo." Zoey rolls her eyes and kicks me again, harder, in the same place. "Is this your plan? To wallow and punish yourself?" Another kick.

I shrug. "There is no plan. It's over. I ruined everything."

Zoey groans and stands up, kicking me one last time. "I usually mean it as a term of endearment, but this time I really mean it, little brother. You're an *idiot*."

"I know that. Do you think I don't know that?" I throw my hands up.

Zoey grabs them, squeezing my hands tightly. "You're missing the point. You're an idiot for not going after her. She went home to stay with her family in Katy, by the way. You're an idiot for not going after her. For thinking that a few unanswered texts and calls is where you should stop. *Dream bigger*."

The words take a moment to roll over me, and when they do, I feel like I've been caught in a sudden downpour of the emotional kind.

*Dream bigger* is what Mom used to say to us, her encouragement, her catch phrase. It was sort of her guide for life. When we'd talk about what we wanted to be when we grew up, or what we were looking forward to about summer.

After celebrating any of our successes, she would always hug us and tell us that we did a great job, and now it was time to dream bigger.

"I am an idiot," I tell my sister, squeezing her hands until she's squirming to escape my grasp.

"Ow! Let go."

I do, but then stand and ruffle her hair in the way I know she hates. "I'm an idiot, and you're the idiot who shares my DNA."

"Only fifty percent," Zoey says, smoothing back her hair and elbowing me in the process.

"Yeah, but you got the idiot fifty percent."

"Shut up. Forget what I said. Abby deserves better."

I nod, catching her eye. "She does. Which means I've got a lot of work to do and I need a lot of balloons."

"Wait—balloons? Not flowers? Chocolates?"

I grin, starting to feel better at just the thought of apologizing, groveling, and winning Abby back. "Yes. Balloons." I pause, considering. "And maybe some coffee too."

# twenty-five

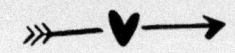

*Abby*

TWO DAYS. That's how long I'm home before I need to get the heck out of here and back to Austin.

My parents seem to have forgotten how to behave with a child at home. Either that, or they're not so subtly hinting that I need to vamoose.

Catching Mama washing dishes in her underwear was one thing. Walking in on Mama and Daddy half-dressed and making out on the couch was another thing altogether. I mean, good for them, right?

I can only hope I still want to make out on the couch with my husband after thirty years of marriage.

*But not with an audience!*

"Are you packing, baby girl? Leaving so soon?" Mama asks, standing in the doorway of my childhood room, which is now a craft room with a daybed unceremoniously shoved into a corner.

I do my best to throw her patented look right back at her. She only laughs.

"I think you've made it clear that you guys enjoy your *privacy*."

She laughs harder. "I can't help it. Your father's new jeans have breathed fresh life into our relationship."

"La la la la la! I can't hear you!" I cover my ears with my hands. Daddy walks by, giving us both a strange look before shaking his head and continuing down the hall.

"It's been a great visit, aside from things of which we shall not speak," I tell Mama, zipping up my bag and rolling it toward the door.

Instead of letting me pass, Mama wraps me in a big hug, the kind that I remember from being a kid when I skinned my knee or came home crying because of a comment some kid made about me.

"You're a fighter, Abby. A fighter with a beautiful heart. I'm sorry you got hurt. Please don't let this keep you from trying again. Or giving him another chance."

It wasn't until her words that I realize that's exactly what I've been doing while home. Fortifying my defenses. Rebuilding the walls I took down for Zane, the ones I haven't been willing to remove for anyone. Not until him.

"It hurts," I tell her, sniffling into her hair.

"Love always does."

I snuggle deeper into her embrace, because whether it's love or not, what I feel for Zane definitely hurts. "I thought love was sunshine and woodland creatures helping with household chores."

She snorts. "Now, I know we taught you better than that. You know love isn't easy."

"This definitely isn't easy," I tell her.

"That doesn't make it love either. The wrong things can be hard too."

"Then how do you know?"

Mama pulls back and grips my shoulders, her eyes holding mine. "When it hurts, but you want to fight through it anyway. That's how you know it's love. When you want to fight." She pats me on the behind and, just like that, our deep talk is over.

I consider her words as I roll my luggage down the stairs. Zane apologized for asking me to change for the dinner with the VCs. He didn't know about the whole high school makeover from hell, and I bet if he did, he would never have asked. Plus, he liked me before that. He saw me messy, first thing in the morning and still kissed me in a closet.

If it were only that, we could resolve things with a conversation. I'm hurt, but he didn't know *how* hurt I'd be. Or why that particular request was so hard for me. But the job thing ...

I believe Zane that Jack was the instigator. But that's the thing: Jack is his business partner. Zane needs to man up and not use Jack as an excuse for his own choices.

Mama said love was real if it was worth fighting for. And Zane didn't fight for me.

I try to swallow down the burn from that realization, but it stays with me, like indigestion after bad tacos.

Daddy intercepts me in the kitchen and takes my bags. "Your oil is changed, and your tires are aired up. I'll put these in the trunk."

"Thanks, Daddy." Knowing him, he also filled it up with gas and got a car wash while he was there.

Mama hands me a paper grocery sack, folded over at the top like a giant lunch bag, then gives me a travel mug that's filled with coffee.

"Snacks for the drive and caffeine. Keep the mug. I bought it with you in mind."

I check out the side of the mug, rolling my eyes when I see the picture. It's got the words "Pain in the" right next to a picture of a donkey's butt.

"Gee, thanks, Mother."

She gives me a kiss on the cheek and shoos me out the door. Daddy's waiting by the car for me, and I give him a big hug.

"Good to see you, sweet potato. Don't be such a stranger."

"You know you could come to Austin and see me."

Dad shudders. "That city's too strange for me. All the men in skinny jeans on bicycles."

I laugh, because he isn't entirely wrong. Though skinny jeans seem to be on the way out for men, thankfully. Very few men could truly pull them off, and the rest looked like they stuffed half their body in sausage casing, only to have the rest explode out of the top.

*"I'm* weird, Daddy." I give his arm a squeeze as I pull back. I shake out my newly blue hair as if to prove my point.

He pats my head, smiling in a way that's like wrapping a cozy blanket around my heart. "No. You're just perfect."

*Hardly*, I think.

"It's happening!"

Mama's shout makes us both spin. She's leaning over the porch railing, waving her arms like she's trying to flag down a cab in New York City. Daddy seems to know exactly what the *it* is, while I'm slow on the uptake.

"What's going on?" I shout at Dad's retreating back.

"The baby! My first granddaughter!" Mama's squeals would rival any pig at the county fair, but the excitement is contagious.

"Which hospital?" I call, already climbing behind the wheel.

"Just follow us!" Mama says, sprinting toward Dad's truck.

Dang, the woman can move. At least, when there's a granddaughter on the line.

I follow Daddy's pickup to one of the newer hospitals that's only ten minutes away. Thank goodness. Houston's Medical Center is renowned, but from out in Katy, it's also a good hour without traffic.

My phone buzzes as we make it through the doors. I check to see a message from Zoey, asking where I am.

**Abby**: At the hospital. My sister in law is having her baby.
**Zoey**: Which hospital?

I text her the name, then ask her why.

**Zoey**: I came for a visit.

I frown at my phone. It's a Monday. Zoey doesn't take off work. That's one thing she and Zane have in common, they're like the Terminator, at least when it comes to work. Apparently not when it comes to me, I think, picturing Zane in his office. Looking so tempting in a dark suit.

Nope. Not thinking about Zane.

I am concerned about Zoey though. I'm not sure Zoey missed a class in college. Any class. Ever. Meanwhile I skipped as many as I could to still manage the grades I wanted. She didn't miss class. She doesn't miss work.

Point being, she shouldn't be in Katy on a Monday. I'm immediately suspicious.

**Abby**: Why aren't you at work?
**Zoey**: Can you please stop asking questions?
**Abby**: No.
**Abby**: What's really going on?
**Zoey**: I'll see you in a little while. Text me where to find you.
**Zoey**: Also, pick a number, one to one hundred.
**Abby**: Lucky number forty-seven.
**Zoey**: You're such a weirdo.
**Abby**: It's a prime number.
**Zoey**: See my above text.

I try to shove my worry to the back of my thoughts as we arrive in the waiting area on some floor. I was too busy texting and letting Daddy guide me into the elevator and through doors to pay attention.

When we arrive, it's like we've left the hospital and are suddenly at one of those big family weddings. I hadn't noticed Mama carrying a bag, but she's like Mary Poppins, pulling out things that should all be banned from hospitals, like pink streamers (which she throws) and pink confetti (which Jessa's mom throws) and pink champagne, which Dad uncorks and starts pouring into pink plastic glasses. Even my nephews are wearing pink shirts that read *Big Brother*. They look as embarrassed as I feel.

I guess everyone's pretty excited about having a girl?

*Note to self: have all boys. Or don't give my family the name of the hospital where I'm delivering.*

Except I'm not going to be having kids because the guy I want, the guy I think I might love, didn't fight for me. Which means he probably doesn't love me back.

Is it fair to assume this, when I haven't answered his calls and deleted all voicemails and texts without listening or reading? Probably not. But I'm doing it anyway.

A nurse rushes over with a security guard, trying to tone down my family's giant pink party. But it's more like tossing a glass of water on a forest fire, especially since Mama and Jessa's mom brought enough champagne and sparkling cider and cake for the whole lobby. Daddy even has an unlit pink cigar between his teeth.

I'm equally embarrassed and proud as the security guard absconds with the champagne but accepts a cigar and a pat on the back from my daddy. We're *that* family. Loud and so far over the line that you don't remember that there's a line at all.

I'm embarrassed, but I also love it. And more than anything, I want to have this for myself. The thing is, I've focused on work, because I didn't think this was possible for me. I poured into my friendships, because my four best friends are amazing. We'll be close until we're old and gray.

It was too scary to risk my heart for a guy who might turn out to want someone different, someone who looked or acted a different way. A Charla, not an Abby.

*But Zane wanted you, not Charla,* an ornery part of my brain is trying to tell me.

*Then why isn't he here?* I argue back. *Why did he give up on me so quickly? Yeah, that's what I thought.*

Despite my longing for the kind of love I see in my parents, in Jason and Jessa, and even in Jessa's family, I don't know if I can open myself up again. I can't imagine going back to square one where I go on one or two dates, then cut and run before they have a chance to leave me.

Because this is what happens when I don't pull the escape hatch. I end up broken-hearted in the hospital lobby, watching the party go on without me.

"Well, aren't you a sad sack? Shouldn't you be celebrating?"

I startle at Zoey's voice, then jump up and grab onto her like I didn't just see her a few days ago.

"Wow, okay." She pats my back, her arms caught at an awkward angle by my hug assault.

"It's so good to see you."

"Are you okay?" she asks when I don't let her go.

"Not particularly."

I love Zoey. I'm viscerally glad that she's here, whatever the reason. But the moment I remember that she's Zane's twin, my stomach sinks like a capsized ship, going belly-up before disappearing under swirling dark water.

"Abby—"

Whatever she was going to say is cut off by a cheer. Jason emerges from a set of double doors, his face lit from within. It's a look I've seen on him twice before. I'm bouncing on my toes with excitement.

"Addie is here," he announces, pumping both fists in the air.

Zoey and I join the melee as all the strangers who shared in the cake and secret stash of champagne security didn't confiscate gather to offer congratulations. Backs are slapped. Hugs are given. Another secret bottle of champagne is popped. This one, the security guard pretends he doesn't see.

I realize that Zoey is squeezing my hand, and I squeeze back, giving her a smile.

"Hey," she starts again, leaning close to be heard over the din.

But Jason's voice rises above all the other sounds. "Where's my sister? Abby?"

I wave my free hand, and Jason's eyes lock on mine. Something passes between us, a current of understanding.

"Come on, squirt. You're first up. Jessa's orders."

Zoey looks conflicted, opening and closing her mouth,

and then she lets go of my hand. "I'll be back," I promise. She nods, her lips pressed together. When I'm not so focused on my very first niece, I need to figure out what's up with her.

For now, my focus is singular: seeing that new baby and holding her in my arms.

The security guard tries to stop us, since Jessa is still in labor and delivery, not in a regular room yet, but Jason insists. They have to put a special band on my wrist that the guard scans. I remember from my nephews' births that security is always tighter when it comes to the babies. I want to ask Jason why the rush, and why me, but I don't actually care. I just want to meet Addie.

I never thought much about having kids until Jason started procreating. The very first time I saw Jace, it was like a lock shattered in some deep place in my heart.

Staring down at his squishy cheeks and puffy eyes, I felt a surge of love so fierce that I would tear off the face of anyone who hurt him. Clearly feeling the same way, Jace made a tiny sound and then spit up all over me.

It was love.

Jason puts his arm around me as he leads me down the hallway, answering the question I didn't ask. "Technically, you're not supposed to come back yet, but Jessa insisted. She's still finishing up."

I have no idea what that means, not even when I walk into the room and see a flurry of activity happening between Jessa's legs, still up in stirrups. This is not the scene I was expecting, and I'm properly scandalized.

I balk in the doorway, but it's too late. Jessa sees me and tilts her head, inviting me in, daring the doctor between her legs to say a word with her fearsome look. Jessa is amazing, and definitely not the kind of woman you argue with ever, but most especially not when she's just pushed a tiny human out of her body. The doctor seems to agree and goes back to whatever he's doing.

"Don't worry about them," Jessa says, waving a hand at the doctor and nurses. "They're just …"

Jessa trails off and grunts, breathing heavily. A tiny squawking cry distracts me, and I realize that I've lost Jason. Near the bathroom door, there's a little rolling cart with a plastic bin at the top. A bright light shines down on the most beautiful creature I've seen.

Not in the typical standard of beauty. Even with the tiny knit cap, her head has that cone thing going on, and her eyes are squeezed shut, shiny with an ointment the nurse is applying. But that baby is still just *gorgeous*.

When the nurse is done, she smiles and carefully hands Addie to Jason.

My heart swells as he curls my new niece toward his chest. My brother, who was an even bigger nerd than me and who teased me mercilessly in the older brother kind of way, has the softest smile imaginable on his face.

To distract myself from the slightly horrifying noises Jessa is making in the bed, I wash my hands in the sink for at least two minutes in scalding water, waiting for my turn to hold Addie.

As if sensing my urgency, Jason hands me my tiny, swaddled niece when I turn around. It's instalove, me and this teeny bundle of a new person.

"Hi, Addie," I whisper. "Love your name. We're almost the same."

"That was the point," Jason says, his hand landing on my shoulder.

I blink up at him. "Seriously?"

He grins, nodding and looking like he's about to say something else when Jessa snags his attention.

"Jase. I need you," she grunts, sounding more Incredible Hulk than human. Jason rushes to her bedside, wiping sweat from Jessa's brow and clasping her hand.

I stare down at Addie, warring emotions rising up and twining together to form a knot in my throat. Tears sting my eyes, and I sway, holding her close, soaking up that new baby smell.

Behind me, there's a groan of relief, and then more activity from the hospital staff. Thinking I probably don't want to know whatever is happening, I focus on the perfect pink cheeks and little bow of a mouth that's mimicking the movements for nursing. If I remember correctly, any minute now she'll start rooting around for milk that I'm not currently producing.

I turn to Jessa, keeping my eyes fixed on the top half of her, and not whatever going on *down there*. I may want kids, but I'm not ready for the gory details of bringing them into the world.

"I'd like to keep it and plant a tree over it," Jessa is saying, locked in an intense glaring battle with the doctor. My brother makes a strangled noise.

*Keep what?*

*Don't ask. Don't ask. Don't ask.*

"It's against hospital policy. I'm sorry," the doctor says. "You can plant all the trees you want, but not with your placenta."

*Yup. I didn't want to know.*

Jessa looks ready to argue but then, she sees Addie and softens. She reaches for her, and I step closer, passing Addie over like the most precious of treasures. Which she is. My arms instantly feel bereft.

"That's okay," Jessa says, in a gooey, baby talk voice that's so different from her usual sarcasm. "The mean old doctor can keep my placenta. I get to keep you. Yes, I do!"

Jason makes another choking noise, and I fight off a wave of nausea. We exchange horrified glances. That's two more times than I ever needed to hear the word placenta. Especially since I suspect that's exactly what the nurse has just wrapped up by the foot of the bed in a medical waste bag.

Babies? Amazing.

Birth? A disgusting miracle.

Two nurses begin man-handling Jessa's stomach area. She winces a little but is distracted by Addie, who is definitely rooting around now, making funny little sounds as her head moves back and forth. She's lost her hat, and Jason tenderly tucks it back over her light blonde hair as she latches on.

"Hey, watch it down there," Jessa says, biting her lip. I'm not sure if she's talking to Addie or the nurses. Probably both.

I give Jason a look. "While I appreciate getting to be the first to meet Miss Addie, I think you'd be better off with some privacy."

Not that they're getting any. Several of the nurses are cleaning things up down below, while one continues to assault Jessa's abdomen.

"Wait," Jessa says, exchanging a look with Jason. "We asked you back first because we want you to be Addie's godmother."

I'm immediately a puddle of tears. "Really?" Jessa nods, also tearing up, and I wrap my arms around my brother, squeezing him as tightly as I can.

"Thank you! I don't know what a godmother does, but I'll google it. Or you can just let me know. Is there a handbook?"

Jason pries my fingers away from his waist when I don't

let go. "Don't overthink it, squirt. We'll talk later. Head back out and tell the rest of them we'll have them back when they move us to a real room."

"Yeah. No one should see this," I say, and Jessa snorts.

"Figured it would be educational for you," she says.

"I'm scared straight now," I deadpan.

Except I'm not. Seeing and holding Addie—*my goddaughter*—only makes the aching loss of Zane hurt more. Thankfully, Jason and Jessa assume my tears are happy ones as I try to follow a nurse into the hallway.

At least, we try to go out the door.

There's a commotion in the hallway. What looks like dozens of helium balloons fill the space, making the hall a kaleidoscope as the overhead lights filter through the rainbow of balloons.

There's a man I didn't even hope to see standing just outside the door, holding a fist full of balloon strings. His eyes are filled with longing, with apology, with love.

"Zane?"

"I'm so sorry, Abby. I love—"

"Sir," the nurse says. "You can't be back here with those. Do you have a wristband?"

Confusion clouds his face. "No, I just followed someone through the doors. I don't—"

"Security!" Another nurse shouts.

"Wait," I say. "He's with me. We're just leaving."

I go to take Zane's hand so I can lead him out of here, when there's a loud bang. Then another.

I know that it's the balloons popping. Not gunshots. But my instinct is to dive for the floor. I'd be in good company. Several people are down on the tile, their hands over their heads. From a nearby room, a woman screams.

Zane's wide eyes meet mine. "Abby—"

And that's when the security guard tackles him.

I'm so stunned that I don't move for a second. Zane loses his grip on the balloons, and they all bob to the ceiling, several more popping. There are more screams, and an alarm is going off somewhere. Babies are crying.

Zane's head jerks up from underneath the guard, eyes wide and panic-stricken. "Abby! Ow!" The security guard pushes his knee into Zane's back, pinning him to the floor. Zane wiggles under the man, trying to meet my gaze. "I need to tell you something!"

"Sir! Stop fighting me. You aren't authorized to be back here. I'm taking you into custody."

"Can you just let me finish this conversation? Then take me wherever you need to."

"No. Be quiet and sit still," the security guard says. I have a sudden urge to kick him in the shins.

"I love you!" Zane shouts, and I swear that I hear someone say, "Awww!"

"You do?" I ask, grinning like the love-sick fool that I am.

"I love you, and I'm sorry I didn't show you that. I know I let you down. I can't promise I won't disappoint you again. But I want to try. I love you, Abby."

"Sir, stop moving!"

Zane's eyes meet mine, and he has that smile that I love. The one that I hadn't seen until recently, and now don't feel like I could live without. The unrest that's been living in my belly for days is gone, and the world feels right again. Except that Zane is about to get zip-tied, and the whole room is weirdly colored from the balloons, giving it a hallucinogenic feel.

"Why the balloons?"

"You're my Ellie," Zane says, referencing the movie *Up* that we watched together at the resort.

And suddenly, this scene makes a lot more sense. It's thoughtful and adorable. And would be romantic if not for the whole hospital security issue.

"At least, I want you to be my Ellie. Without the whole, dying too soon thing. And maybe without the house flying to South America."

"I love you too," I tell him, and then cringe as the security guard pushes Zane's face to the floor.

My brother steps out of the room behind me. "What is going on?"

The guard finally gets Zane's wrists secured with white zip ties.

"My boyfriend is getting arrested," I tell Jason, grinning. "This is Zane. Zane, meet my brother Jason."

"Hey," Zane grunts.

Jason looks down at Zane, up at the balloons, then nods at me. "Well, I guess congratulations are in order for the both of us."

# twenty-six

*Zane*

As far as grand gestures go, I think mine was a little bit too grand. Maybe if I'd had four balloons, not forty-seven. Or waited until I had the right security bracelet for the labor and delivery ward. My actions were suspicious. That's the impression I got from the security guard's knee in my back. And while I was being detained in what I'm pretty sure was his break room, being yelled at for not following hospital policy and causing pandemonium and panic.

After I spoke with several hospital administrators and an actual cop, explaining that the balloons were a gift, and not a way to block the security cameras to sneak in to kidnap a baby, they let me go with several strong warnings.

Abby is waiting outside the room, and my whole body reacts. My mouth is already smiling, my heart kicking up a fast rhythm, and my hands itch to touch her. Without waiting for permission, I wrap her up in my arms, lifting her feet off the ground and holding her to my chest. She's the perfect size.

"You okay?" Abby murmurs, snuggling even closer, her lips grazing my neck. "Any police brutality to report?"

"I'm going to have bruises on my wrists and back, but overall, I think I got off easy for my crime."

"Which was?"

"Not chasing you down to apologize sooner."

Abby turns and presses her lips to mine. I'm caught off-guard, but it only takes me a minute to catch up. Maybe a little too much, but I'm feeling desperate for any assurance that this is real. After a moment, Abby giggles and pulls back. We're both breathing way too heavy for a hospital hallway. I release her a little reluctantly but keep her hand in mine.

"Zane, I messed up too. Maybe more than you. *Probably* more than you." She sighs, and before I can argue, she continues. "Sam told me that I sabotage things, and I think that she's right. I got scared, and I assigned too much blame to you. I reacted impulsively, and I ran scared. Will you forgive me?"

I lean closer, until our foreheads touch. "I do. We both made mistakes. Do you still want to run?" She shakes her head, and I press a quick kiss to her lips. "How about we forgive and move on? Full trust. No more being scared. Or, if we are, we talk about it."

"I think I can handle that," she says. "Now, the big question. Want to go meet my *goddaughter*?" she asks.

I pull back just enough so that I can look at her. "Your goddaughter? That's amazing. Yes. If ... I'm allowed?"

Abby nudges my shoulder. "We'll leave the balloons in the waiting room and get you an official bracelet." She holds up the white plastic band on her arm.

I should be nervous about meeting her family—I'm not counting the moment her brother saw me getting manhandled by security—but I'm just excited. And ten minutes later, introductions have been made, and I'm sitting on an uncomfortable plastic couch with Abby nestled into my side. Where she belongs.

A little noise has me staring down at the baby in Abby's arms. I can't see her hair color under the little cap, but her cheeks are flushed and full. Her little fingers escape the top of the blanket she's swaddled in. I've never seen such a tiny fingernail before. It fills me with awe, and something deeper, a sense of love and connectedness to Abby. A desire for more.

My experience with newborns up until today has been nil, but I'm shocked at how natural this feels. Me. Abby. A baby.

*Get her a ring first, idiot.*

That's the Zoey voice in my head, and I don't disagree. In fact, I'm already thinking about asking my sister what Abby would want. Because I suspect that Abby's not a platinum and diamond kind of girl. Maybe something blue, like her current hair color, which I might love more than the pink.

Addie's lips begin working and she grunts, her head starting to whip back and forth. "She's hungry," Abby says. "I hate to wake Jessa."

"But she asked you to," I remind her. "She wanted to feed on demand, right?"

I'm pretty proud of the new vocabulary I've adapted in the few hours I've been at the hospital. Things like feeding on demand, latching, and rooming-in. Whenever it is time, I vow to know all the terms, and be the best support I can be. Much like Jason, who appears in the doorway with a coffee for Abby and Chinese takeout for Jessa.

I help pull Abby to her feet and watch as she gently wakes Jessa, who looks exhausted but more than happy to have

Addie back in her arms. She's also excited about the Chinese takeout. But compared to ice chips and hospital food, who can blame her?

Jason passes the coffee to Abby like a baton before becoming immersed in his new family member, and then we're out in the hallway, I think headed to Abby's parents' house to help watch her nephews. Zoey is already there.

My arm is around Abby, where it's been for the last few hours. It would take the jaws of life to remove me at this point. I screwed up the first time I let her go, and I'm not planning to do it again.

"What time is it?" Abby asks, yawning.

"I don't even know."

Abby grabs my shirt and pulls me to a stop in a little alcove with soda and snack machines. My mind immediately goes to kissing, but she's got a worried look on her face.

"Why don't you know what time it is? Why aren't you at work? You and Zoey both skipping is like apocalypse-level stuff."

I laugh, feeling a freedom that I didn't know I was missing until right now, hearing her concern. Despite being at the hospital with Abby for hours, I haven't had the chance to explain much to her. We went straight from security to making out, to meeting Addie.

I lift my hands, cupping Abby's face, loving the softness of her skin against my palms. Her hands find their way to mine, holding me in place.

"I'm leaving Eck0."

Her eyes bug out, and she tries to shake her head. I hold her in place.

"But you can't! That's your thing!"

"No," I tell her, stroking my thumbs over the apples of her cheeks. "It wasn't hard to let go of. I don't want that life.

I don't want to work with Jack. We wrote in a clause just for this kind of thing. I'm going to help through the launch, but more like a contractor. More flexible hours."

"But the money ... all your time you spent!"

"I won't walk away empty-handed. I'll be fine. And my time wasn't wasted. I learned a lot. I've made money. Maybe not as much as I would if I stayed long-term. But I especially learned what's most important to me, and what's not."

Abby blinks her big hazel eyes at me. I find myself studying them, noting the colors and the way they change. Today, they're more of a light brown with some olive around her pupils. She's so beautiful, and I get the feeling that she won't ever understand how much. Even if I tell her often. Which I plan to do.

"You are so beautiful," I tell her. "And I like the blue."

"Better than the pink?"

I shake my head. "I love all your colors, Abby."

Though I hate to waste the smile spreading on her face, I can't wait to kiss her any longer. Using my body to crowd her deeper into the alcove and out of sight, I press my lips to hers, needing the connection. Needing her.

I planned to be sweet and soft, wanting Abby to know and feel how much I treasure her, how much I missed her even in these few days apart. But she seems to share the same hunger I feel, and the press and brush of our mouths becomes desperate, like we've just crossed a desert and found the oasis after passing mirage after mirage.

My hands slide around to tangle in her soft hair and her fists grip the front of my T-shirt, keeping me in place.

As if there's anywhere I'd rather be.

When we break apart, both of us are breathless. I feel no less desperate for this closeness with Abby, but there are still so many words that need to be said.

"Have I told you yet today that I love you?" I ask.

Abby grins. "I can't seem to remember. You might need to tell me again. Just in case."

I let my hands fall to her waist, holding her close, feeling possessive and needy and also somehow completely content. Like being with Abby is just right.

"I love you," I tell her, bending so our foreheads touch. "And I plan to tell you every single day."

"I love you too. I never would have planned it. But it's the best surprise."

It really is. Closing the distance between us, I kiss the end of her nose, lightly, teasingly. My eyes scan her neck. The edge of her chameleon tattoo peeks out near her collarbone. I have so many places to kiss and to claim. So much to explore.

*Don't rush. Slow and steady wins the race.* I'm thankful that I'm not hearing this in Zoey's voice, because kissing Abby is the last place I want to be thinking about my sister.

"I have an idea," Abby says. "Are you game?"

I almost ask her to tell me before I agree, but this is Abby. It's probably something that I would never have thought of, something that will push me out of my comfort zone and that later, I'll love.

"With you? I'm always game?"

Her eyes light up. "You might regret that later."

"I don't plan to have any more regrets when it comes to you."

She kisses the corner of my mouth, pulling away before I can capture her lips. I groan, and she giggles. "That wasn't my idea. Though let's file that one away for later. For now, I thought we could take however many balloons are left in the waiting area and brighten up the children's ward in this place. What do you say?"

"I say that you're full of good ideas," I tell her, stealing one more kiss before I take her hand and pull her out of the alcove. I'm afraid we might be tempted to stay all afternoon if we don't.

I link our fingers, then bring her hand up to my mouth. "I'm sorry that I keep kissing you in strange public places."

"I'm not," Abby says. "I think that's maybe something we should keep on the list."

"We have a list?"

"I'm making it up right now, as we go. First on the list: saying I love you every day."

"And the second is kissing in public places?"

The elevator dings at that moment, and suddenly Abby is pulling me inside. It's empty, and she gives me a grin that makes some deep part of my body feel like it's gone cliff diving. The doors close behind us.

"How about *mostly* private public places?" she asks.

But before I can answer, Abby is up on her tiptoes with her hands locked behind my neck, pulling my smiling mouth down to hers. I could stay in here all day.

As the elevator comes to a stop, I break the kiss only to put my lips next to her ear so I can whisper in my sexiest voice something only Abby will understand, "Hypertext Markup Language."

Giggling, she squeezes me tightly. "Aw, Zane. You always know just what to say."

# epilogue
## Abby + Zane Yeva

*Zane*

I'M STARING at the ring in my palm, turning it over and over, watching the princess cut black onyx catch the morning light as it comes through the tall trees at the edge of her family's property.

All I can think about is the third-grade spelling bee.

As a finalist, I had to stand on a stage in the cafeteria, the hot lights causing a sheen of sweat to form on my face, as Ms. Mulch called out word after word. I was last in the row, and honestly feared that I might collapse. Or sweat into a puddle that would drip off the edge of the stage.

I spelled *apron* wrong on purpose, just so I could be done with the torture. My nerves disappeared instantly, but the rest of the day, my shirt was slightly damp from sweat.

That's nothing compared to my nerves now. And it's unfortunate, because I don't want to propose to Abby drenched in sweat and smelling like a high school boys' locker room.

It's not that I expect her to say no ... but, then, does anyone who proposes really think they'll get turned down? No. But according to the internet, which we can always trust for accurate data, one fourth of women turn down proposals.

*Focus on the positive,* the Zoey voice in my head says. *That means three-fourths say yes.*

Easy for her to say. First, she's my subconscious, so she doesn't count. Second, the real Zoey isn't likely to be in my position, unless she flips the script and proposes to her boyfriend. Doubtful.

"I almost fainted when I proposed to Jessa," Jason hisses from the bushes where he's hiding. Also in the bushes are Jessa, Jace, Joey, Addie, and Abby's mom. They're good sports, especially since it's pretty cold on this Christmas morning. Yesterday, it was seventy degrees. Today, it's forty. That's Texas for you. Abby's dad is inside, ready for his role, which is getting Abby out of bed and out here. It's not a job I envy. Except that it's warmer.

"It's true," Jessa says. "And he fainted at both boys' births. He faints at anything."

"Hey!" Jason says.

"It's true. And I love you anyway. Don't worry, Zane. She's gonna say yes."

"Okay," I say, but I have to wipe my forehead with the back of my hand.

That's when I hear Abby's sleepy voice from inside and the heavy clomp of her father's boots.

"Why are we"—a yawn interrupts the question—"going outside? And why so early? Can I at least have coffee first?"

"Hush, sweet potato. Just get yourself outside."

The whine and screech of the screen door makes my heart

thud in my chest. Abby's father steps out onto the porch, his breath forming a quick cloud that dissipates almost immediately when he smiles at me.

"Ooh!" Abby squeals, still out of sight. "Is it a Christmas puppy? A baby goat! Did you finally get me a baby goat?"

Dang. The platinum and onyx ring is amazing. But a ring with a baby goat …

It's too late to second guess this goat-less proposal because Abby is at the top of the steps, staring down at me where I'm kneeling.

She blinks sleepy eyes, one hand going to her hair, which has halfway fallen out of a long braid, the purple highlights vibrant in the morning sun. Her pajamas are fuzzy and pink with lines of computer code on them, a birthday present from me a few months ago. It's the first time I've seen her in them. Suddenly, the ring feels so heavy in my hand. I want to very badly to wake up every morning to see Abby adorable and half-awake.

"Abby," I say, my voice steady.

I've found my resolve. There are no more nerves. I want Abby to be the first and last one I see every day, for the rest of my days.

"No," she whispers, and someone in the bushes, maybe Jessa, gasps.

"No?" A black hole opens in my stomach, but before I let it suck me into a vortex of disappointment, I remind myself that this is Abby. She loves me. Last night, we made out on her parents couch under a sprig of mistletoe that she ducttaped to the ceiling. I wait for her to explain.

Abby lifts a hand to her hair, then crosses her arms over her chest. "Zane. You can't propose to me when I look like this! Not in the morning! Not before coffee! Just … hang on and let me change!"

Before I can move, she's bolted like a skittish calf, running back into the house, leaving an awkward silence in her wake.

It wasn't no to the proposal.

It was no to being proposed to *in pajamas.*

Her father stands on the porch, looking half dumbstruck and half amused. When he sees the determined flint in my eye, he throws open the screen door to make way for me.

I bound up the porch stairs in two big steps. "Abby! Get back here! I'm trying to propose!"

From upstairs, I hear her call. "I know! And I won't be proposed to looking like this! My answer is no until I've at least brushed my teeth and put proper pants on!"

I catch her in the upstairs hallway, just before she ducks into the bathroom. She shrieks when she sees me, dropping the clothes in her arms and covering her mouth.

"Morning breath!" she shouts through her hand. "I can't kiss you with morning breath!"

I grab her firmly by the hips, keeping the ring tucked in my palm with two fingers.

"I don't care about morning breath," I say, my fierce eyes meeting hers, which are still puffy. Just like that morning in the resort, when my feelings graduated from a crush to something much larger.

"Zane, *please.*"

It's the *please* that gets me. "Fine." I release her, and she scurries into the bathroom, slamming the door. I lean my forehead against it. "But only brushing your teeth! One minute!"

"Dentists recommend a full two minutes!"

"I'm not a dentist! One minute or I'll bust down the door!"

Abby squeals again and I hear the water running. A throat

clears at the bottom of the stairs. Her father lifts an eyebrow at me, a scarily similar look to the one my dad gives. The rest of her family is crowded at the bottom of the stairs, watching. Her nephews look slightly horrified, and Addie has fallen back asleep wrapped in a fuzzy blanket with a knit cap pulled down over her head. Abby's mom has her hands clasped to her chest as though a hallway proposal after an argument about pajamas is just the most romantic thing she's ever seen.

"I'll pay to repair it, of course," I explain to her father. "But I *will* break it down if she doesn't come out in thirty seconds."

Her father nods. "All right."

The door swings open, startling me.

Abby has managed to brush her teeth, but also has smoothed her hair into a ponytail, washed her face, and applied lip gloss.

I narrow my eyes, even as I feel a smile trying to break loose. "I said *only* brush your teeth."

Abby shrugs. "I kept on the pajamas. Now. Shouldn't you be down on a knee?"

The woman has a point. I drop to both knees, glad for the soft rug running the length of the hall. The gravel outside will leave bruises.

I take Abby's hand. "Abs. I know you're not a morning person. But there's a reason I'm doing this now."

"Because it's Christmas morning?"

I shake my head. "Nope. It's because I need you to understand that I want to marry this version of you. The one fresh from sleep with messy hair and tired eyes and grumpy before coffee. I love Abby in the wild. And I love Abby the brilliant hacker and programmer. Abby being too competitive at game night."

"I'm not—"

"You are," several voices from downstairs echo.

"You cheat," Jace says, and Abby's cheeks go pink.

"I don't ... okay. Sometimes I do cheat. Fine."

Jace nods, as though he's done his part.

"I love the Abby that has to win at all costs. Who decorated my house to make it a home. Who cares for my sister and would fight to the death anyone who might threaten her friends or family. I love all your hair colors and I love your heart. Your face is the one I want to go to sleep beside and wake up seeing."

Fat tears pool in her eyes, which are a bright green this morning, with only a hint of golden brown. "Even before coffee?" she whispers.

"Even before coffee. Abby, will you make me the happiest man alive and marry me?"

I lift my other hand, holding the ring between two fingers. Her eyes drop for half a second, then snap right back up to mine. The tears are still poised in her eyes, ready to spill at any moment. Still, she holds my gaze.

I frown. "Do you not like the ring?"

"I'm sure it's beautiful. But I'm looking at the only thing that matters right now."

I swallow hard, emotion tightening my throat.

"Yes, Zane. Yes! I would love to marry you." Twin tears finally fall, skipping right over her cheeks and falling on my hand.

And then I'm up and wrapping her in my arms, picking her up and swinging her, the sound of her laughter and her family's cheers from downstairs making the moment seem bigger, more festive.

"I love you, Abby," I say, pulling her lips to mine. She's

warm, and she tastes like her cool mint toothpaste, new and fresh.

"I love you too," she says against my lips. We kiss until there are gagging noises from her nephews and a wolf whistle from Jason.

When I pull back, it's to slip the ring on her finger. A perfect fit, thanks to Zoey giving me inside information.

"It's beautiful," Abby whispers, staring at the ring. She looks up at me, and the love in her eyes is like a flame igniting something in me. It never gets old.

"I love you," I tell her again. I can't seem to stop saying it.

She squeezes my arm. "I love you too, Zane. But please. Please. Get me some coffee."

I grin, because I'd thought of this. And I was up early, at the one coffee shop I found open at this hour Christmas morning.

"Your flat white is downstairs."

Abby grins, kisses me quickly, and bolts down the stairs. "You really are the perfect man, fiancé."

**THE END**

---

*Don't miss Zoey and Gavin in Falling for Your Boss!*

# bonus epilogue

>>>—♥—→

Zoey

... To sum up, *they say you can't help falling in love. It just happens. Like big hair in humid weather or dropping salsa in your lap when you're wearing white pants.*

*But when it comes to your best friend's twin, you want to proceed with caution.*

*As with any best friend's sibling situation, you need to understand that a romantic relationship could impact the friendship. Maybe end it.*

*Dating a twin takes things to the next level. It's like ordering a burger but getting the whole combo as a free upgrade. There is something special about the twin relationship. Sure, it may be a stereotype, but in my experience, twinsense is a real thing. Just realize what you're getting into. Look before you leap.*

"What are you reading?"

I practically fall out of my chair at the sound of Gavin's voice behind me. I was so caught up in reading the draft of Sam's chapter that I didn't hear my boss come in. I slam my laptop shut before Gavin can see that I'm not reading office memos or answering client emails.

I keep my voice cool, my expression blank. It's my armor, my only line of defense against my feelings for my boss. Total overcompensation.

"Nothing. Why? Do you need something?"

*Like me?*

I grit my teeth, wishing that my thought life could be as easy to control as the rest of my life. I am the queen of scheduling, the COO of productivity, and the president of organization. But my inner self? Has other ideas. Like the one where I should crush on my boss.

"Nope. For once, I'm just checking on you."

Gavin grins with his dimples on full display and drops a hand on my shoulder for a quick squeeze. My entire body wakes up at the contact. It's like the starter's gun from my high-school track days, and all my hormones take off sprinting.

*False start! Come back! The race is off!*

But my pulse leads the charge and is already halfway around the track at a record-breaking pace. I must have stiffened under his touch, because Gavin's dark eyebrows knit together, and he drops his hand. He takes half a step back and I'm thankful but also want to follow him in my rolling office chair.

"Sorry. Are you okay?"

*Define okay. Because if the fact that my body has decided to abandon all good reason and rational thought is okay, then yes. I'm great.*

"I'm fine. Sorry. I guess I'm just a little distracted."

*By your strong, clean-shaven jaw and your thick dark hair that I want to run my fingers through. And by the laugh lines by your eyes that tell me you may have ten or more years on me, but you've spent them smiling.*

"I'll let you get back to work. But I do have a project that I think would be perfect for you."

*Perfect for me like you're perfect for me?*

Oh, my good gracious, I am going to murder my subconscious. I make a mental note to search for online courses that teach you to keep your thought life in check. I need to stick mine in prison. Better yet, solitary confinement.

Gavin looks at his watch, and I look at the little bit of muscular forearm revealed when he pushes aside his sleeve.

"How about you stop by after lunch? Say one o'clock?"

I nod, not trusting my words. In the true crime podcasts Dad got me hooked on, they talk about something called leakage, where a guilty party unwittingly speaks their guilt. If I say too much now, I'm going to be leaking all over the place.

"I've got a better idea. I'll order us lunch. We can talk over a meal. How does that sound?"

*Like a date. It sounds like a date.*

Except for the whole *work* part.

"Sure."

On the outside, I'm composed. Someone observing might even say I look bored. Inside, there's a whole marching band now in the center of the track.

I should probably go home sick. Or develop an incurable disease. Maybe it's time to quit and move to another firm. I can update my resume before lunch. It's not like working in market research was my end goal. I'm barely more than an executive assistant to Gavin. He has one of those, and then he has me. Nancy takes care of his schedule, and I work alongside Gavin with projects and attend meetings, which allows me to learn and do more than any assistant would.

I wanted to work in marketing or advertising firm, but this is the job I found after school. The pay is good, and I've gotten a ton of hands-on experience. But also ... Gavin. I stay for Gavin, something I suspect everyone in my life knows, but I'll never admit.

"It's a date," Gavin says, and it's like all the hormones sprinting through my body swoon at one time. I swear my heart makes a tiny skip, and the breath leaves my lungs. "I mean, a work date," he says quickly. "A working lunch. You know what I mean." Laughing, he runs a hand through his hair.

I want that to be my hand, touching the soft locks, feeling his scalp beneath my fingertips.

I want *him*.

"I got it."

My tone is too short, the words clipped. If I freeze Gavin out, he can't see my feelings. I'm convinced this is why he chose me to work alongside him instead of the other women I work with. They're obvious in their crushes, irritatingly so. Syrupy voices. Flirtation. Innuendo. Batted eyelashes, buttons undone on blouses. I can't count the number of times I've had to deal with homicidal thoughts towards my coworkers.

I'm the only one who seems unaffected by Gavin's good looks and the confidence that oozes from him like some kind of pheromone. *Seems* being the operative word. It's not simply his looks, though that would be enough. For the past few years, Gavin has topped lists as one of Austin's most eligible bachelors *and* one of the wealthiest men under fifty in the state of Texas.

Not that I care about those accolades. I mean, they aren't

anything to sneeze at. But my feelings for my boss didn't develop based on his wealth (though it's not exactly a turn-off), his success (though I respect it), or his good looks (which I definitely admire).

My crush on Gavin built up slowly over time in the last two years I've worked here. The more time I spend with him, the more my feelings took root, like one of those invasive, creeping vines that are so hard to get rid of. Dad has one that keeps recurring, growing right up the side of our house and loosening the mortar of the bricks.

Gavin has been loosening my tight control bit by bit by bit, even though I'm sure he has had no intention of doing so. It's just who he is.

He's a good man. Funny. Thoughtful. Kind. But not in a sappy way. He still totally rocks that Alpha thing when it comes to closing deals. Seeing his eyes flash and his jaw harden as he takes charge has made me want to fan myself with a file folder in a meeting.

"Do you want me to order for you, or would you like to pick?" he asks.

"Surprise me," I tell him, though I'm not sure why. I loathe surprises. Give me the steady, the expected, the sure thing every day of the week.

Gavin rubs a hand over his chin in mock thoughtfulness. "Hm. What would Zoey want?"

*You. I want you.*

I feel like he is making this whole crush thing worse with every word he speaks. I really am serious about updating my resume. Maybe Zane knows some places that are hiring. I know he's been looking for more of a nine-to-five since he fell for Abby and decided to leave not only his startup, Eck0, but the whole startup life.

"Good luck," I tell Gavin. Immediately I want to slap a

hand over my mouth. I know my cheeks turn pink. For a tiny second, I didn't keep things under control and look what slipped out: flirtation.

Gavin looks surprised by my comment, then gives me a wide grin that feels a delicious sort of torture. "Oh, I think I can figure you out, Zoey. And I'm sure I will make you happy."

Seriously! Could the man say any more things that I can take another way? This lunch meeting is going to be sweet, sweet torture.

I turn away, not bothering to say goodbye as Gavin leaves my small office. If he thinks I'm rude, that's fine. Better he think I hate him than know the truth: I've fallen head over heels for my boss.

---

*Keep reading for a Bonus epilogue featuring Abby & Zane OR dive right into Falling for Your Boss, Zoey & Gavin's story!*

# bonus scene
## the hot tub
### (following chapter eleven)

*Abby*

THE ONLY THING that could possibly be worse than Zane seeing me in a bathing suit already happened. There's nowhere to go but up when someone has seen you naked.

I mean, I assume he saw at least SOMETHING when I rolled off the massage table and ended up right below the face-hole in *his* table. Even if he said he didn't. To his credit, Zane did keep his eyes on mine. I could practically see the strain of resistance making his eyeballs twitch.

He was about as gentlemanly as a man can be with a totally nude woman in front of him. I appreciated his concern, the way he didn't look OR laugh.

It only made my teeny, tiny crush a little more difficult to ignore.

In any case, I should work off the assumption that Zane saw at least some of my lady parts out of the corner of his eyes. At the very least, a vague blur of skin in places the sun doesn't shine.

So, why I am I standing in the dressing room, begging the Gibbs in my head to tell me I look fine?

"Gibbs, come on man. Don't leave me hanging."

But Gibbs remains silent. Probably a good thing, considering the age gap between me and the actor Mark Harmon is significant.

Do I really want someone who could be my dad telling me I look awesome in a bikini?

"Good call, Gibbs. I'll handle this assignment on my own."

Step one is to stop overthinking, stop being self-conscious, and step out of the dressing room and into the hot tub area channeling Lady Gaga's confidence.

I wrap the short, silky spa robe over my black and pink polka dot bikini. It's a fifties style with ruching in all the right places—giving my cleavage a happy hug—and a high-waisted bottom Zoey tried to tell me no one could pull off.

"I was wrong," she admitted when it arrived in the mail after I made a late-night impulse buy from an Instagram ad. "*You* can pull it off, Abs."

"Heck yeah, I can," I said then.

In addition to looking good on my figure, it passed all my bathing suit tests. Which include (but are not limited to) bending over in front of a mirror to see if anything—*anything at all*—escapes.

Jumping up and down to make sure we don't have any nip slips.

I mean, I'm NEVER going to voluntarily jump around in a bathing suit, but what if I had to? Like some kind of life-or-death bathing-suit hopping moment? I need to be prepared and fully covered by a suit that holds all my parts in a viselike (yet still comfy) grip. This one definitely fits the bill. No more malfunctions! At least not today.

"You've got this," I tell the Abby in the mirror.

She looks less confident than I feel, so I try standing in one of those power poses people are always going on about. It only makes me giggle. But I feel a little of my stress and insecurities fading away.

*Peace out, insecurities. You are henceforth banished.*

With a last look in the mirror, I grab one of the spa towels and open the door.

Zane is already in the hot tub, and his head snaps up as I enter. Before he politely looks away, I don't miss the way his eyes do a fast perusal of my bare legs.

And was that ... appreciation?

He clears his throat, still looking toward the wall. "Hey."

"Hey."

Silence descends. A particularly loud silence, only punctuated by the sound of the bubbling water.

Well, isn't this nice and awkward?

I fuss with my towel, placing it on one of the teak wood chairs. The lighting is low, mostly coming from flickering electric candles. Steam makes everything feel soft and dreamlike. Soft music plays through speakers in the ceiling. The whole vibe is—

"Romantic, huh?" Zane asks, pulling me out of my head.

I give him a small smile. "Definitely not a place for business meetings."

"Then I guess we'll have to avoid talking about business."

Is Zane being ... flirty?

I still don't feel like I have a good read on him. Despite knowing him for years. Despite seeing him so much this week. This trip has gone a long way toward peeling back some of his tough outer layers. But I can't say for sure. I really, REALLY hope it's not my wishful thinking.

"Are you getting in?" Zane asks, and I realize I'm still just standing here, like I'm part of the spa decor.

Guess this means it's time for the ceremonial disrobing and bathing suit reveal. "Yep."

Before my insecurities can escape from the basement where I've locked them, I slip out of the robe without checking to see if Zane is watching. It's better not to know. Instead, I focus on gracefully stepping into the hot tub.

Which, of course, doesn't quite work.

I miss the steps and instead, sort of plunge with a splash. At least I don't fall on top of Zane, which would have been one more humiliation for my day. But I don't have time to celebrate because HOT SWEDISH MEATBALLS THIS WATER IS SCALDING.

Instead of scrambling out of this boiling death trap like I should, I settle in deeper, hoping it will get better as I sit down.

It doesn't.

I'm feeling very sympathetic toward lobsters right now.

The raw places on my knees from where I fell in the massage room sting, but within a few seconds go strangely numb. I look down to make sure my legs haven't melted. Nope. Still there. Barely visible between the bubbling water and turning a brighter pink than my hair—but there.

"Zane! It's so hot!"

He tilts his head. "It's a *hot* tub, not a lukewarm tub."

"Hot tub, not boiling pasta water tub," I tell him, sitting up a little straighter to feel the relatively cool air on my skin. But that puts my breasts right on the surface of the water in a way that's hard to ignore, so I sink back down.

"Is this not ... normal?" he asks.

I look to see if he's joking, and only then notice the beads of sweat dotting his forehead and the redness in his cheeks.

"I'm not some expert level hot tubber. But this doesn't feel healthy. Did you really not notice?"

"Oh, it's painful. I just thought this was how hot tubs work."

"Have you never been in a hot tub?" I ask.

Not like I spend TONS of time in them. I don't go prancing around the city from hot tub to hot tub. But it feels like a sort of normal adult thing to get in them *sometimes*.

Or at least to recognize this is NOT the normal temp.

"I have," he says. "It's just been a while. Do I still have the top layer of my skin?" Zane halfway stands, leaving everything from his belly button up on display.

I hesitate, but he's *inviting* me to look.

He ASKED.

And since he's my boss right now (sorta), I HAVE to do it, right?

*Don't mind if I do!*

I push away my concern when I notice a line of red ending near his clavicles. Ouch.

I could say something about this or suggest we both escape before being teriyakied, but instead, I get a little lost looking at Zane's chest. It may be mildly scalded, but it is still a thing of beauty.

The man is like a midnight snack. Not to be confused with the regular kind of snack. Oh, no.

Zane is the delicious treat you crave so hard, you can't resist it at midnight—even though every woman knows midnight calories go straight to her problem areas.

*No midnight snacks, Abs.*

This is NOT the time or place for Gibbs to show back up

in my head. Nothing like an imaginary father figure showing up and putting a damper on all the fun.

I ignore him and tell my brain to be normal for once. No voices. No Gibbs.

Just me ... and the man I'm currently and unabashedly ogling.

"Like what you see?" Zane smirks, then crosses his arms over his chest.

Don't men know this kind of move makes all their muscles pop?

Based on Zane's expression, he knows. Oh, he KNOWS.

I shrug. "You're the one who asked me to look, boss. I wasn't sure if this might count toward my job performance."

"I thought we agreed no business in here."

No need for a reminder. There is zero business happening in my head. It's ALL personal.

Meanwhile, I'm still staring. I should look away. Or make a snarky comment. Or point out that his skin is bright red up to his clavicles, a clear sign the water is too hot. But my body and brain are like two cars that disconnected while the train was hurtling down the track.

Guess which car got left behind?

The brain car. Goodbye, brain.

Zane's chest is all the things I like. Not that I've spent hours obsessing over chests or making a system for rating them. But if I DID, he'd get a solid ten for how broad he is, another ten for the sharp—but not like steroid creepy—cut of his muscles, and a nine-point-three for his chest hair.

Don't get me wrong—I'm not looking for a bald-as-a-baby smooth chest. I'm deducting points because I could take a little MORE hair. I'm not wanting enough to, like, grab in case of sudden turbulence—which may never apply in actual life—but long enough to run my fingers through.

And if this all makes me sound shallow, I don't date based solely on looks. I don't going around rating guys on their chests. If I did, though, most guys I've dated are fives at best. I'm fine with fives and a good personality.

But a near-perfect ten and Zane's personality? Deadly combo.

"Eyes up here, Abby."

Because I've already been caught looking too long AND because I hate being told what to do, I peruse Zane for a few more seconds just out of PRINCIPLE.

That's the only reason. My very strong principles.

Hopefully, my expression is more like that of a scientist studying the surface of Mars rather than a woman about to reach out and see if the subject I'm studying feels as good as he looks.

I also hope Zane doesn't notice the blush I know is rising in my cheeks. Or is that just the heat from this boiling cauldron we're in?

Zane's abs are likewise ... perfection. Chiseled blocks of muscle stacked in neat rows. Orderly. Defined without being TOO defined. I highly approve. Five Stars. Two enthusiastic thumbs—and heck, my big toes too—up.

More than just being nice to gaze upon, these muscles show something of his character.

Zane is driven. Disciplined. Intense. He works hard.

Even though his uptightness often irks me, it's part of a bigger set of qualities I admire.

A lot of guys our age complain about college debts while spending their paychecks at bars and new shoes instead of paying down their debt. Or they're still living with parents while working part-time for a rideshare or grocery delivery service. NOT that there's anything wrong with those jobs. It just seems like every dudebro in town hanging in bars and hitting on women is living some version of this life: part-time job, foolish spending, big debt.

Case in point: I had a date a year ago with a guy who paid for dinner with his mom's debit card. When he caught me looking at her name on the card, he said his mom gives him "date allowance" because his part-time job money all goes toward his credit card bills and—wait for it—his comic book collection.

Nothing against moms. Or comics. Again—not even part-time jobs.

But there's something about a man like Zane who works hard NOT to need someone else to pay for dates. A guy like Zane who has big, scary dreams of a startup and goes hard after what he wants.

I wonder if he goes this hard after everything he wants? Oh, to be the one he's going after …

I allow my gaze to track back up his body in a leisurely fashion—*that'll teach you to tell me where to look, Zane!*—like I'm taking a Sunday morning stroll. My gaze finally reaches his blue, blue eyes. The same color as Zoey's.

Which is a cruel, rude—but needed—reminder that I shouldn't be doing this. I can't look at Zane like this. I can't flirt.

I need to be his employee. His sister's BFF. The person NOT harboring a secret, unrequited crush.

NOT a woman who'd like to do a graduate dissertation on Zane's perfect musculature. Which would, of course, require LOTS of hands-on study.

Needing to change the tone of the moment, which feels like it's shifted from light to charged and intense, I utilize one of my favorite go-to movie quotes. "That'll do, pig. That'll do."

Zane sinks back in the water with a little hiss of pain.

"Did you just quote the movie *Babe* to me? Or—rather, *about* me?"

"Hey, there are worse things than being compared to bacon."

"I hope you like bacon because I definitely feel cooked."

I LOVE BACON. Literally and, in this specific situation, figuratively as well. The best answer here is to plead the fifth.

"You were supposed to be checking for second degree burns, not checking me out. But I guess after what happened in there"—Zane points in the general direction of where we had our massages—"we're equal."

"We will NEVER be equal. That in there was a high-level moment of complete humiliation. A one hundred on a scale of ten. I was simply examining you for second-degree burns."

Zane snorts. "Is that what you were doing?"

"Yes. And there's a spot on your right side looking like it's about to blister."

Zane glances down, then twists, trying to find the nonexistent spot I'm talking about. I take advantage of this distraction and splash water his way. Which was a mistake, because it's no fun playing in boiling water. When it splashes up over his neck, he winces.

"Sorry," I say. "Maybe we should get out?"

It's a half-hearted suggestion. Because I AM IN A HOT TUB WITH ZANE. I'm not cutting this short. Even if my skin feels like it's covered in fire ants.

"Are you ready to get out?" His blue eyes burn into mine, and I slowly shake my head, trying not to jostle the water. "Maybe we should treat it like a challenge," he suggests. "First one to get out is the loser."

"I'm game. What's the prize?"

"Bragging rights?"

"No, let's make it interesting," I tell him. "How about …

the loser owes the other person coffee when we get back home?"

My heart is a quivering mess, but I manage to keep my face as cool as I can, given the current temperature. Does that sound too much like a date? Coffee is less date-y than drinks, and definitely less date-y than dinner, so—

"Let's make it dinner, and you're on."

Dinner, huh? Zane nixed coffee, skipped over drinks, and went straight to dinner?

I don't want to get my hopes up—imagining Zoey glaring at me slightly helps—but confetti cannons are being shot off in my heart.

Zane holds out his hand for me to shake. I clasp his hand firmly, and he squeezes right back before letting go.

"Guess we're doing this, then," I say, wishing I could enjoy this moment rather than honestly questioning if it's possible to damage one's internal organs from being submerged in too-hot water.

Zane smiles, then pants a little before clearing his throat. "Yep."

For a few minutes we sit in a silence that's comfortable, not like the awkward pause after I came in. Either I'm starting to get used to the heat, or I'm moving into a pre-boiling state of euphoria, because I don't feel the burn as much now.

Or ... maybe my nerve endings were seared off? I'm good with whatever though, because Zane stretches his arms out on the tiled edge, one hand brushing my shoulder. It stops to rest there, a tease of a touch.

It's a tiny thing, but it feels HUGE to me. Every cell in my body is suddenly hyper-focused on just that spot.

Can Zane tell how much he's affecting me? I can always claim heat stroke.

Honestly, with the way my head is spinning, I may not just be CLAIMING heat stroke. Did someone turn the temperature up? Because it feels like the water just jumped another ten degrees.

"I think it's getting better," Zane says, his fingertip moving slightly over my skin. "Once it burns through the epidermis, it's not so bad."

"You know, you're pretty fun when you lose the suit," I tell him.

He slowly raises one eyebrow. "When I lose the suit, huh?"

I realize what I said sounded like Zane taking off his clothes. Not what I meant! But now I'm remembering that he didn't have a bathing suit.

Which means I'm sitting next to Zane, and he's in his underwear.

The moment I think about it, I have to fight off a wild surge of curiosity to know what kind and what color.

*Not my business! Bad Abby! No!*

I can't be privy to this kind of information! I won't be able to look at Zane in regular clothes again without the knowledge of what's under them. And that is NOT good.

I force my eyes to a canvas with a waterfall painted on it. Probably should be soothing, but only makes me wish for cold, spring-fed water like a lot of Austin's swimming holes. What I wouldn't give to be tossed into Barton Springs right now.

"That's, uh, not what I meant," I say, when I realize Zane is still waiting for an answer.

"What *did* you mean?" Zane asks.

"What I meant is that you're different when you step out of the office and let your guard down."

He makes a humming sound, and that finger brushes my

shoulder again, like he's drawing light circles on my skin. My body shivers, which should be an impossibility in the heat.

To distract myself from Zane's touch, I keep running my mouth. "Hey, I bet if you sent a text right now, you might even use contractions. Or NOT feel the need to sign your name."

"Are you poking fun at my texting abilities?" Zane gives my shoulder a shove.

I should let the momentum carry me away from him, away to safety. Instead, I push back with my shoulder. But his hand has moved back to the edge of the tub, so my momentum carries me a few inches closer to Zane.

We're not just sitting together now. We're practically cuddling.

Zane's arm slides down until it rests on my shoulders, still a little hesitant. It's not quite around me like a scarf; more like a light pashmina draping there. I happen to LOVE a good pashmina.

Though … right now either one sounds too hot, and it's hard to enjoy Zane's touch when my blood is turning to lava.

"Is it getting hotter in here?" Zane asks. A bead of sweat drips down his nose.

"Giving up so soon?" I tease.

But no really—he should give up. Then I can give up, and we can see if there's an ice bath somewhere.

"Nope." But he shifts a little, pulling more of his torso out of the water.

Steam billows around us, and I'm starting to feel slightly woozy. Is that the effect of having Zane nearby, or is the heat really getting to me?

"You don't look so good," Zane says.

"I'm fine." Fine, but black dots dance in my vision.

"You are not fine."

And before I can register what's happening, Zane has scooped me up and is stepping out of the tub.

"Hey," I say, but my head lolls against his chest. "Now who wins the bet?"

"Don't worry about that right now," he says, gently placing me down on a lounge chair with a waterproof cushion.

Don't worry about that?

That's ALL I'm worried about.

Not whether my internal organs are shutting down or I've killed brain cells.

No—I need to know if I get my dinner with Zane! I don't even care who pays.

I'm going to turn into the paper route kid from *Better Off Dead*, an eighties movie my parents love. Except instead of chasing Zane down asking for my two dollars, I'm gonna chase him down asking for my dinner date.

It was going to be a date, right?

"Just rest. I'm going to get you some water. I think we're both dehydrated."

If only that were something a little good old fashioned mouth-to-mouth would fix. I almost suggest it—which sets off alarm bells that I really MIGHT be suffering from heat stroke—when Zane turns to cross the room.

In his fitted black boxer briefs.

DANG IT!

I cannot unsee this! I will forever know exactly how Zane's butt looks in super fitted, wet fabric.

I squeeze my eyes closed, trying to imagine the least sexy things I can.

The gross spills that always end up crusted below the bottom fridge drawer.

Babies crying on an airplane.

The combo of a shag carpet and multiple dogs with intestinal issues.

Too bad none of these are effective in dimming my current attraction to Zane. And while his back is turned is the best chance I'll have to escape.

I lumber to my feet. I'm totally Frankensteining, but at least I make it to the door without looking Zane's way.

"Hey!" he calls. "Abs! Come back. You need—"

I need SPACE.

Slamming the dressing room door, I grab my clothes and make a run for it through the door leading back where we came from. This means I run right into another couples massage and my favorite masseuse.

Four heads snap up at the sight of a soggy, pink-skinned and pink-haired woman bolting by in a bathing suit.

"Enjoy the massage!" I call over my shoulder as I make it to the exit. "My best advice: stay on the table!"

## a note from Emma

You made it to the author note! Give yourself a nice high five.

I have been planning this book and this series for over a year, waiting until I finished (or got close to finishing) other series that needed to come first.

It has been SO good to finally start writing! The rest of the books will follow Zoey, Delilah, Harper, and Sam as they deal with more love tropes. I can't wait!

Comedy is a scary thing to write.

I feel like you really have to put yourself OUT THERE in a way that's even more vulnerable than just telling stories to begin with. I know not everyone finds the same things funny. I also know every book isn't for every reader.

My other books are a little *sweeter* in tone, but most have humorous elements, even my most serious books. This won't be for everyone, but I hope that you have loved it. As I'm writing in 2020, I think we could all use a little comic relief.

A quick note about epilogues.

I know that TYPICALLY they're showing the wayyyy happy every after with a proposal or wedding or baby. Because this series is related, I'm wrapping up the book with a transition to the next. This series will go through all five friends- Abby, Zoey, Harper, Delilah, and Sam.

I hope you keep reading!

Want to connect? I'd love for you to join my Facebook Reader group:

https://www.facebook.com/groups/emmastclair/

If you haven't left a review on this book (or my others), that would mean the world to me! Thank you so much for being a reader!!

-e


PS - If you want weekly emails with book updates and romcom recs, sign up here:

https://emmastclair.com/romcomemails

PPS - If you want to find Zoey and Gavin's story, go here:

https://emmastclair.com/zoey

# thank you!

A huge thanks to all the people behind the scenes for making this book happen.

To Rob, for always telling me when placenta jokes need to NOT be in my books.

To Sarah Adams, an amazing author who made me feel like this might work.

To Stephanie, for your honesty. You have no idea how much I appreciate it!

To Judy & Devon, for catching my errors.

To Jillian, Lori, Leslie, Rita, Judy, Lisa, Anna, Amberly, Marsha, Lissa, Sandy, and anyone else I missed in this list who read early for me! You guys really are amazing.

## ALSO BY EMMA ST. CLAIR

### Graham Brothers
The Buy-In
The Bluff
The Pocket Pair

### Sweet Royal Romcoms
Royally Rearranged
Royal Gone Rogue

### Oakley Island (with Jenny Proctor)
Eloise and the Grump Next Door
Merritt and Her Childhood Crush

### Love Clichés
Falling for Your Best Friend's Twin
Falling for Your Boss
Falling for Your Fake Fiancé
The Twelve Holidates
Falling for Your Best Friend
Falling for Your Enemy

Sign up for weekly emails and book news—
http://emmastclair.com/romcomemail

## ABOUT THE AUTHOR

Emma St. Clair is a *USA Today* bestselling author of over twenty books. She lives near Houston with her husband, five kids, and a Great Dane who doesn't make a very good babysitter. Her romcoms have humor, heart, and nothing that's going to make you need to hide your Kindle from the kids. ;)

You can find out more at http://emmastclair.com or join her reader group at www.facebook.com/groups/emmastclair.

facebook.com/thesaintemma
instagram.com/kikimojo